What Readers are Saying

I needed a seatbelt for *Imperfect Trust*. And oxygen. If you like edge-of-your-seat, chiller reads liberally sprinkled with humor, romance, and modern-day cowboys, this is a good book for you.
~ Betty Thomas Owens
Author of *Sutter's Landing*

Romance, mystery, action, humor—*Imperfect Bonds* has it all. I've now read all three in The Imperfect Series and have fallen in love with Elizabeth Noyes's writing style. She's one of the best authors I've come across in a long time, and I look forward to reading more of her stories in the future.
~ Amanda Sue King
Author of *Hidden Scars* and *Not Ever*

If you love stories with action, adventure, suspense, and a splash of romance, the Imperfect Series is for you. *Imperfect Wings* is a page-turner and very hard to put down.
~ Vicki Mobley

Imperfect Trust is the "perfect" read. It joins adventure, romance, and intrigue. I found the book engaging and near impossible to put down.
~ Lynn Sewell

Imperfect Lies

ELIZABETH NOYES

Write Integrity Press

Imperfect Lies
© 2017 Elizabeth Noyes

ISBN-10: 1-944120-41-6
ISBN-13: 978-1-944120-41-2
E-book ISBN: 978-1-944120-42-9

Published by Write Integrity Press, 4475 Trinity Mills Road, PO Box 702852, Dallas, TX 75370
Find out more about the author, **Elizabeth Noyes,** at her website: **www.ElizabethNoyes.com** or on her author page at **www.WriteIntegrity.com**
Printed in the United States of America.

Library of Congress Control Number: 2017944756

Cast of Characters

MAJOR CHARACTERS

MALLORY CAMERON - fourth in age of the Cameron siblings and oldest of twin girls, a freelance journalist with aspirations to work for one of the major news organizations.

SHERIFF JAMES EVERS - former Army Ranger, former member of a covert Bureau of International Intelligence special operations team, and newly elected sheriff of Hastings Bluff.

GARRETT CAMERON - oldest of the Cameron siblings, a former Army Ranger, former member of a covert Bureau of International Intelligence special operations team, and current overseer of the Triple C Horse Ranch operations in Hastings Bluff, Idaho. Married to TJ McKendrick.

TJ MCKENDRICK CAMERON - former accountant, now an elementary school teacher. Married to Garrett Cameron and expecting the first Cameron grandchild. She and Garrett have their story in *IMPERFECT WINGS*.

WADE CAMERON - second in age of the Cameron siblings, former Army Intelligence/Signal officer, creator of a revolutionary computer language and its accompanying suite of security applications. Started his own security business in Hastings Bluff. Engaged to Lucy Kiddron.

LUCY KIDDRON - former Bureau of International Intelligence analyst, video game entrepreneur, and computer hacker extraordinaire. Engaged to Wade Cameron. She and Wade share their story in *IMPERFECT TRUST*.

JONAS CAMERON - third sibling in age, a former Special Forces sniper, and the current director of breeding service for the Triple C Horse Ranch.

SHEA TOWNSEND - trained chef, current cook for the Calico Diner, on-call substitute elementary school teacher, and part-time caterer. More of her story will emerge with the upcoming book, *IMPERFECT PROMISES*.

CASSIDY CAMERON - youngest of the Cameron siblings, a recent graduate with a degree in physical therapy; she recently returned to the Cameron fold.

DEPUTY DEREK NAUGHTON - former Navy SEAL, former member of a covert Bureau of International Intelligence special operations team, and current deputy in Hastings Bluff. Derek and Cassidy begin their story with award-winning *IMPERFECT BONDS*.

CODY CAMERON - Owner of the Triple C Horse Ranch in Hastings Bluff. Married to Cate. Father of Garrett, Wade, Jonas, Mallory, and Cassidy.

CATE CAMERON – Wife and bestselling author. Married to Cody. Mother of Garrett, Wade, Jonas, Mallory, and Cassidy.

SUPPORTING CHARACTERS

DIRECTOR KEVIN FOWLER - career agent with the Bureau of International Intelligence in charge of North and South American operations with oversight into Africa, the Middle East, and Europe. Mission Leader for the covert operation into Nigeria.

DEPUTY KYLE ABBOTT - former Marine; former member of a covert Bureau of International Intelligence special operations team, and current deputy in Hastings Bluff.

OLIVIA ASHCROFT (EVERS) – childhood friend and alleged wife of Sheriff James Ever.

JARED KINSLOE – senior section editor for the Seattle newspaper.

JAMES EDGAR FITZHUGH EVERS, III – ailing father of

Sheriff James Evers.

JOHN ARCHER – former Special Forces sniper, current covert operative for the Bureau of International Intelligence on assignment as bodyguard for Mallory Cameron.

SISTER AGATHA – nun at the Sisters of Mercy refugee camp in Nigeria.

SISTER MARY MAGDALENA – nun at the Sisters of Mercy refugee camp in Nigeria.

MAYAƙAN – an offshoot of the Nigerian Boko Haram terrorists.

THE EXTRACTION TEAMS

Alpha Team	Bravo Team	Charlie Team
"HOUDINI" (Kevin Fowler)	"ROMEO" (Kyle Abbott)	"TREEKILLER" (John Archer)
"DAWG" (James Evers)	"GHOST" (Jonas Cameron)	"COWBOY" (Garrett Cameron)
"MADMAN"	"COCHISE" (Wade Cameron)	"RUBY"

Helicopter Pilots

"CRASH"

"SPIDER"

Dedication

IMPERFECT LIES is dedicated to my readers,
because you're the reason I do this.
It's your kind words, encouragement,
suggestions, and support
that make the journey worthwhile.

Chapter One

"Yes!"

Mallory clapped a hand over her mouth, startled by how loud her shout sounded in the empty house. She wanted to giggle, jump up and down, and shout to the world. The New York Times had seen her article! They knew her name. Chicago and Seattle, too. They wanted her to come for job interviews. Her. Mallory Cameron, from Hastings Bluff, Idaho.

A dozen twirls around the kitchen left her a little breathless, but did nothing to slow the adrenalin rush. She flopped onto one of the tall barstools, jumped up again, and paced the kitchen. Of all the times for her family to disappear on her. Here she'd just received the biggest news of her life and had no one to share it with.

She could talk to TJ, but her brand-new sister-in-law

wouldn't be free until late in the afternoon. The principal of the elementary school in Challis where TJ taught frowned on cell phone use during class hours.

Jonas was an option. Mallory considered a run over to the big barn, but decided against it. The youngest of her brothers had left out before dawn that morning, concerned about one of the mares due to foal. *If* he took the time to listen to her, all he would offer was a caveman grunt, and then they'd both feel weird.

Her thoughts turned outside the family to her friend, Shea, who worked at the diner, but a quick glance at her wristwatch nixed that idea. By the time Mallory finished her chores, got cleaned up, and drove into town, the lunch rush would be in full swing there. Shea wouldn't have time to breathe between orders, much less sit down and chat.

Mallory tapped her lips with an index finger and smiled. Hazel eyes came to mind. "James, it is," she said aloud. "Even sheriffs have to eat sometimes, right?"

Her oldest brother, Garrett, had brought him home more than two years ago to recuperate from an injury. A shudder went through her at the memory of the ragged gunshot wound in his side. He'd been grumpy at his helplessness, but also grateful for help in his vulnerable state. She'd fallen a little in love with him that day, and sank deeper with every day that passed.

Regardless of whether he reciprocated her feelings, James was a friend. She tapped out a quick text and hit send. *Free for lunch?*

His reply came back seconds later. *Sure. Come by the office.*

Her stomach lurched. Would it upset him to know she might move away, or would he wish her well and say goodbye? She'd find out soon enough.

Be there at 11.

Chores first. Rascal, their foreman and her dad's oldest friend, had asked her to feed and water the animals in the small barn adjacent to the house this morning. She didn't mind, but it worried her a little. Rascal never asked for help. The foaling mare must have a problem.

In the mud room off the kitchen, Mallory slipped her cell phone in her jeans pocket and donned a heavy jacket. She stomped her feet into well-worn boots and stepped outside into the brisk morning air.

A flock of birds drew her attention as she walked to the barn. The black mass swooped and wheeled in complete synchronization, until they lit among the treetops behind the barn. Bare limbs swayed in the light breeze. Denuded branches coated with hoarfrost glistened in the weak sunlight and framed the dark clump against the gray sky.

A moment later, the birds erupted from the branches in a furious cloud, and disappeared beyond the forest.

Uneasiness made her skin crawl. Ravens had long been considered harbingers of bad luck, probably because of their glossy black plumage.

She shoved the superstitious thoughts away. Anything could startle a flock of birds—rustles in the underbrush, a glint of sunlight on metal, a sudden wind … or perhaps the primal instinct all animals possessed when danger loomed.

The same intuition that made the hair on her arms stand on end.

Unnerved by where her imagination led, she ended that train of thought and entered the heated barn through the small door on the side. The big sliding doors stayed closed in the winter months, opened only when the horses were taken out for riding or exercise.

Soft whinnies greeted her. The horses knew breakfast was late.

Mallory chattered, aware of how her voice soothed the animals. "I know, I know. I'm late. Bet you guys are hungry, huh? Well, hold your horses." A laugh burst out at the pun Rascal always used.

Using the scoop in the barrel, she measured oats into one pail and fortified feed into another, enough for all seven horses. Let the feeding frenzy begin. Thank goodness, one of the hands would come over and muck the stalls later.

When she reached the empty stall at the end, her throat tightened. Buffy's loss had hit her sister, Cassie, hard. All of them, really. Such a senseless waste.

Mallory blinked away unexpected tears and headed

outside to tend to Edwina, the ornery old billy goat she and Cassie had rescued once upon a time. With everything stored away again, it was time for a much-needed shower.

Three steps outside the barn, the stillness made itself known. The wind had died down, but everyday sounds should still remain—bird titters, rustling branches, small animals in the underbrush, whinnies from the pastured horses.

That same awareness she'd felt on her way out here returned, a sense that if she turned at the right moment …

Wow, her imagination had a mind of its own this morning. She put a clamp on the wayward thoughts, but did a slow, three-sixty sweep of the surroundings anyway.

All of nature seemed to hold its breath.

Unnerved again, she hurried for the safety of the house.

Inside, the deadbolt on the kitchen door complained from lack of use. The family seldom locked up given the distance of the ranch from town. They'd even given up on the state-of-the-art security system that her middle brother, Wade, installed two years past. No one came this way unless they had a reason to. And when they did, the locked gate at the property's entrance announced their presence.

Mallory considered rearming the security system as she shrugged out of her coat. Garrett always said you should trust your gut. She pulled off her boots, patted her pocket to make sure she had her phone, and started toward the front of the house. Whether imagined or real, she would feel better with locked doors and windows between her and whatever lurked out there.

The quiet snick of the front door lock and chain fed her uneasiness. She finished a sweep of the first-floor entry points, windows included, and decided to rearm the security system.

Jonas would probably set the alarm off when he came home. He'd get mad, and then make fun of her.

Tough.

She headed upstairs.

The grandfather clock in the foyer struck a double four-count of Westminster quarter chimes. Half past ten. Feeding the horses had taken longer than she expected.

She made short work of checking all the upstairs windows and hurried through her shower. Time for her battle gear. The black skinny jeans should get the job done, the ones Dad called 'vacuum-sealed.' Paired with her new Lively boots and the sapphire turtleneck that made her eyes pop, James wouldn't stand a chance. He was, after all, a man.

Fifteen minutes later, Mallory pulled on her new Shearling jacket and a pair of leather gloves, and started for the barn again. Alert and wary, her eyes strayed from side to side, in constant motion.

She covered the distance between house and barn in record time, surprised when her anxiety didn't return. What also surprised her was the big F-150 Super Crew Raptor in all its shiny black and chrome Ford beauty parked next to her sister's little Ranger.

Jonas must have come back while she showered.

Mallory changed directions and stepped inside the barn. "Jo?"

No answer.

"Jonas?"

Her footsteps slowed. Diablo's stall stood empty. Jonas had taken his horse and ridden into the mountains again. Which meant something bad must have happened.

Wade claimed Jonas had nightmares and sometimes just needed time alone, to find peace and quiet. Curious how her two oldest brothers had seen a ton of deadly action in the Middle East, but didn't feel the same need for solitude that Jonas did.

These solitary jaunts of his had increased in frequency. Lately, his jokester nature made fewer and fewer appearances. How long would he stay away this time? Two days? Three? That thought made her worry grow. Jonas knew how much she hated staying alone in the house.

She whipped her cell phone out and pressed pound-five, the speed dial number for Jonas.

The call went straight to voice mail.

Of course, it did. She dialed pound-eight next.

Rascal answered on the first ring. "H'lo."

"Why is Jonas's truck parked at the house?"

A long silence. "We lost them both, the dam and the foal."

Both? The news crushed her. How much worse for her brother. Jonas put his heart and soul into the Triple C breeding program. "He took Diablo."

"Figured he would. Let him be, honey. If he's not back in a couple of days, I'll go check on him."

"Thanks, Rascal. I'm so sorry."

"Me, too, little girl."

The thrill of the phone calls she'd received that morning disappeared. Her eagerness to see James receded. She almost sent him a text to cancel, but then wondered why. Not seeing James wouldn't bring the mare or the foal back. And she still wanted to share her good news.

She climbed in her sister's truck. After Cassie lost her driver's license and Mallory totaled her Honda, there didn't seem to be any urgency in replacing her car. A quick twist of the key and … nothing. Not even a click. A second attempt yielded the same result.

"Are you kidding?" Dad took it in for the 60,000-mile service last month. It should work fine. She pounded the steering wheel. "Aaaagh."

Okay, now what?

Had the weather not turned bitter cold, she'd consider riding one of the horses into town. But that would take too long, plus she'd end up smelling like Eau de Horse Sweat. Ugh.

She could call James. He would come get her, but she wanted her own way home if things turned awkward between them.

She turned her head and stared at Jonas's truck.

These jaunts of his typically lasted one or two days, sometimes more. He'd kill her if he found out. Jonas had named the darned thing, for Pete's sake. He didn't let anyone, not even Dad, drive *Darcie*.

But he wouldn't know.

With a silent promise to be uber-careful, Mallory entered the small office inside the barn and twisted the combination on the lock box. An array of keychains hung on hooks inside, one for each of the family vehicles—a horsehead for Dad, a tiny BMW logo for Mom, and giant letters for the rest of them. She grabbed the "J" and hurried back outside. One click and … *beep-beep.* The doors unlocked. Lights flashed.

It took her several minutes to readjust the seat and mirrors to fit her more diminutive five-feet-five height. Jonas took after their dad and the other brothers. At well over six feet, they all had legs that stretched into tomorrow. "Please, Lord, help me remember all the settings so I can put everything back the way it was."

Darcie's roar made her little Ranger sound like a sewing machine. Mallory reached for the gearshift. She hesitated. What if Jonas did come back?

An old gas receipt nestled in the cup holder between

the seats. A pen that had teeth marks on it lay on the floor. She scribbled a quick message and made a mad dash to secure the note under the Ranger's windshield wiper.

Guilt assuaged, she climbed back inside and shoved the truck into gear. Time to go.

The drive from the house to the main road spanned not quite two miles. She slowed as the double-entry neared, and punched every button on the visor until one triggered the opening.

The left gate jerked, out of sync with the other one.

She made a mental note to tell Rascal, and then drove through in the middle of the lane.

A thump and a crunch sent a shockwave through the truck.

"No, no, no." Mallory glanced in the rearview mirror and saw the faulty gate rebound off the rear of Jonas's truck.

Once clear of the entry, she hopped out to check the damage. The glass bulb of the taillight remained intact, thank goodness, but a pile of red plastic shards lay on the ground, all that remained of the cover.

"Agggh!" She threw her hands up in the air. "Jonas will kill me."

Her mind jumped into problem-solving mode. Toby, down at Wrangler's Auto Parts and Service, could order a replacement. She'd pay to have it overnighted. Maybe he would deliver and install taillight cover, and take a look at

Cassie's truck while he was there.

Behind her the defective gate closed flush with the other one, but then it drifted ajar a good two-feet. A swift kick wouldn't accomplish anything, except maybe bruise her foot. She squatted and gathered up the plastic fragments instead. Now, she was late, and Mr. Punctual, a.k.a., Sheriff James Evers, would give her grief about it.

Imperfect Lies

Chapter Two

James looked out the window for the third time in as many minutes. Mallory was late. It didn't take much to make him worry about her.

A faded blue jalopy of a truck chugged down Main Street, the rounded bonnet and clunky grillwork reminiscent of the 1940s. He tracked the ancient vehicle until it disappeared from sight, a thick plume of exhaust was all that remained. How many trucks did Judd Wheeler have out behind his barn? Eight or ten, at least, some of them older than the old geezer himself. And they all still ran. Sort of.

His cell phone buzzed with a text message.

He didn't recognize the number, not that it mattered. He recognized the single word on the screen. And what it meant.

Gestalt.

Time stopped. Everything faded away. Some commitments never ended.

James and his former teammates had left the government organization that controlled their lives for years. They were all civilians now, and yet the team remained one of the parts that summed up the whole. Always would. One of those imperfect truths you learned along the way. Or was it an imperfect lie? Only Fowler would dare demand action from a now defunct covert militia.

From the locked bottom drawer of his desk, James retrieved his personal laptop. Top of the line, as secure as any computer out there, it came equipped with amnesiac software that eliminated footprints and tracking cookies, and blocked stealth malware attacks that targeted the user's background movements. He typed a web address in the browser, a domain that made no sense to anyone not in the know. Nine security layers and fourteen checkpoints later, James entered his own unique, eighteen-character, alpha-numeric, nonsensical password phrase, and opened another secure domain where a protected mailbox resided.

He hated the apprehension that unfurled in his gut. None of the messages Fowler sent via this protocol ever contained good news.

The little hourglass on the screen spun for a few seconds, and there it was. A single email appeared in his inbox. Subject: Report. Status: *ThreatCon Charlie.*

His lungs resumed breathing.

The *Charlie* designation reflected a non-specific but viable threat validated by two or more credible sources. A potential danger, but not imminent.

A *Bravo* label, on the other hand, indicated an imminent or already in progress threat that required immediate response. *Alpha* was reserved for the direst circumstances, as in action required yesterday. Such a threat would in all likelihood result in Fowler's arrival on their doorstep, unexpected, uninvited, and with an army in his wake.

Now that he thought on it, he recalled a couple of recent visits where Fowler had done just that.

James double-clicked on the attached report, read through the first paragraph, and skipped to the Summary Analysis at the end.

The threat is a militant jihadist group, an offshoot of Ansaru, which itself is a splinter group of the larger Boko Haram organization. As yet unnamed, the threat operates near the northeast border of Borno State in Nigeria where the strip of land called Cameroon's Neck and the country of Chad all come together.

New terrorist factions cropped up every week. The established groups either absorbed the upstarts into their organization, or eliminated them. How did this new group slip through?

The threat's target is unidentified at the time of this report. However, communiques of inquiry were intercepted specifying target's location—the western United States, specifically the town of Hastings Bluff and surrounding areas of Custer County, Idaho.

Well, that wasn't good. He needed to brief Garrett, Derek, and Kyle as soon as Garrett returned from wherever the heck he'd gone. Might as well include Wade and Jonas since his gut told him the target was one of their group.

Another thought struck him as he logged out and re-secured the laptop, one that chilled his blood. Two other potential targets he hadn't considered—Mallory and Cassie—had a tenuous Nigerian connection.

James tucked that tidbit away for later consideration. Right now, Mallory claimed his full attention, even if he couldn't act on his desires.

Soon, though. The expensive, high-powered Nevada attorney he'd retained promised he'd have his life back in a month, two tops. Which meant a future he could offer with a clear conscience. That's when he'd show Mallory how he felt. And—oh, brother—share his intentions with her daddy.

The front door squeaked open. His head jerked up.

"Hey, Lorraine. The sheriff in?" Mallory's voice had a smoky quality that punched him in the gut.

A cross between a growl and a whimper clawed its way out of his chest and, right on cue, a swarm of bumblebees took flight in his stomach.

"James, Mallory's here."

Lorraine's screech made him cringe, but years of enforced social decorum prevented him from yelling back. Instead, he walked out and tried to hold his grin in check. Mallory had arrived at last. "Good morning, princess."

She removed her jacket, slung it over one shoulder, crossed the office. Those tight jeans, that sweater ... the woman could conduct electricity in those clothes.

He swallowed hard and yanked his gaze up to her face. Mallory knew what had gone through his mind. He could see it in her blue eyes, in the way her lips twitched. Naughty girl.

"I wonder, can a girl buy a hardworking sheriff lunch as a token of her ... appreciation?"

She wanted to play? Okay. He knew this game. "An observant bystander might construe your offer as an attempted bribe, Miss Cameron."

"What, for a little act of community gratitude like lunch?" She sashayed toward his desk in a slow, liquid glide. Mallory had perfected the look of wide-eyed innocence. "A bribe would require ... more. Don't you agree?"

More?

She dipped her chin and looked up at him.

His brain waves spiked. James wiped a hand over his mouth and prayed he'd find no drool. Time for safer

waters. "You, ah, mentioned news. Want to discuss it now? Or wait until we get lunch?"

Her taunting smile blossomed into a huge grin. "I can't believe it. You know that article I wrote on human trafficking? Did you ever read it?"

He nodded. "Of course, I did. It was great. You captured the desperation and despair, and made it come alive."

A pale pink blush stained her cheeks. "Thanks. It's received a lot of attention on a national level, and quite a bit of international recognition, too. In fact, I had two calls yesterday, and one this morning, all inviting me for job interviews. Practically my whole family is out of town, though. I needed to share my good news with someone, so I picked … you."

"That's great, Mallory. Give me the details."

Her voice trembled with excitement, but somehow that same enthusiasm didn't find its way into her eyes.

"The first call came from the Seattle Times, the second from the Sun-Times Media Group in Chicago, and the third, the New York Times. It's still so unreal. I can't imagine living in a big city."

He watched her mouth form the words, saw her tick off each call on a finger. The woman seemed to have no idea of the effect she— "Wait. Where?"

"You aren't listening. I swear, you're about as attentive as Jonas. Seattle, Chicago, and New York City.

Seattle wants me there next week, the day after Thanksgiving. The other two want to schedule me sometime before Christmas."

"But ..." Words didn't often fail him. They did now.

"The New York job is almost all travel. All over the world. I wonder if I'd have my own cameraman and an expense allowance. The Chicago position is a city beat, so I'd have to move there, but Seattle sounds promising. There's some travel involved, and I think they might let me work from home when I'm not off on an assignment."

"Uh ..."

"I keep pinching myself. I can't believe they want me."

He couldn't believe she would leave. "Of course, they want you, Mallory. You're smart, intelligent, and you have a remarkable talent, but are you sure?"

She grew pensive. The light in her eyes faded. "I've lived here all my life, James. I've only been to one other state, and that was for a family vacation in Jackson Hole, a whopping four hours away. I'm pitiful. I've never even flown on a plane."

And just like that, the bees in his belly took a nosedive. He'd known she led a sheltered life, just not that sheltered. New York City would chew her up and spit her out.

"You sure? I mean—"

He threw his hands in the air. What did he mean? He had no clue except if she left it would decimate him. But

he sure hadn't given her any reason to stay.

A sad facsimile of her earlier smile touched her mouth. "I hoped you'd help me sort through the pros and cons, help me decide which one to take. Or not."

He looked away. No way he'd help her make that decision, not if it meant she left him.

"James?"

He met her gaze, fell under her spell. Without conscious thought, he took a step closer, caressed her cheek. "I don't want you to leave, princess."

She pulled that plump lower lip between her teeth and bit it … and then swayed toward him.

Magic ignited. Inch by slow, languid inch, he moved in. Stared at her face. Her mouth. His hand found its way to the back of her neck and pulled her closer.

"My, my, my, Jameson," a sugary-sweet voice broke in. "Did I interrupt something?"

Mallory recoiled from him. Her pretty pink blush turned dark red.

James stared over her shoulder, unable to move or take a breath. He'd been pinned under heavy fire, knocked down by shock grenades, deafened by mortar rounds, shot twice, and survived insurmountable odds, but nothing had ever unmanned him like the woman in his doorway. His nightmare past was alive and well, and determined to make him pay.

Mallory whirled around. Confusion knit her brows

together, and then she tilted her head to one side. "Who are you?"

Every runway-perfect inch of Olivia Ashcroft glided inside the room. With a practiced flick of long ashen hair, she lifted her patrician nose. No one did haughty better than the Ashcrofts. He should know.

Powerless to stop the impending disaster, James had a terrible premonition of what hell must feel like. Every instinct screamed run, hit the dirt, hide, get out of Dodge. He sank into his chair instead.

His biggest mistake had caught up with him, one he should have rectified a long time ago. Never in any scenario did he imagine Olivia would show up in Idaho. Pitch a tantrum? Yes. Cry for her daddy? Yes. Maybe even approach his own father for reinforcement, but the consummate socialite and heiress he'd grown up with didn't do rural. Nevertheless, she'd come here despite her delicate sensibilities. For blood. His blood. Olivia wanted payback for having her served with papers in front of her friends.

Olivia's amused chuckle raised his hackles. "Secrets, Jameson?" She stared at Mallory, disdain dripping, but she pointed a long, red-lacquered nail at him. "That, my sweet, naïve little country bumpkin, is Jameson Edgar Fitzhugh Evers, the fourth. And I am Olivia Ashcroft Evers, his wife."

Imperfect Lies

Chapter Three

Wife?

The word stuck in Mallory's throat. Her mind sputtered like a missing sparkplug, but her heart had caught on. Proof came from the out-of-beat clamor inside her chest.

She stared at the goddess in the doorway. High cheekbones, delicate nose, perfectly sculpted lips, a porcelain complexion—all framed by long, Nordic-blonde hair. Beautiful seemed a woefully inadequate description. Until those pale blue eyes impaled you. Ice chips. Cold. Disdainful. No beauty there.

But … *wife?*

With effort, she tore her gaze from the hostile woman. "James?"

He'd slumped in his chair, elbows on knees, head in

his hands. "I'm sorry."

The arrogant warrior was gone. No sign existed of her brothers' friend or the adoptive son her parents had taken in. Not a hint remained of the honorable man the people of Hastings Bluff had elected as their sheriff. Just an empty, defeated husk.

Seeing him broken cleared her confusion. James had a wife. He'd lied. To everyone.

No, not James. Her James didn't exist, only Jameson Fitz-whatever-Evers the fourth. She'd fallen for a fake. A fantasy. A lie.

A fine tremor started at the tips of her fingers and built until her whole body shook. Something fragile and precious shattered inside her. Then, Cameron DNA came to the rescue. Mallory lifted her chin and straightened to her full height. Pride, a fierce stare, and a snarled, "Excuse me," got her past the woman and out the door.

Outside James's office, a wide-eyed, open-mouthed Lorraine bumbled out of the way. Perfect. The epicenter of all Hastings Bluff gossip had heard every word. Everybody in a hundred-mile radius would know of her humiliation and rejection by sundown.

"Mallory, wait," James called. "Please."

Surprise made her falter. She'd never heard James plead, not that it made a difference. She'd already wasted three long years waiting for him. No more.

The front door opened and Agnes Tillberry stepped

inside.

Could the day get any worse?

The birdlike woman, once the principal of the high school she and her siblings had attended, took two seconds before a frown appeared. "What's wrong?"

"Sorry," Mallory choked out. Oh mercy, not here, not now. Not in front of James.

She darted past Miz Tillberry and ran out the door.

The tears wouldn't be denied much longer. Even so, Mallory held her head high and marched across and down the street past the diner. Blurry eyes and shaky hands made it difficult to find and extract the key from her purse. And then she dropped the darned thing. The giant silver "J" skittered under the truck.

The tears would have fallen then but for several hard swallows, a spate of furious blinks, and a throat squeezed so tight it threatened to choke her. Mallory dropped to her knees and patted the ground under the truck in search of the elusive key.

"Mallory, dear? Why don't you come home with me for tea?"

A pair of sturdy black granny-style shoes stood close by. Thick woolen hose covered thin legs that peeked out from beneath a long tweed skirt. Miz Tillberry was a nurturer, a fixer, and not at all what Mallory wanted right now. But she couldn't ignore the kindly woman who'd known her since birth.

Rudeness wasn't an option, either, so Mallory grabbed the wayward key, swiped at a rogue tear, and looked anywhere but at Miz Tillberry's wrinkled face. "Uh … I … can't."

To Mallory's mortification, raw emotion made her voice crack. How much more could she endure?

"Nonsense. Bite your lip, pinch your arm, slap your face—do whatever necessary, but pull yourself together and come help me climb into this ridiculous rig. You can park behind my house. You'll have the whole afternoon safe from prying eyes. Come along, now."

Miz Tillberry's shock tactics worked. With a meekness foreign to her, Mallory followed the scrappy old woman around the truck and opened the door for her.

They both stared at the chrome step that stood a good eighteen inches off the ground.

Mallory looked at the truck, and then at Miz Tillberry. They'd need a miracle to get her inside.

"Okay, let's do this." With a death grip on the door, Miz. Tillberry somehow got one foot on the step. Unfortunately, flexibility was not one of her strong suits. Her body canted to one side.

Frantic the frail old lady might fall and break something, Mallory wrapped her arms around the older woman's waist.

"Push, girl," Miz Tillberry instructed. "I'm almost in."

Hardly. Mallory grunted from the strain of holding the

other woman upright. She blew out a breath to clear the hair out of her eyes. "This won't work, Miz T. Put your foot back on the ground."

Mallory held onto Miz Tillberry until the old woman had both feet firmly on the ground again. Both of them leaned against the truck and panted like they'd run an uphill mile.

"You don't … think anyone … saw us … do you?" Miz Tillberry sucked in air as though it might be her last.

That earned a chuckle. Mallory looked around for inspiration. "We need another plan."

"I quite agree." An embroidered hankie appeared in Miz Tillberry's hand from who knew where. She proceeded to make dainty dabs over her wrinkled neck and forehead.

A dusty red pickup pulled into a space a few places down.

"Wait here," Mallory instructed her determined friend before marching over to the new arrival.

Fred Robison, a handyman who did odd jobs around town, and even better, was an old friend of her father's, got out of the truck.

"Hey, Fred. Got a minute? We could use your help.'

Fred removed a grimy ballcap and resettled it on his bald head. Sharp, brown eyes peered out at her from behind thick black-framed glasses. "Sure thing, Miss Mallory. What do you need?"

Mallory stretched up on her tiptoes and peered into Fred's truck bed. He had a reputation for hoarding, and always carried a lot of junk. She saw two-by-fours stacked in the back, rope, a battered gas can, rakes, shovels, a chain saw, a monstrous tool case ... and two cinder blocks. "We could use one those. Miz Tillberry needs a step."

The handyman looked over to where Miz Tillberry waited. "Jonas let you drive his new truck?"

"Just this once." A guilty twinge made her look away, even as she crossed her fingers behind her. Did a white lie count against you? "I've been using Cassie's truck, but it died this morning."

Good enough for Fred. He hefted one of the cinder blocks over the side, carried it over to where Miz Tillberry stood, and set it on the ground. "Let me help you up, ma'am."

Miz Tillberry gave him a gracious nod and accepted the offered hand. "You are a true gentleman, Fred Robison. Thank you kindly." She made it inside without a problem, tucked her skirt around her ankles, and buckled the seatbelt.

Mallory covered a snicker by coughing, and then pressed her lips together. Tight. "Can I keep it?" She pointed at the cinder block. "We'll need it for her to get down."

"Sure. I'll load it for you." Fred closed the passenger door and hoisted the cinder block into the back of Jonas's truck. "Hope it don't scratch the paint. Wouldn't want your brother mad at me."

"Thanks, Fred. Don't you worry about the paint. Any scratches will be on me. I'll return your cinder block."

"Not worried. You take care." He re-seated his cap once more, and then waved as he headed for the diner.

Mallory almost smiled again. Five minutes with Miz Tillberry had chased her tears away. For now.

A heavy metal tune greeted her when she opened her door.

"I believe your purse is singing, dear. Mr. *Bad to the Bone* is quite insistent."

"Not important." She already knew the identity of the caller, and couldn't deal with James right now. If ever.

A chime sounded. He'd left a voice mail. A few seconds later a different chime sounded—a text message alert. And then another. She picked up her phone and glared at the string of "missed call" notifications.

The beeps and tones continued through the duration of their ride. Mallory pulled around back of Miz Tillberry's house as instructed, but had to climb into the truck bed for the cinder block. No way she could lift it over the side like Fred. A long rasp along the floor made her flinch.

Jonas was so gonna kill her.

Miz Tillberry's descent, though a bit harrowing, went much easier. Inside, both women flopped into chairs at the kitchen table.

The frou-frou handkerchief reappeared in Miz Tillberry's hand, used as a fan this time. "Next time I'll walk."

Mallory's giggle contained a hint of hysteria. She clapped a hand over her mouth and squeezed her eyes shut.

"It's okay, dear. You're safe here. You can let it out now."

Banked tears held too long in check spilled over. A wretched sob worked its way up from the depths of her soul. Mallory crossed her arms on the bright yellow table cloth, buried her face, and surrendered to the destruction of her world.

Miz Tillberry hummed and puttered about the kitchen, filled the tea kettle, and rattled cups and saucers. No pity, platitudes, or false assurances. No demands.

In time, the tea kettle whistled. A steaming cup of tea appeared on the table, along with a box of tissues. At least the incessant phone calls had stopped.

Several tissues later, Mallory took a sip of the fragrant tea, and dared look at her companion. Miz Tillberry's expression held sadness and compassion, even understanding. But no pity. Age had no boundary for two strong women in sync with each other.

Mallory attempted a halfhearted smile through the residual sniffles. And then her phone buzzed again. She pulled it from her purse, saw James's name again, and choked on another sob.

"He worries about you. Any man worth his salt would."

Mallory snorted. Not a good move. She reached for another tissue.

"He won't go away, you know," Miz Tillberry went on. "He needs to explain, and you deserve an explanation."

A wise woman. Knowing James, he'd tear the town apart looking for her if she didn't answer.

"He's married." Her voice broke again. "How do you explain away a *wife*?"

Miz Tillberry nodded and refilled their teacups. "I'm not sure you can, but he seems to think it's necessary."

"I can't. Not yet. Not like this."

"I agree. You should stay with me tonight. Send James a message. Tell him you'll talk tomorrow, and then turn your phone off. That will give you time to wrap your mind around everything. Send TJ and Rascal messages, too. So they don't worry."

"I don't want—"

Miz Tillberry's hand shot up. "Not another word. "I have an extra toothbrush still in its packaging and a nightgown you can borrow. Nothing fancy, but it's clean and serviceable. Now, pull yourself together, send your texts, turn your phone off, and come help me put fresh sheets on your bed."

"Thank you, Miz T." Just when she thought the tears were done, the waterworks started again.

"No thanks necessary, dear." Kindness filled the older woman's hug.

James had seen horrors that made a grown man cry, done things no man should ever be asked to do, and never once wavered in his duty. But Mallory walking out of his office—out of his life—destroyed him. He wanted to howl from the pain he'd caused her.

"Mallory, wait." She couldn't leave, not without hearing the truth.

She didn't stop or even slow down. Had Olivia not stepped aside, Mallory would have plowed over her.

In that moment, he realized how formidable the battle ahead of him would be. All the Camerons had an ample portion of fierce pride. Add a hair-trigger temper and ... yeah, a fix wouldn't be simple or easy.

"Please."

Olivia blocked him from following. "Let her go, Jameson. We have more important things to discuss."

His fingers curled into fists at his side. The little girl he'd played with as a child, the privileged teenager with braces, even the shy college girl he'd once trusted was gone. The woman in her place had all the beauty money could buy, but she'd grown cold and ruthless.

Fury at the damage she'd inflicted strained his control.

He crowded her space, forced her back a step. "Have your attorney call mine."

"You embarrassed me."

He didn't bat an eye.

"What you did was low," she went on, but uncertainty lurked in her eyes now. "We're legally married whether you like it or not. And you've made your father furious."

"My father has no say in my life. You both should know this by now."

A flash of a plaid fluttered at the door. He looked over and saw Lorraine nearby, and Miz Tillberry, of all people, slipping out the front door.

James yanked Olivia into his office and slammed the door. Lorraine probably had her cronies on speed dial. The whole town would know all the ugly details before the lunch hour passed.

Olivia yelped at his rough treatment, which only fueled his anger.

"Sit." He shoved her toward the chairs in front of his desk. No more nice. She didn't deserve nice.

"James—"

"Be quiet a minute. Are you capable of that one small mercy?"

Thinly arched eyebrows flattened into a glower. Her rosebud lips pressed tight in displeasure. She sat down with a huff.

James paced the room. He stopped at the window and

stared out at nothing, unable to un-see the devastation in Mallory's eyes.

The tap-tap-tap of long fingernails on the wooden chair arm broke through his panic. Mallory would have to wait. First order of business: evict his *wife* from his life once and for all.

Steeling himself, he turned and confronted his past. "Okay, talk. Why, Olivia? Why did you do it?"

Emotion flitted across Olivia's face, gone before he could give it a name. Guilt? Remorse? No matter. She'd mastered the art of feminine wiles, and called on those skills now. Her lower lip trembled into a pout. She placed a hand over her heart. The capper, though, came with the crocodile tears.

"I see you're still obsessive and controlling, but you can't possibly blame me for your drinking problem."

"Ah, but I've always had a two-drink rule. You didn't know that, did you? It's part of my obsessive controlling personality. I don't drink at all anymore, not since that night. So, help me understand how one, two drinks at most, put me on my face?"

"Obviously, you broke your own rule. Look, I'm not at fault here. Limits or not, you're the one who drank too much. You're the one who proposed."

Her over-confidence and the calculation in her eyes irked him.

"You know, Ollie—"

"Don't call me that," she snapped. Angry wasn't a pretty look for her.

He smiled without a smidgeon of amusement. "I don't remember much of our so-called wedding night, but I do recall how I ran into you and your cousin, Richard, at the Venetian. One drink there, and then we hit Tao." Visions of the Asian-inspired bar filled his mind. Strobe lights. Crazy-loud music. A water feature. He'd ordered a club soda. And then his memory blanked.

Olivia's expression hardened. "You can't possibly remember anything. You were so drunk by the time we left Tao, you couldn't walk without help."

"I know I would never willingly marry you, drunk or sober."

A flash of hurt became a seductive smirk. "You were more than attracted to me on our wedding night."

"I doubt it. Was that before or after you dumped me on the floor of my hotel room?"

Confusion filled her face. And then concern. "You can't possibly kn—" Her fingers covered her mouth.

"What? Know your pals dragged me through the casino? Into the elevator? Tell me, if it was my idea, why'd you go along with it?"

A shadow of uneasiness wiped away her confidence, right before she lifted her patrician nose in the air. "I've always loved you, Jameson. I wanted to marry you. Our night was amaz—"

His bark of laughter shut her up. "No. It wasn't. We didn't. You say you love me, and yet I woke up in my hotel room, alone, fully dressed, and covered in vomit."

"What?"

"The maid found me the next morning and called 911, which in all likelihood saved my life.

Pure unadulterated shock froze her features. "911?"

"You wouldn't know, now would you? Because you'd hopped the first flight out."

Her eyes darted around the room as she floundered for a comeback, and then repugnance took over. "Ugh, what did you expect? You were disgusting, vulgar, and rude, and then you passed out on me. I left because I knew you'd be embarrassed. I expected you to follow me home and make amends."

He laughed again, a real laugh this time. And then his voice went deadly soft. "I have the lab reports from the hospital, you know. The surveillance tapes, too, one from every place we went. You, your cousin, and some other goon carried me into the Elvis Chapel and then to the Venetian."

"I don't know what you mean."

Disgust unleashed a wave of nausea. "Give it up. I know my father is behind this. He pumped a hundred thousand dollars into your account. You thought you'd get access to my trust fund, didn't you?"

Her eyes went icy. "It's her, isn't it? The country

mouse I ran off."

"Stop the games and sign the annulment papers."

The flush in her cheeks faded, leaving her porcelain skin much too pale. "Never."

"Then I'll file for divorce and see you in court. Do you really want your dirty laundry aired in public? The drugs? The gambling? The underground club? However this goes, I'm done with you."

Her eyes filled with shock. Her nostrils flared. Panic edged her voice. "We can make it work, I know we can."

"I don't love you. I don't even like you. And I want you out of my life. Is that clear enough?"

Agitated, Olivia flounced from the chair. "Well, it's obvious I caught you by surprise today. I'll give you time to calm down. We'll talk again."

The door opened.

"Olivia?"

She looked over her shoulder.

"Sign the papers, or I will ruin you."

And he would, too. But right now, he had fences to mend with Mallory. He just hoped she'd let him.

Chapter Four

James rolled over and looked at the red numbers aglow on his clock radio. Quarter past way too early, and only thirty minutes later than the last time he looked. Daylight wouldn't show its face for a long time yet.

With a tired sigh that gave up on sleep, he swung his legs over the side of the bed and stretched. A shower, shave, and fresh uniform first, and then coffee.

Snow had fallen while he'd tried to sleep. Not enough to call out the plows, but sufficient to give the world a fresh, clean look. Buried under his heavy jacket, James set off on foot for the half-mile walk to the office.

Soon now, the town would start to stir. Cars, trucks, and school busses would leave their marks on the roads. Pedestrians would plant footprints in the landscape, and shop owners would venture out to sweep the sidewalks in front of their stores.

The people who lived and died here were an integral part of the land, every bit as much as the rivers, creeks, and mountains. Like the Western White Pine that covered most of the state, the locals not only survived, they thrived in the harsh environment.

His chest swelled with pride. Hastings Bluff was his town now. His responsibility. His home. And he'd do everything in his power to protect them.

Yesterday's threat alert from Fowler concerned him, as did the damage wrought by Olivia's unexpected appearance. He kept visualizing Mallory's face, the way her features came alive with excitement. The softness when desire heated her eyes. Cheeks pink with embarrassment when she thought they'd been discovered. And then, the stunned disbelief. The betrayal.

He swore the bullet he'd taken in Honduras hadn't hurt nearly as bad as the way Mallory looked right through him before she walked out.

The diner loomed ahead, looking exactly like a place called The Calico Diner should. Curtains with a flower-pattern adorned the windows, and inside—how many times had he sat on one of the red vinyl booths, or eaten at a table with the signature red-and-white checkered tablecloth? He could almost smell the bacon sizzling.

Two men loitered outside, waiting for Dee Dee to unlock the doors. One jabbed the other and gave a nod toward James.

Now, even the old codgers were giving him the side-eye. One day, Lorraine would go too far with her gossipy ways.

"Howdy, Sheriff." Percy Barnum's pack-a-day rasp sounded rough for this early in the day.

Both men tipped their ball caps.

"Morning, Percy, Earl." James touched his Stetson in return. He could feel their stares on his back.

He crossed the street and unlocked the front door of the Sheriff's Office, stepped inside and switched on the lights. The smell of beeswax, gun oil, and fresh paint from last week greeted him. The only thing lacking—coffee.

While the first pot brewed, James brought up the *ThreatCon* email from Fowler and reread it.

The report represented a variety of both foreign and domestic intelligence, gleaned by those who did nothing but listen to radio and telephone chatter day in and day out, pre-programmed internet bots that trolled the web 24/7 in search of key words used in online communications, informants who had their own axes to grind, and our own undercover boots on the ground.

The compilation analysts—those who pulled the pieces of the puzzle together—were typically genius-geeks who lived their entire lives behind a computer screen. They reviewed all the intel and used a proven matrix to discredit or validate every piece of data collected. The result? A

comprehensive and compelling summary. In this case, some very bad guys in Africa were looking for someone here in Hastings Bluff.

This particular report offered no assumptions on the identity of the target, but the detail, combined with James's own firsthand knowledge of the residents, helped him rule out the majority of men in the area. He had a growing suspicion the target might turn out to be one of his inner circle of friends.

He needed to brief his deputies. Garrett, too. The four of them had been teammates on the same special projects team for years, performing off the record services in undisclosed hotspots around the world. All without official sanction, of course. They didn't keep secrets from each other.

Might be a good idea to include the two younger Cameron brothers. Wade had gone the traditional military route and served two deployments in Afghanistan before an ambush ushered him out of the Army. He was a good man in a pinch. And then there was Jonas, who had so many deadly skills despite his one enlistment stint in the Army.

James went to the kitchenette to fill his cup. Not even six yet. Still too early for a visit to the Triple C. He'd scare Mallory to death if he pounded on her front door at this hour. Might as well take a look at the military record he'd requested on the younger brother from less than proper sources. It came a week ago, but he hadn't yet read it.

The very first line of the chronological record gave Jonas's enlistment date. That started James thinking. Both Garrett and Wade finished college, Garrett with a business degree and Wade with a double degree in Software Engineering and Communications Technology. Both went into the Army as officers, and ended their military careers with captain's bars.

Jonas chose enlistment over a commission, despite having earned a degree in Mathematics.

Nothing seemed unusual about his early assignments—Fort Benning for Basic Combat Training. Fort Bragg for Advanced Individual Training. Knowing Jonas, it would have been odd had he not been selected for AIT.

The next assignment took him back to Benning for Jump School. A PFC by then, Jonas requested and was admitted into the pre-selection process for special forces training. Back he went to Bragg.

James was both surprised and yet not surprised when the next assignment on the record listed Camp Mackall, the special forces training ground. It suggested that Jonas's intentions as well as the Army's expectations had changed.

A significant time lapse occurred before the next assignment was posted, most likely because of the extensive training required of all Special Operations Command soldiers.

At least the sniper stuff made sense now. What else had that boy learned?

Laying the report aside, James rubbed his temples. How much of this did Garrett know or perhaps suspect? Or their father, for that matter.

He flipped the page and saw Jonas's first real assignment, almost two years after his initial enlistment date. A Sergeant E5 by then, Jonas snagged a slot with the 10th Special Forces Group in Bad Tolz, Germany, and the center of the universe for special forces activity in Europe, Africa, and the Middle East. Six months later—

James sucked in a harsh breath. Jonas didn't get out when his enlistment period was up. He received a medical discharge.

Of all the horrible luck. Spec Ops guys invested blood, sweat, dreams, and every facet of their lives into the job. To go out like that … after all the work … and never let on.

He flipped to the last page and found the Medical Summary Report, a lone paragraph, sandwiched in between Jonas's performance reviews and DD-214, the Certificate of Release or Discharge from Active Duty.

DIAGNOSIS: Right knee subluxation.

RECOMMENDATION: Medical discharge.

REASON: Unfit to perform required duties.

"What the heck is a …?" With a growl, he swung around to his work computer, brought up Google, and mouthed the word as he typed. "Sub-lux-a-tion."

The definition that came up on the screen didn't make sense. He'd known men released for medical or psychological reasons, or for conditions that compromised their ability to do the job, conditions like amputation, PTSD, head injury, hearing loss, blindness, lots of reasons. But not for "a slight dislocation."

Leaning back in his chair, James let his mind roam while he tried to digest what he'd read.

Ranching was hard work. Jonas muscled horses around, some of them tipping the scales at more than a ton. He rode in the saddle for long stretches of time, and put in ten- and twelve-hour workdays, but not once had James ever seen him limp, rub a knee, or favor one leg over the other. Not even a complaint.

Something Garrett once said came to mind. He'd been grumbling about his baby brother trekking around Europe instead of coming home to help with the ranch. "Dad needs his help, but Jo can't be bothered with more than an occasional postcard. Not even a call or an e-mail."

For two years? That didn't sound like Jonas. Family meant everything to the Camerons. The land was in their blood.

So, what was he missing?

Grabbing a piece of paper, James wrote out a rudimentary timeline for Jonas's service history. Everything pointed to the medical discharge and those missing two years after his discharge.

On a new sheet, he started with Jonas's final assignment with the 10th Special Forces Group, and sketched an org chart up the chain of command to SOCOMM, the Special Operations Command, to Department of the Army, and then Department of Defense. The only level above DoD was the Commander in Chief himself, the President.

He started down the other side with departments that reported to DoD, and stopped at … the Defense Intelligence Agency. His heart rate hit a gallop. DIA ran the Defense Clandestine Service and its sister department—the *Bureau of International Intelligence.*

A deep belly laugh echoed in the empty office. It didn't take a forensic scientist to see Fowler's fingerprints all over this. The DCS ran covert espionage activities all around the world, often in conjunction with the CIA. And the BII. Fowler had somehow managed to steal Jonas from the Army and put him to work as a covert operative. "You went off grid, didn't you, boy? I'll bet my next paycheck your family didn't know anything about your work, you sly dog. They probably still don't."

The back door opened and closed. Heavy footsteps trudged inside. "Morning, Boss. You're in early. Couldn't sleep?"

James eyed his deputy with suspicion. Kyle had a wicked sense of humor and wouldn't hesitate to bust his chops if the opportunity presented itself. But whether he was ragging on James about yesterday or not, he couldn't tell. Not a blink, not a twitch gave his thoughts away. He'd be a killer at the poker table if he ever wanted to play.

James gave Kyle the benefit of the doubt this time, but not much else. "Coffee's ready. I slept fine, thank you, and I always come in early."

"Not on your day off," Kyle smirked.

James glared at his deputy. "You forget this job is 24/7." He stuffed the report on Jonas back in its folder and locked the file away. He'd call a meeting later in the week after Garrett returned from the horse auction and Wade got back from his bison-wrangling trip. They needed to know about the ThreatCon, and he could explain it one time.

Kyle shot him a quick glance that said, "I feel for you, brother," right before he disappeared back into the kitchen.

So, it was official. The whole town knew his dirty secrets. So be it. Yesterday was done, thank goodness, and though regret still chafed as bad as a stiff tag in a new t-shirt, he would move on. First up, to have any chance of making this right, he owed Mallory an apology and an explanation. *If* she'd hear him out.

The clock ticked closer to seven before his patience ran out. James grabbed his keys, hat, and jacket, and started toward the back door where they parked their vehicles. "I'm heading out. Got some things to do."

Kyle looked up while stirring his coffee and nodded. "Roger, that. I'll hang here until Lorraine gets in."

James didn't remember much of the fifteen-minute drive to the ranch. His mind remained stuck on the coming confrontation with Mallory, and the knowledge that nothing less than a good knee-on-the-ground grovel would do. Whatever it took, he'd do it for her.

The turnoff to the ranch drew near, and the first thing he noticed were the tire tracks in the new-fallen snow. They turned onto the Camerons' private drive from south on Route 93, and again on the way out. Likely TJ's, since she and Garrett lived a scant five minutes down the road. She must have gotten up extra early this morning for a round trip. School teachers had to be at the school in Challis by seven-fifteen.

He steered the Yukon up to the security call box and punched in the code. The gates began to move, the one on his right swinging well ahead of the other one. That's not good.

With a tap on the accelerator, he started forward … and slammed on the brakes just in time. "What in the—"

The malfunctioning gate crashed closed, rebounded, and finally came to rest two feet shy of the locked position.

James backed up, re-entered the code, and cheated to the far left this time. The Yukon slipped through with room to spare.

The fork appeared a half-mile in. Right led to the house where the family lived. Left took a winding path to the big breeding barn and training corrals, the heart of the

Triple C Ranch operations. Not five hundred yards beyond the right fork, the tire tracks veered off the road in a U-turn.

Puzzled, James started on by, but then slammed on his brakes, threw the gear into park, and got out. He released the retention strap on his handgun with a flick of his thumb and picked his way through the slush and snow to where the unknown vehicle had pulled off the drive.

For a moment, he wondered if Fowler's alert had him looking for shadows where none existed. But then he found tracks that caught his eyes. Footprints. One set. Large. Leather shoes, not boots or sneakers. They led to the fence. And then toward the house.

James pulled his cell phone from his pocket and dialed Jonas's number. His concern escalated when the call rolled to voice mail. He dialed Mallory and prayed she'd turned her phone back on and would answer this time.

She didn't.

The main number at the ranch house, the land line Cate refused to give up, went straight to a recording. *The number you have dialed is temporarily out of service. Please hang up and try your call again later.*

Something was wrong. He punched in Kyle's number.

"Yo, what's up?"

"How fast can you get out to the Triple C?"

The rustle of papers in the background stopped. "Ten minutes. Let me switch the answering machine back on. Where?"

"Main drive. Just past the fork. Watch out for the gate, it's screwed up. And Kyle, no lights." He didn't think whoever left the footprints was still around, but no sense taking chances.

A door slammed. An engine cranked. "Roger," Kyle said. "Want me to stay on the line?"

The beauty of a close-knit team was they answered when called, came when needed, asked no unnecessary questions, and always had your back. "No."

Weapon in hand, James followed the suspicious footprints until the sprawling home Cody Cameron had built with his own two hands came into view. Sitting on a slight rise that overlooked the long valley, the house faced a southern vista of wide open pastures as far south as the eye could see. The red barn stood at a distance behind the house, framed by a stand of aspens and larch.

Worry for Mallory consumed him, but to go busting in without backup was stupid. Finding nothing, he returned to his vehicle, the jog mercifully short.

Kyle's black Jeep Cherokee with the magnetic Hastings Bluff Police Department logo on the side appeared almost immediately. His deputy pulled up beside James with the driver's window lowered. "What do we have?"

"Tire tracks. Came in from the south, left the same way. Thought they might be TJ's at first." He pointed off to the side. "They pulled off the road here. Footprints are too big for a woman. They lead to the barn."

Kyles eyebrows disappeared under the brim of his hat. "You call one of the Camerons?"

"Everybody's out of town except for Jonas and Mallory. His line went straight to voice mail. The main line has a recording that says it's out of service."

"And Mallory?"

Heat filled his cheeks. "She's, ah, not taking my calls right now."

"Let me try." Kyle grabbed his cell phone and dialed. A few seconds later, he shook his head. "Straight to voice mail, too. Guess we do this the hard way. Got a plan?"

"Yeah. We drive up to the front of the house. You knock on the door, and I'll cover you."

A grin cracked Kyle's stony countenance. "Never thought I'd see the day our mighty sheriff was scared of a little bit of fluff."

"Don't underestimate the fluff factor. I'd rather go hand-to-hand against a whole squad of Ali Babas than face off with Mallory when she's mad, or worse, when her feelings are hurt."

Imperfect Lies

Chapter Five

With the first hint of gray spilling around the edges of the lacy curtains, Mallory rose and hurried on bare feet down the hall to the bathroom. As promised, a new toothbrush lay on the sink, along with a tube of toothpaste, fresh towels, and a bottle of aspirin.

She swallowed two of the caplets. They probably wouldn't do much for her swollen eyes—thanks to staying up half the night to bawl and spill her guts—but they should help settle the drum banging inside her head.

A short time later, face washed, teeth cleaned, hair somewhat tamed into a messy bun, and dressed in yesterday's clothes, Mallory gathered her things and tiptoed to the kitchen.

"Good morning, dear." Miz Tillberry stood at the sink wearing a thick velour robe that covered her from chin to

ankle. She filled the kettle from the tap and set it on the stove.

"Sorry, Miz T. I didn't mean to wake you."

"Age is a funny thing. People who've reach my advanced years either sleep a lot, or hardly at all. I fall into the second category. Do you have time for breakfast, dear? It won't take but a minute to heat the water and make the toast."

Tea and toast. Ugh. They'd shared a supper of sandwiches last night—crustless bread with a smear of butter and a thin slice of ham cut into perfect little triangles. Mallory pressed her lips together at the thought of those beauties in her brothers' paws, but she had to bite her lip to hold back giggles at a vision of what her father's reaction would be to the dainty tidbits. Camerons, both male and female, had hearty appetites.

"Um, no thanks. I left too many chores undone yesterday. I really need to get going." After the previous day's emotional drain, it felt good to laugh, even if only internally.

"I understand."

"I planned to leave you a note, but I'm glad I get to say this in person. Thank you for yesterday. You took me in when I needed a friend, and listened while I blubbered half the night. You were right. The world didn't come to an end. My heart might be broken, but I'm strong. One day this will all be a bittersweet memory."

If she told herself that a hundred times a day, she might begin to believe it … in another ten years.

Miz Tillberry's eyes took on a suspicious sheen behind her wire-rimmed glasses, which summoned Mallory's own tears. And here she'd called herself a prune last night, thinking all the moisture in her body used up.

After a quick embrace and a promise to call soon, Mallory left.

The cold air chased away the dregs of her headache. Three inches of new snow had fallen overnight, whitewashing the outside world, and leaving a promise of that most rare of events, a cloudless winter day.

Filled with new resolve, Mallory cranked Jonas's truck, turned the defroster to high, and grabbed the ice scraper. Unable to reach more than a small portion of the windshield, she went back for the cinder block. Ten minutes later, the defroster and ice scraper had worked their magic. She could see through the windshield again, and waved to Miz Tillberry as she drove away.

The trip home claimed her full attention. Even though the morning traffic had already turned the snow-covered roads to slush, hidden icy patches posed a danger, and the last thing she needed was to put a dent in Jonas's truck and add his wrath to her burdens.

At the turnoff, she remembered the replacement part she needed for Jonas's taillight. Should she go back, or go home? With her luck, James would spot her on the way

back to town and write her a ticket for the broken taillight. Though, technically, was it broken if the bulb still worked? Knowing him, he'd lock her up to ensure she stayed put long enough to listen to whatever he had to say.

A touch on the remote set the entryway in motion. Too many conflicting thoughts ricocheted through her head to deal with James right now. She'd call Toby from the house and let him figure out what was needed. She still had a chance of Jonas not finding out.

The gate still had a quirk, so she rumbled through the entrance on the left side to avoid another bump.

She believed what she had said to Miz Tillberry this morning. Life throws curves, and keeps right on moving. You either hang on with both hands, or get run over and left for dead.

Later, she could face James and hear what he had to say. Whether they could remain friends didn't concern her anymore.

The truck slid a little as she passed the fork in the road. That's when she noticed the tire tracks that had turned the dirt road to slush.

The house came into view around the last bend, but relief at being home fled when she spotted the two vehicles parked in front. Kyle's Cherokee and James's Yukon. Great.

With her foot off the gas pedal, the truck slowed to a crawl. Should she pull up to the front? Or head to the barn and make them come to her?

She opted for the barn, wanting every available second before she had to deal with James and his wingman.

"Mallory?"

Well, that little respite lasted all of a minute. She ignored him, returned Jonas's keys to the lock box, and started toward the house.

"Hold up. Why are you driving Jonas's truck?" James grabbed her arm and pulled her to a halt.

Why did everyone seem more concerned about Jonas's truck than her?

Mallory lifted one eyebrow and stared pointedly at the hand on her arm.

He let go and stuck his hands in his pants pockets, a recalcitrant expression on his face.

"Cassie's truck wouldn't start, not that it's any of your business."

His eyes took on that right-before-a-storm look she knew so well. James didn't do distraught, but darned if a dozen emotions didn't flit across his face in those few seconds. Holding his tongue cost him, but he did it.

"I sent a text last night, James." Mallory's hands landed on her hips. "I said we'd talk today. Why are you here?"

The question must have hit a nerve. The look he gave her would deep-fry a turkey. A moment later, he sighed. His shoulders slumped. "I was worried. Where were you?"

Just when she thought she could toss his arrogances back at him, his voice went all soft and full of concern. The tears she'd thought were bottled up made a new bid for escape.

Unable to look at him and keep her composure, Mallory started for the house. "Come inside. I'll make coffee."

James followed a few steps behind, with a reluctant Kyle dogging his steps. Poor Kyle. He must be wondering how he got pulled into this mess. Which raised the question—why he was here?

That thought dried up any notion of tears.

She stamped her feet on the rough boot-scraper door mat and flipped the lights on as she stepped inside.

James and Kyle cleaned their boots as well.

With her jacket half undone, she thought better of taking it off. The house was cold. Too cold.

"Man, I think it's warmer outside. You forget to turn the heat on or something?" Kyle blew on his hands.

"I don't know. I'll check—"

James had already gone over to the thermostat on the wall between the kitchen and the dining room. "It's set at sixty-eight, but registering forty-four. That's not good. Kyle, check the unit out back. See if it froze up. Mallory, turn on the faucets. See if the water's okay."

Right on schedule, Mr. Bossy Pants returned.

"I don't think it got low enough last night to freeze the

pipes." She turned the kitchen faucet on anyway. Water flowed without any hesitation, but James had disappeared.

Mallory filled the water reservoir on the coffee maker, added grounds, and hit the start button.

"Found your problem," James called from the far side of the dining room. "Window's open."

She snagged three mugs from the second shelf … and went still. "What did you say?"

"Need a couple of towels," he called. "Snow melted on the floor."

Setting the cups on the island with care, she followed his voice and, sure enough, the curtains billowed around one of the windows.

"Mallory? Towels?"

She stared at the mess on the floor as fear crowded into her mind.

Kyle chose that moment to open the kitchen door. "James. Need you outside a second."

Goose bumps pebbled her arms. A chill that had nothing to do with temperature settled inside her. The itchy feeling, that sense of someone or something just out of sight, overwhelmed her.

"Be right there," James yelled, but then his tone softened. "Princess? You all right?"

She sagged against the wall, but somehow forced her voice to remain steady. "Go see what he wants. I've got this."

James left with Kyle, while she went to the laundry room for rags to mop up the water on the floor. Last night the whole male population was on her hit list. This morning, she'd never been happier to have a couple of Y-chromosome types close at hand. Fortunately for her, none of the men in her life discounted gut feelings. All she had to do was explain in a convincing fashion why'd she'd been so creeped out yesterday.

CCC

The first snow had laid the pattern for what to expect in the coming months. High winds and ice abrasion from winter storms helped sculpt the landscape, often resulting in wedge-shaped stands of trees. Add in a good-sized structure like a barn and you had yourself a windbreak. Or in this instance, a snow-break. At least until the deflected winds found the leeward side and a nice open space to deposit their loads of snow.

James looked from the barn across the open space to the house. The little four-inch dusting that had fallen between midnight and three a.m. left foot-deep drifts against the northwest side of the house. Which is why houses here almost always faced south or southeast.

The locals called this 'snow creep.' Another two months and the creep would cover the windows, which was a good thing, as it offered an added layer of insulation against the fierce cold. And another layer of security.

For now, the snow presented a canvas for the trail of footprints that led right up to the dining room window. Either the intruder was a bumbling idiot, or more likely, he wanted the Camerons to know of his visit.

James frowned at the tiny scrapes on the window frame and shook his head. "Too easy. All you need is a flathead screwdriver and a mallet to pop these locks. Wade should know better."

"The footprints went straight to her truck and then inside the barn," Kyle said. "From there, he followed the trees until he could come at the house from the west. Maybe you should talk with Garrett and Wade about upgrading their security."

"Security is only good if you use it. The Camerons have a false sense of security. They think since they've never had an incident, the distance from town, and the gate across their drive makes them safe from whatever. You find anything in the barn?"

Kyle shook his head. "No, but I'm probably not the one to say if anything's missing or out of place. We need Mallory to look around the barn and the house."

"Take a look at Cassie's truck. She took Jonas's truck because the Ranger wouldn't start."

Kyle nodded and jogged off.

Inside again, he found Mallory on her knees in the dining room, cleaning up the mess. "Any damage?"

She reared back and clapped a hand over her heart. "Don't do that."

"Do what?"

"Sneak up on people. It's stalkerish." She tucked a strand of hair behind her ear. "The rug will dry out, but the wood under the window might stain."

Still too pale. And her hands trembled when she resumed swabbing the towels over the floor.

"Mallory?"

"Yes?" She kept her focus on the floor.

"I know you're upset about yesterday. I am, too." He kept his voice soft and reassuring. "We'll talk about that soon, but right now I need to ask you a couple of questions. Something's not right. Where's Jonas?"

Her chest shuddered with a deep breath. "We lost the mare. Her foal, too. Jo takes these things … hard. He needed to get away for a while."

"So, he took his horse and ran off to the mountains again. Left you here alone."

Her troubled blue eyes looked up. "It's not like I need a keeper."

James walked over and shut the window none too gently. "No?"

Her chin dropped again.

"Look at me, princess."

Her head didn't move.

"Please. I need to know what's got you spooked."

She seemed to deflate, but met his gaze. "I'm not sure I can explain."

Goading wouldn't work with Mallory. If he pushed too hard, she'd shut down, so he waited.

"Yesterday morning, after I got the call from New York, I went outside. I like the cold air. It clears my head. Anyway, I thought ..." She shrugged. "I sensed ... Ugh ..." Frustration resonated from her. "I felt like someone was watching. It creeped me out, so I went back inside and made sure *everything* was locked down tight, doors and windows, upstairs and down. I even re-armed the security system. Why didn't the open window trigger the alarm?"

One more question to add to the growing list. Why didn't her truck start? Why did the main gate malfunction? Why was the landline out of service?

The back door flew open.

James whirled, his gun in hand.

Mallory jumped to her feet with a little screech.

The devil himself stormed in without pausing to stomp the snow from his boots. Rage seeped from every one of Jonas's pores. "What in the name of Jack Daniels happened to my truck, Mallory?"

James wanted to laugh at the guilty as sin look on Mallory's face and at the same time bloody her brother's nose for putting it there. He re-holstered his weapon instead and shoved Jonas away. "You left your sister alone, jerk face. Someone broke into your house. You're supposed to protect her."

Jonas staggered back, his fury gone. "Wh-what?"

Okay, maybe he could have softened the blow a little.

Mallory pushed past James. "Stop it, both of you. Jonas, it's okay. I'm fine."

Party boy, jokester, all around funny guy, none of those designations fit at the moment. They all had demons to battle, but it sure looked like Jonas had taken on more than his fair share and was losing the fight. Pain etched deep lines around his eyes and mouth, aging him by ten years.

Kyle opened the door, took in the tension, and held his hands up in a defensive gesture. "Did I interrupt something?"

James sighed. Things were moving way too fast. They all needed to take a deep breath and relax. "Mal, is that coffee ready yet?"

Chapter Six

Mallory got the creamer from the refrigerator, another mug from the cabinet, added some spoons, and set them all on the island while James grabbed the coffee pot.

"Not that unleaded stuff, is it?" Kyle settled on the stool next to Jonas. His expression made no bones about what he thought of decaf.

"Nope," Mallory answered. "Dark roast rocket fuel. You in or out?"

He held his cup for James to fill. "In. Don't suppose you got anything to go with it, maybe some of your mom's muffins?"

James and Jonas looked up at the mention of food with hope in their eyes.

"I'll check."

The extra freezer in the mud room yielded a large

Ziploc bag of blueberry muffins. Perfect. She arranged them on a plate, covered them with a paper towel, and zapped them in the microwave. "Jonas, grab the butter from the fridge and some extra napkins, will you?" She reached for a butter knife in the silverware drawer.

"Mm, this smells wonderful. Your mom rocks." Kyle inhaled and stuffed a whole muffin in his mouth.

"Actually, I think Lucy made them."

Kyle choked.

James stopped mid-chew, his cheeks stretched and rounded. He pounded Kyle on the back.

Jonas, who'd been about to take a big bite, closed his mouth and set his muffin back on the plate.

"C'mon, guys. She's getting better." Mallory pulled her own muffin apart and popped it in her mouth. They'd all partaken of Lucy's culinary adventures, some of them quite memorable, but like she said, Lucy the perfectionist had indeed improved. "Mm-mm."

One-by-one they started eating again, albeit with smaller, more cautious bites.

After pouring the last of the coffee, James set the empty pot in the sink and took his seat again. "Okay, let's talk."

Half an hour later, Mallory felt she had a good understanding of what had transpired, though not the who or why of it.

James, still in charge, handed out marching orders.

"Kyle, I want a full report on the gate, Mallory's truck, the phone lines, and the security system. Dust for prints, though I doubt we'll find anything usable. Jonas, you check out the barn, see if there's anything missing or disturbed. And alert your hands, maybe set up a schedule so the ladies aren't left alone ... from now on."

An unnatural stillness descended on Jonas. His chin dropped to his chest, but only for a moment. Iron found its way into his backbone. He hadn't missed James's hesitation or the unspoken "again" any more than she had. Spine straight, shoulders back, he met her eyes. "Sorry, Sis. Won't happen again."

Mallory had to swallow hard to keep her throat from closing up. Her family had been blessed—or cursed, depending on how you looked at it—with an overabundance of moral fortitude. As a child, Jonas had idolized his older brothers, especially Garrett. He used to follow him around, aping what he said and did. And to Garrett's credit, irritated or not, he never belittled his baby brother.

She suspected Jonas still held Garrett high up on a pedestal. And was still trying to live up to his standards.

"Good," James continued. "Now that's cleared up, I'll get a meeting set up to brief Garrett, Wade, and Derek when they get back."

"I want to be included in the meeting," Mallory informed him. These guys were nuts if they thought she'd

sit quietly by and forget about the violation of her home.

James looked at her for a long, drawn out moment before he spoke. "Call TJ. Have her stay here with you until Garrett returns. Neither of you should be alone."

"That's it?"

"No. I want you, TJ, Lucy, and your sister when she gets home, to stay close to home. Don't go anywhere without me, Kyle, or one of your brothers. At least not until I can get a handle on what's going on. Right now, I want a closer look at these footprints and tire tracks." James buttoned his coat.

Jonas's head swiveled back and forth. One eyebrow lifted in speculation as he watched the verbal tennis match between her and James.

Kyle, at least, had the good sense to find something interesting to study on the floor.

James paused in the threshold of the kitchen door. "And Mallory? You and I *are* going to talk. Soon."

Not waiting for a response, he motioned for his deputy to follow, and the two men departed.

"Well, that was … insightful." Jonas's mouth had quirked up on one side.

Mallory glared at him.

"Just saying." Jonas followed James and Kyle outside.

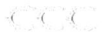

Mallory blotted her lipstick, her ears perking up at the sound of gravel crunching in the driveway.

"Wade's out front," Lucy called from downstairs.

"We're coming," Cassie yelled in reply before pausing at Mallory's bedroom door. "Get a move on, Mal. Daylight's burning. We've got shopping to do."

It was good to have everyone home again, or almost home. TJ had stayed at the ranch with Jonas and her until Garrett arrived home on Friday. Lucy and Wade came back on Saturday, and her parents were due in later tonight, just in time for a two-day cooking marathon for Thanksgiving. If she wanted to look professional for her interview on Friday, she had to find the right clothes today.

With a last look in the mirror, Mallory grabbed her oversized purse and felt for the hard bulge of the Smith & Wesson Lady Smith revolver inside. She'd balked at first over the idea of one of her brothers pulling escort duty for her, Cassie, and Lucy while they shopped. She and the other girls had concealed weapon permits now, and they all carried a handgun more often than not. But then she remembered how quickly everything had spiraled out of control during the incident with the human traffickers a few months back.

Wade had already lifted Lucy into the front passenger seat of his blue-gray GMC Sierra by the time Mallory made it downstairs and out the front door.

"Wait for me," Cassie called as she rearmed the

security system, and then piled into the back seat of the extended cab. They'd all become more security conscious since the intruder incident.

Having a man along or not, the trip promised to be great fun. Mallory had her gun, a credit card, two of her besties, and a weather forecast that promised clear roads, sunshine, and a high of forty-four degrees. What more did a girl need for a grand shopping adventure? Certainly not thoughts of the annoying, arrogant, deceitful sheriff who said he 'wanted to talk.' Like he could explain away a *wife*.

She checked her cell phone, a frustrating habit she'd fallen into since she last saw James. He hadn't come by, called, or even texted since then. Did he plan to wait until Thanksgiving? When they had eighteen people around the table? For someone who wanted to apologize, he sure had a funny way of doing it.

Or had he changed his mind and no longer cared enough to explain? He had to know she'd hear of his breakfast at the diner with Olivia on Friday. And the hours they'd spent in his office on Saturday. With the door closed. Not to mention the late dinner at the steakhouse in Challis last night.

A long, slow inhale relieved some of her tension. The softly hissed exhale helped even more.

"What's the big sigh for?" Lucy asked.

Mallory laughed, a soul-cleansing chuckle that freed her spirit. "I just realized how much I hate being in limbo.

Here I am, unwilling to move forward until I let go, and unable to let go until I move forward. I've decided—or re-decided—I'm breaking out of the hamster wheel, and today is my new start. And you guys are my accomplices and my guardians. In other words, men suck. No offense, Wade."

"None taken. I happen to agree with you. Just don't put me in a position where I have to take sides, because I won't." He gave her a smirk in the rearview mirror.

"Here, here," Lucy championed.

"You know I'm on your side," Cassie added.

Poor Wade. He'd drawn the short straw for today's outing. A small blessing. Of her three brothers, he grumped less than Garrett and had more tolerance for feminine chatter than Jonas. Plus, any bad guys would think twice with someone his size tagging along.

The two-and a half-hour drive to Idaho Falls passed in no time with rich conversation on many diverse topics. Wade remained mostly quiet during the trip, but made one growled demand as they approached the outskirts of the city. "We are not going to any underwear stores."

Silence fell for a good thirty seconds.

"But, honey." Lucy reached over and stroked his arm. "You have such exquisite taste. Remember the trip to the lingerie store?"

Mallory leaned forward and made a "T" with her hands. "Whoa, girl. This is my brother you're talking about, and this subject is forbidden, verboten, prohibido,

taboo. Unless you want me scarred for life."

"We only have one lingerie store on the list, Wade," Cassie added. "You can wait outside. We won't take long."

Wade looked out the side window and grumbled something under his breath.

Mallory decided against asking him to repeat what he said.

Eight hours later, after hitting fourteen stores non-stop, they stopped for a late lunch, or more like an early supper, at the SnakeBite Restaurant. Mallory's mouth watered when the waiter set a thick T-bone steak in front of Wade. The sizzle alone made her second guess her own order of fish tacos.

Lucy's salad was a thing of beauty, if you liked grass and such. Cassie's burger and fries on the other hand had everyone's nose sniffing the air. Ah, the pleasures of food.

Cassie finished eating first, licked her fingers, and stood. "Nothing like a greasy burger. I'm off to wash my hands."

"Hang on," Lucy said, pushing back from the table. "I'll come with you."

Wade nudged his plate aside and leaned his elbows on the table. "So, Mal, you're really gonna to leave home and go work in the city?"

The last fish taco lost its taste. Mallory dropped it on her plate, wiped her mouth with the napkin, and leaned back. She'd successfully avoided facing this very question for four long days. Leave it to Wade to cut to the chase. Of course, she had worked for him for a year prior to Lucy's arrival, so he knew her well. He also understood how much she disliked confrontation.

"I don't know yet. Maybe. I have interviews to get through first. Who knows? They might not like me."

He snorted. "Be honest with me, Mallory."

"You want honesty? Okay, I love this land. I love the ranch and our family. Everybody knows me here and I have nothing to prove, but it's not enough. I want a forever kind of love like you and Lucy have. I want a husband one day, and children to raise right here in Hastings Bluff. So, no, leaving is not my first choice."

She looked away. "But I won't find any of that here, not if I shatter watching James live out his happily-ever-after right under my nose. These job interviews represent a chance for me prove myself out there. Leaving will let me move on and, hopefully, find a new future."

"I get what you're saying, but I don't think it's like that with James. He's a good man, Mal. You need to talk to him, hear him out."

"I know he is, and I will." She let her head fall against the back of the booth and willed the tears not to fall. Her voice broke anyway. "Just not yet."

Wade covered one of her hands with his, but she snatched it away. Sympathy, compassion, whatever, would be her undoing. She fought for control, and won. "James

never promised me anything. He never gave any indication that he returned my feelings. This is all on me, but I have to protect myself from now on. I can't stay here. I can't watch him with her."

"It's not like that, Mal."

"Then what's it like, Wade?"

Her brother opened his mouth to say something, thought better of it, and hung his head. "Not my place to say. It's James's story."

Mallory stood. "No problem. I already know the story. James is married. He has a wife, and doesn't need a girlfriend. Excuse me. I think I'll hit the facilities before we start back, too."

Chapter Seven

James pulled up to the call box at the gate to the Triple C and lowered his window. The number pad stared back at him, passive yet demanding.

He'd promised to call Mallory, and then didn't. Now, here he sat on her doorstep, afraid to face her family, afraid to see the hurt in her eyes, hurt that he put there, and even more afraid of losing her.

The holiday season held a conglomeration of memories for him, some good, some not so good, and others simply unremarkable. It wasn't until he met the Camerons that the true meaning of Thanksgiving revealed itself. He didn't want to ruin it for them today.

Before he could act one way or the other, Garrett's voice bellowed over the speaker. "Don't even think about leaving."

He grinned and waved at the new camera as the gates began to move. How well these guys knew him. Wade had taken his suggestions for upgrades to their security to heart. With CCTVs at the gate, along the drive, on both barns, and at several positions around the house, anyone inside would know who approached and when. Wade had also taken the entire system off the phone and power lines, and moved them to a secure underground cable with a backup generator.

The iron gates swung inward without a hitch. He drove under the big arch adorned with the three big intertwined horseshoes turned on their sides to form the letters of the Triple C—for Cate and Cody Cameron.

Those two were legends in the area. They'd married young and against their families' wishes, but through hard work, determination, and sheer cussedness they'd carved a life out of a patch of worthless land and scrub brush. Forty-odd years later, the ranch spanned twenty-five-hundred acres, and had a reputation as one of the best quarter-horse breeding and training operations in the state.

No more snow had fallen since the dusting last week, though the weatherman projected six more inches tonight. The drive had been recently graded, which eliminated the ruts from last week. Nothing to slow him down.

James poked along anyway, worried about the reception awaiting him. Garrett, Wade, and Jonas had met with him several times since the intruder incident, mostly to discuss strategy and to brainstorm the identity of the target in Fowler's warning. Garrett had blistered him plenty for not confiding in him about Olivia, but neither he nor Wade mentioned Mallory.

Jonas, on the other hand, had delivered a terse, "Fix this with my sister, you hear?"

If an infinitesimal chance remained, he would make this right with Mallory if it killed him.

He hadn't seen Cody or Cate, though, not since his past became the hot gossip topic around town. Would they think less of him now?

The Cameron vehicles were all crowded around the barn, but four other vehicles lined the drive-in front of the house. He spotted Kyle's Cherokee and Derek's Blazer, and recognized the Honda CRV Dee Dee Guthrie drove, but not the older model piece of junk behind it.

Strays. All of them. Cate Cameron collected strays the way some people adopted cats. The thought warmed his frozen insides. He liked belonging to Cate and her family.

A quick count had him guessing there'd easily be more than a dozen people at the table today.

As he sat there trying to drum up the nerve to get out of the car, the front door banged open. Garrett barreled down the steps toward him. "Why are you hanging around out here? Mom's been hounding me for the past hour to hunt you down. You know how she is about having dinner on time."

"Sorry. I'm still wondering if this is good idea."

"Don't be stupid." Not one to mince words, Garrett all but yanked him from the car.

James followed him inside where a mélange of aromas made his nose lift and his mouth water—roast turkey, hickory smoke from the fire, sweet mulled cider, bread fresh from the oven, cinnamon, vanilla, and lots of sugary smells. His stomach roared with appreciation, even as his lungs tried to hyperventilate. "Man, that smells divine."

"Well, that's a compliment if ever I heard one." Cate Cameron bustled forward and reached for him. "The belly growls, I mean. Not your pretty words. Now, bend down so I can hug you proper. You boys are too tall."

James removed his hat and did as she commanded. He loved the chokehold she wrapped him in that passed for a hug, but took care not to squeeze too hard in return. Like her husband and her sons, he was a lot bigger than Cate or the girls. Their smaller statures made him feel awkward, and very aware of his strength.

"Hey, James," Cassie called from the dining room where she arranged plates and silverware. "'Bout time you got here. Now we can eat."

The big table had been turned sideways so it extended into the hallway, with a long folding table extension. Derek followed behind Cassie carrying a stack of plates and a basket of silverware. He looked sheepish, but kept a smile on as he handed her the different items she asked for.

Mallory appeared in the doorway from the kitchen, her hands covered in oven mitts and holding a large bowl of—

Before he could see what was in the dish, she lost all color, did an about-face, and vanished back into the kitchen. All the air in the room seemed to disappear with her.

"What a wuss," Cassie muttered. "Don't worry, James. She'll come around."

He wasn't so sure.

"Forget the brat." Garrett tugged on his arm. "Come say hi to everyone."

It took several minutes to work through all the people crowded into the family room. Dee Dee Guthrie, who owned the diner, yelled across the room to him. "Howdy, Sheriff. Catch any speeders today?"

Shea Townsend, who worked for Dee Dee at the diner, shushed her and offered him an apologetic smile.

Jonas and Kyle were there, as was Miz Tillberry. "Afternoon, ma'am. Good to see you again."

She sniffed, not at all charmed. "Sheriff."

Jonas motioned a teenage boy forward. "You remember Casey? He works for Wade after school. Kid's a computer whiz."

Thin, with shaggy hair—yeah, he remembered the kid. "You the one who hacked into the school's computers and deleted a few records?"

James couldn't resist busting his chops. All in all,

Casey's little prank had worked out rather well. The boy restored the files, but the bullies learned a valuable lesson that day. When they realized their football scholarships were at risk, they apologized and never bothered Casey again.

Casey surprised him by sticking a hand out, and then surprised him again with a firm grip. "I have no idea what you're talking about, Sheriff," he said with a straight face. "I'd like you to meet my mom, Patricia Petersen."

"Sheriff." Mrs. Petersen, fortyish and already prematurely gray, smiled but didn't offer her hand.

"Ma'am." James nodded, remembering what Lucy told him about Casey last summer. No dad in the picture. Mom worked long hours cleaning houses, a fact confirmed by the dark shadows that framed her tired eyes, and rough, reddened hands.

"Patricia, how good to see you," Miz Tillberry appeared out of nowhere and took the quiet woman under her wing. "Come with me. I want to introduce you to Shea Townsend."

James leaned toward Casey. "I saw Derek got shanghaied into helping Cassie, but where's Wade?"

The boy lowered his voice to a conspiratorial whisper. "He got roped into helping in the kitchen. Be glad you got here late. Mrs. Cameron *volunteered* all us men for different jobs. I had to carry the chairs from the barn. She says it's good for us to feel included. You might want to keep a low profile. Otherwise, you'll probably get tapped for cleanup."

Kyle clapped the boy on the back. "You learn fast, kid."

"What's so funny over here?" Rascal Sutcliff, Cody Cameron's oldest friend and his ranch foreman, sidled over and reached for James's hand. "Glad you could make it sheriff."

Cate took that moment to announce dinner. "Hope you're hungry. Lucy will tell you where to sit."

James found himself at one end of the table next to Cody with Miz Tillberry on his right. He couldn't believe his luck when Mallory sat directly across from him.

Cody clinked a knife against his glass, and quietened the chatter. He bowed his head, and like dominos, those seated around the table followed his example. "Lord, we gather here today in thankfulness for the abundance of Your provision and grace. Bless this food, bless those who prepared it, and bless those who keep our country safe, and grant our leaders wisdom. We pray this in Your Son's name. Amen."

"Amen," James repeated along with several others.

Pandemonium reigned for the next several minutes as bowls and platters made their way down the table and back.

Mallory refused to look his way, no matter how hard he willed her to.

When a measure of calm returned and the eating

began, he leaned forward and raised his voice. "Mallory, would you pass the salt?"

Was it his imagination, or did the room go quiet?

The forkful of dressing she'd lifted to her mouth halted in mid-air. With controlled deliberateness, she set the fork on her plate and reached for the salt shaker, taking care to set it on the table in front of him instead of handing it over. And still she didn't look at him.

Breaking through her defenses might prove more difficult than he'd thought. Not that he ever backed off from a challenge. "And the pepper, please."

No doubt about the silence this time. Her fork clanged against the plate like a gong.

His efforts earned him a look this time. Mallory's dark blue eyes raged like twin storm clouds, all but daring him to push her again. It was amazing her hair didn't stick out given the way the air practically crackled around her. Yeah, he should've called her like he promised.

The pepper shaker slammed down on the table in front of him. "Anything else?" Saccharine sweetness infused her voice enough to give him diabetes.

Choosing prudence for now, he salted and peppered his food. "No, thank you."

Conversations swirled around the table. Sometimes he participated, sometimes not, but he kept an eye on Mallory all the time. And didn't miss the surreptitious glances she cast his way. That was good, right?

Halfway through the meal, under the guise of a dropped napkin, James surveyed the underside of the table. Prim and proper, just like her momma taught her, Mallory's feet sat flat on the ground, knees pressed together, hidden by the long tablecloth. Perfect.

Straightening up, he waited until she raised her glass and took a drink before sliding his long legs forward to bracket hers.

The look of utter shock was worth it. She sputtered, choked, got her napkin over her mouth in the nick of time, and still managed to set the glass down without spilling it. It also earned her a heavy-handed pat on the back from Casey, who sat next to her, and a concerned look from her dad.

Not one to let an opportunity pass, he rubbed the smooth top of his boot up and down her calf and tried hard not to grin when she choked again.

That's when she landed a solid kick against the inside of his thigh.

James winced, more from the damage she might have done than the actual pain inflicted. He withdrew his legs.

Was that …? Yep. The corners of her mouth twitched, that or she had muscle spasms. Maybe his princess would talk to him after all. With a wink that promised more, he left her in peace, for now.

At the other end of the table, Cate stood and announced dessert. "We have pecan pie, pumpkin pie,

applesauce cake, a raspberry trifle, brownies, and cookies, so no football yet."

Wade folded his napkin, pushed his chair back, and cleared his throat as he got to his feet. "I … uh … want to say something."

Conversation stopped. All eyes turned to him, and to a blushing Lucy as she took his hand.

"I … we … thought today would be a good time to share our news. Lucy has agreed to marry me."

Cate catapulted from her chair and raced around the table, where she hugged them both. Handshakes, back pats, tears, laughter, jokes, and more hugs followed as Lucy flaunted her new diamond ring.

"Does it have a security chip in it, too?" TJ teased.

"She won't need one since I have no intention of letting her out of my sight for the next fifty years," Wade quipped back.

When the excitement died down a little, Cate drafted a trio of helpers to serve the desserts, and gave orders to pass the dirty plates to the end of the table.

James seized the moment. He walked around the table, grabbed Mallory's hand, and tugged her to her mother's side. "Cate, would you mind if Mallory and I skip dessert? There are some things we need to discuss in private."

A dicey move on his part, but no risk, no reward.

Mallory's mouth fell open. She started to object when a buzzer rang in the family room.

"Someone's at the gate?" Cate turned away, choosing the distraction over giving him an answer.

"I'm on it." Jonas bounded from the room and disappeared through the hall.

"Okay, let's talk," Mallory said, her lips pressed into a thin line. "You owe me an explanation, but somewhere private."

Jonas rushed back in, his eyes searching until they found Mallory ... and then settled on James. He stopped just inside the door, one hand rubbing the back of his head. "Uh, it's ... uh ..."

"Well, who is it?" Cody prompted.

Jonas looked like he'd swallowed a bug. "It's ... She says her name is Olivia. That you invited her, James. I buzzed her through."

Mallory went stiff beside him.

The air in the room dropped to ten below. This couldn't be happening, not again. The beating of his heart became a roar in his ears. The front door opened, and the clickety-clack of high heels on hardwood started his way.

"There you are, darling." Olivia's strident voice turned his stomach. Worse, when she reached him she stretched up on her toes to kiss his lips.

He jerked away.

She settled for a pat on his cheek before looking around the room. "Sorry I'm late, everyone. James didn't tell me what time to be here, so I had to guess. Oh, you've

finished already, and here I haven't had a thing to eat all day."

All around the table, the Camerons and their guests, some standing, some still seated, stared in fascination at the farce playing out.

James felt nothing but horror. How could she do this again?

Staunch Cate, ever the lady, came to the rescue. "I'm sorry, I don't believe we've met. I'm Cate Cameron."

Olivia wound her way to where Cate stood and held out her small, well-manicured hand. "I'm Olivia Ashcroft Evers, Jameson's wife. It's so nice of you to have us over."

Always gracious, Cate rose to the occasion. "I've heard. Well, there's plenty of food. You can catch up while we enjoy dessert. Jonas, be a dear and fetch another chair for Olivia. We'll make room right here next to me. Cassie, get another place setting."

"Oh, I'd prefer to sit next to my husband, if you don't mind. He's my security blanket, if you know what I mean."

James couldn't take anymore. "Cate, thank you for your hospitality. I apologize for Olivia's outrageous behavior. We'll leave now."

He took Olivia's hand and pulled her toward the front door.

Not content until she ruined the day, Olivia dug her heels in for a final poison dart. "Sorry to leave so soon. We've been married for years, but never had a honeymoon.

Slow down, sweetheart. We have the rest of our lives to catch up."

"Shut. Up." Venom laced the two words he spat out for all to hear.

Her laughter set his teeth on edge. He'd never hurt a woman, had no desire to now, but he couldn't take much more of her stomping all over his life. Seething didn't do justice to the volcano inside him. He slammed the door behind them.

Chapter Eight

The slam registered with enough force that it seemed to suck all the air out of the house. The windows rattled. And then, silence. Not the comfortable kind where peace resided, either. This collective void had the prickly texture of awkwardness mixed with embarrassment.

Mallory closed her eyes, but the damage was already done. The pictures were seared into her retina, fated to play over and over. James holding Olivia's hand. Tugging her outside. In a hurry to leave. Olivia laughing as he whispered to her.

All the flirty comments at dinner, playing footsy under the table, his great need to talk in private. And she'd fallen for his guile again.

She turned to flee, had to get away—and came face to face with fifteen pairs of eyes, all filled with varying degrees of pity, sympathy, anger, and outrage.

The pain, unexpected and wicked, made her lungs seize. Tiny hairline cracks infiltrated her composure and spread in a spider web network of tiny fissures.

Not here.

Breathing became a luxury she couldn't afford lest she become a living replica of a cracked desert landscape.

Not in front of everyone.

Adopting a faraway look that allowed her to see without seeing, Mallory turned toward the stairs. "Excuse me, please."

No one spoke. No one stopped her. A path opened, and she took it.

Safe inside her bedroom, she leaned against the door. Cassie would come later, but for now no one would bother her. They would respect her need for privacy.

A long time later, once all the moisture had been cried from her body, Mallory clawed her way up from the despair. Everything ached, her eyes, nose, head, and most of all her heart. "Fool me once, shame on you," she quoted in a broken voice. "Fool me twice, shame on me." There wouldn't be a third time.

Mallory gathered her nightclothes, grabbed her iPod, and slipped into the bathroom she and her sister shared. Scalding hot water to thaw the block of ice in her chest, bubbles, jasmine-scented bath salts, candles of the same fragrance, and soft, bluesy music. A sensory distraction and a balm for her ravaged heart. She refilled the tub twice before pruney fingers pulled the plug.

Cassie was waiting on her bed when she finished with the bath. "Hey, you okay?"

"No, but I will be."

"I know you're hurting."

"What gave it away? The bloodshot eyes, or my red, swollen nose?"

"I'm sorry, Mal."

Pity? Or sympathy? She wanted neither. "Why apologize? You're not at fault here."

"James isn't either."

Mallory stared at her twin, searched for the horns that had surely sprouted after that last statement. Had she taken his side? "He lied, Cass."

"No, he didn't. His private life is his. Just because he chose not to tell you or anybody else doesn't make him a liar. He doesn't owe us an explanation."

Her words reeked of accusation and betrayal.

"I get it. You're on his side." Mallory shook her head and turned away to avoid saying something she would regret. Cassidy was her twin, her confidante. They were supposed to have each other's back.

Her sister apparently didn't have the same compunction. Cassie hopped off the bed and got in Mallory's face, hands on her hips. "I don't think you get it at all. You're not the only victim here. James is Garrett's best friend. How do you think all this drama makes him feel? He's Wade's and Jonas's friend, too. My friend. And Mom and Dad love him like one of their own children. You can't shut him out the way you—"

Cassie looked away.

The way you did to me.

The unspoken words raised Mallory's pain to a whole new level. Past collided with present, like salt on the open wound of her heart. "He was my friend, too," she whispered.

"Was?" Cassie rounded on her. "Newsflash, Sis. Friendship doesn't come with an on/off switch. Love either."

"He's married. Did you miss that part?"

Color tinted Cassie's cheeks. "No, I didn't miss it. But that happened before he came here. And you said yourself he never encouraged you."

"He didn't. But he knew how I felt, and friends don't let you make a fool of yourself."

"You can't know that."

Mallory snorted. "The whole town knew. He couldn't possibly *not* know."

"Look, I don't want to hurt you, Mal," Cassie pleaded. "You've hurt yourself enough for a lifetime. But we promised to tell each other the truth, and sometimes truth hurts. I'm asking you to step outside yourself long enough to see what James is going through. The embarrassment, the humiliation of having his dirty laundry debated by every gossip in town. He didn't want this for you or for him. He was trying to fix it—"

"You can't fix a mistake by covering it up. That makes it a lie."

"If you count privacy as lying, then you need to 'fess up, too, because you never told him how you feel."

This time the tears burned. How foolish could she get? Despite having his marriage rubbed in her face, she'd held onto hope. And tonight, she'd misconstrued his playfulness. She thought he wanted to make things right with her, when all he really wanted was to salvage his relationships with her family.

Her naïveté died a hard death. James had no room in his life for her, other than as his best friend's little sister. She had to let him go before he inflicted more damage.

"You're right. I can't punish everyone else for my misguided fantasies. But I can't hang around and watch their happily-ever-after unfold either. I'm not that strong or forgiving. I'd wind up in jail for throwing cow chips at them."

Cassie hugged her. "I'm so sorry. I thought he felt the same way you did. And for what it's worth, I'd be sitting in jail right beside you."

Enough with the pity party. She broke free of the embrace, but held onto Cassie's arms. "Go on now, get out of here. I have a job interview tomorrow, and Dad wants to leave for the airport by three-thirty. I need to get to bed."

◌◌◌

Six inches of snow fell during the night as forecasted and for once Mallory was glad her father insisted they leave way early.

"Thanks, Dad." Mallory leaned over and kissed his leathery cheek when he pulled up in front of the Idaho Falls Regional Airport. "I'll call if my flight is delayed."

"You get in at midnight, right? I'll be here. Be safe, Pixie-girl."

"Always am." She closed the truck door, and smiled at his pet name for her. Sprite and Pixie-girl. She hadn't heard those names in years. Hitching the strap of her new black leather messenger bag over one shoulder, Mallory headed inside, glad she wouldn't be gone overnight.

Whoever booked her travel put her in coach on the leg from Idaho Falls to Salt Lake City, but had arranged a first-class seat from Salt Lake to Seattle. Four hours later, she stepped off the plane at Sea-Tac International and stopped in the first ladies room she saw to freshen up.

She'd worn her hair loose, but took time to fashion it into a tight, low bun for her meeting. The calf-length charcoal skirt hugged her waist and hips, but had just enough flare at the hem to allow for an easy stride. The black cashmere shell, topped by the swingy collarless sweater jacket looked chic, accented by the patent leather belt. The only part of her ensemble that worried her were the three-inch heels on the black leather boots. Heels and icy pavement didn't mix well. Still, they were comfortable. And they made her legs look a mile long.

She spotted her name on a sign held aloft at the entrance to baggage claim.

"Hi, I'm Mallory Cameron."

The gray-haired man smiled and lowered the sign. "Welcome to Seattle. My name is Frank. Do you have any bags? No? Well, then I'll take you straight to your car. It's about a thirty-minute drive to the office."

A car? Had they gotten her a rental? She was in trouble if they had. Seattle was a lot bigger than Idaho Falls or Pocatello, and maybe even Boise.

He led her outside to where a black Lincoln had just pulled up to the curb. The driver, an older black man dressed in a dark suit and white shirt, hurried around to open the rear passenger door.

"Here you go, Miss Cameron. This is Curtis. He'll take good care of you." Frank helped her in, nodded, and closed the door.

Relieved she wouldn't have to find her own way, Mallory looked out first one window and then the other, not wanting to miss a thing.

"First time in Seattle, Miss?" Curtis asked from the front seat.

Oh, dear. He must think her a hayseed, the way she'd been scooting from side to side. "Yes." She didn't bother telling him it was pretty much her first time anywhere.

"We have some time before they expect you," he said with a knowing grin. "How about I give you a quick tour of the city?"

She couldn't hold back a clap of delight. "Oh yes, please. I didn't think I'd get to see anything."

Curtis chuckled and launched into a vivid narration as they drove toward downtown Seattle. He pointed out Pike Place Market, a couple of museums, the Olympic Sculpture Park, the historic Smith Tower, Safeco Field where the Mariners play, the iconic Space Needle, the Great Wheel, Pioneer Square, Chinatown, and finished down by the waterfront.

Mallory managed to snap a few pictures with her cell phone and promised herself, whether she got the job or not, to come back one day and play tourist.

The Lincoln pulled to the curb in front of an intimidating skyscraper. Curtis got out, came around to open her door, and helped her out.

"Is this …" She peered up at the tall building, sure it wasn't what she'd researched.

"No, ma'am. The new building is still under construction. Meanwhile, the different departments are spread. Your meetings are here. Take the elevator to the sixteenth floor and Mr. Kinsloe will meet you there."

"Thank you, Curtis. I can't tell you how much I enjoyed the tour." She fumbled in her bag for her wallet, mindful of Lucy's tipping advice, but the driver shook his head.

"No need, Miss Cameron. I'm well compensated. I'll return later to take you to the airport. You have a good day."

A well-dressed man of moderate height greeted her the moment the elevator doors opened. "Mallory Cameron. It's a pleasure to finally meet you. Welcome to Seattle. I'm Jared Kinsloe, Senior Section Editor. Call me Jared. Come, I'll show you to the conference room we've put you in for the day."

She walked beside him down the hall, and ticked off his attributes. Garrett's age. Nice looking. Well-groomed, right down to his buffed fingernails. Trim. Great suit that looked like it was tailored for him. Perfect manners, good voice, intelligent, and witty. But no buzz. No attraction beyond 'like.' Not that she was in the market for a rebound. Miffed, she decided to let time take care of her problem.

They passed several offices and one huge open area filled with a city of cubicles and the low-level hum of employees on telephones, chatting with each other, and working in small groups. "Wow, how many people are here?"

"In the company, or this department? Doesn't matter. Honestly, I have no idea. We're scattered all over the place

for the foreseeable future, until the new building is completed. In the Investigations Department alone, we have about fifty full-timers who come into the office, plus those who work remote."

Mallory perked up. "Remote, as in work from home? You allow that?"

He chuckled. "We like our reporters chasing stories, but we also require an occasional appearance. You'll meet a few of my colleagues today. Here we go. Make yourself comfortable. The Ladies Room is two doors down, and there's water in the fridge behind you. Lunch should be here in about fifteen minutes. I'll be back with your first interviewer then."

Mallory set her shoulder bag on the conference table and shed her coat, folding it neatly over one of the chairs. One entire wall was made of glass and looked out over the city. The view was spectacular. She looked down at the pint-sized people scurrying along the sidewalks and felt small and insignificant. Could she navigate this world, or would she lose herself in the enormity of it?

With her portfolio at her fingertips and a pen and notepad ready, she schooled her features into a mask of confidence, and took a seat. After all, they had sought her out, not the other way around.

Hours later she'd run the gauntlet of senior reporters, a news editor, two copy editors, a secretary, a photo journalist, someone from HR, and even a lawyer. Mental exhaustion became a concern, but she had one more interview to go, with the Bureau Chief. Jared had participated in all of the previous sessions, but he left with the others. She was on her own with the big boss.

The door opened, and a hurricane swept into the room. Short and somewhat stout, with a receding hairline, the Bureau Chief looked like he could run circles around her.

Mallory stood to greet him with extended hand.

"Miss Cameron, I'm Robert Deerborn." He gave her hand two quick pumps and turned away. "Please, have a seat. Can I get you anything? Coffee? Water?"

She smiled. "No, thank you. Your staff has been very attentive."

He took his chair, slapped a folder on the desk, and leaned on his elbows. "I know you're tired, so let's get straight to it. May I call you Mallory?"

"Yes, of course."

"Mallory, I have to admit I was skeptical of bringing you in. You're young and have only freelance work under your belt. You've never worked for a news organization—or any organization from what your resume shows. And you have zilch in the way of practical media experience. Jared wants you here, though. He thinks you have potential, and your work on the trafficking article reflects it. The others you met today think the same."

Dread turned into disappointment, and then to incredulity. She had to pinch herself to control the giddiness so she didn't miss the rest of Mr. Deerborn's words.

"Jared's been with me for twelve years. I've learned to trust his instincts. Anyway, what I'm taking the long way around to say is, I'm excited to discover such raw, fresh talent as yours. You're bright, decisive, intelligent, inquisitive, determined—all qualities we look for on our team. The job is yours if you want it, with conditions."

Conditions. Her ego plummeted. "What conditions?"

He smiled. "Caught that, did you? Sharp girl. Here's the deal." He flipped open the folder and extracted a stack of papers.

"This is our standard contract. It has a ton of legalese guaranteed to put you to sleep. Nonetheless, I caution you to read it through, and then reread it. Might even want to have your lawyer take a look. To boil it all down, your acceptance of this offer means you move to Seattle for no less than six months. Jared will be your supervisor and mentor. He will arrange training and assignments, show you the tricks of the trade. In other words, he'll teach you how an investigative reporter performs to our standards. This is non- negotiable. You're a rookie. As such, you need time with those who know the ropes. With me?"

She nodded. The stipulation didn't come as a surprise, but still … six months. Somewhere in the back of her mind, she'd hoped for a way around leaving home.

"You'll start out with small, local assignments. Scut

work. Once Jared is comfortable with your competence, he'll send you out or go with you on more demanding projects. If you don't have a passport, get one."

His words ignited a hunger in her. She wanted to push her boundaries and broaden her horizons. It would mean leaving James well and truly behind her. "I haven't traveled much, but only because of limited opportunity. I'm more than eager for new experiences."

His stare seemed to drill right through her. Several moments passed before he stuffed the papers back in the folder and handed it to her. "Call me the week between Christmas and New Year's with your answer. If you say yes, you'll start the second Monday in January. Any questions?"

"Wow. I'm not sure I can pull off a move and find a place to stay in that amount of time."

"Then you better get started. It's been a pleasure, Mallory." He stood and shook her hand again.

Jared appeared as though by magic. "Curtis is downstairs. He says if you want to make your flight, you have to leave now." The Cheshire cat couldn't compete with Jared's grin, especially when he opened the door for her and bowed her through. While he might not be dazzling in the looks department, he had charisma in spades when he turned the full force of his charm on her.

He escorted her downstairs to meet her ride. "I know you're in hot demand right now, but I hope you'll give our

offer serious consideration. You can have a fantastic future in Seattle, one I hope to foster." He took her hand, removed the glove she'd just pulled on, and pulled her hand to his lips for a soft kiss. "I look forward to showing you the sights of my city."

Curtis held the car door for her, waited while she tucked her legs inside, and closed it behind her.

Jared waited and watched until she couldn't see him anymore. Definitely suave, maybe even a player … and nothing like the man back home.

Chapter Nine

Mallory looked down at her buzzing phone. James had left several voice mails and texts in the four days since her return from Seattle. She hadn't read or listened to any of them, and didn't intend to start now. Instead she turned her attention to planning her second shopping trip. She'd even managed to strong arm Derek into being their escort since Cassie planned to tag along.

The look of relief on Wade's face when he heard he'd been absolved from shopping duty still had the power to make her laugh.

"So, Derek," she asked on the drive to Idaho Falls. "Please explain why men find shopping with women so painful."

His answer came with a derisive snort. "Shopping is a necessary evil. You deal with it, but you don't revel in it."

"Okay," Cassie said. "I'll bite. How do you deal with it?"

"Men know what they want going in. We find it, buy it, and leave. Done. You girls have to wander through every department, touch everything, and smell everything. You hold stuff up to check how it looks on you, even knowing you won't buy it. You wander around in aimless, every-widening circles like you're waiting for the dress fairy to jump out and zap you with her magic wand, and say, 'Buy this one. It's perfect for you.' You try it on, let your friends tell you lies about how great it is, buy it, and then never wear it because …" He raised his voice to a falsetto. "It doesn't fit right. I thought it did, but now it doesn't."

Was he talking about Cassie? Cause if he was ….

"Wow." Lucy's mouth hung open. "Just … wow."

Cassie leaned over and knuckle-punched Derek's arm, right where his bulky bicep dipped below the shoulder.

"Ow." He flinched away. "What'd you do that for?"

Cass turned her face to the window and ignored him.

Mallory leaned in and whispered in a loud voice. "Take a warning, Romeo. My sister rocked anatomy in school. She knows every vulnerable part of the human body."

"I'm not Romeo. That's Kyle." He pointed a thumb at his chest and inhaled to expand its impressive width. "I'm the Iceman."

"Oh, puh-leeze." Deliberately obtuse. As if the

military nickname bestowed on him while in service was a badge of honor. He knew good and well she'd been referring to his hound dog ways before Cassie.

"Okay, no more squabbles. I have a plan and we're sticking to it." Lucy brandished the list she'd compiled. "Behave yourself, Derek, and we might feed you before we head back."

He made a strangled sound, but lapsed into silence for the rest of the drive.

It took four hours to find everything on Mallory's list, plus a few other non-essential items. Taking pity on Derek, who'd acted as their unsmiling pack mule and lugged all their bags for them, they stopped for a late lunch at Jalisco's Mexican Restaurant.

Their choice nudged Derek right back into his happy zone. "Best Mexican food I've had since I left Texas," he said with a smile and patted his belly.

Mallory leaned toward Lucy. "Have you and Wade set a date yet?"

Lucy stared over Derek's shoulder, intent on something across the street. Her eyes narrowed with that look of concentration she sometimes got when working at her computer.

"Lucy." Mallory nudged her shoulder.

"Oh, sorry." Lucy snapped her attention back to the group, but pulled her phone from her purse and began to fidget with it. "No. No date yet. I think soon, though." She angled the phone to one side and tilted it.

"Are you taking pictures?"

"Yeah."

"Of what?"

"People."

"Well, daylight is on the downslide. I say we head home." Derek grabbed the bill from the waiter.

On the return drive, Lucy stayed busy with her phone, but now and again, she'd twist around to look out the rear window.

"What's going on, Lucy?" Mallory asked her in a low voice.

"Nothing. Just working a few things out."

Mallory's phone pinged, chasing away her concerns about Lucy. Another text message from James. She opened this one.

> TALK TO ME. GIVE ME A CHANCE
> TO EXPLAIN. DON'T SHUT ME OUT.

Pushy and demanding as usual. How could she move on without him when he refused to be left behind? Maybe one day, in a year or two, they might rekindle their friendship. Then again, probably not. Like Cassie said, love didn't have an expiration date. And she didn't know if she could forgive, must less trust him again.

A shuddering sigh wrenched free, taking a piece of her heart with it. Time to end whatever this was between them for her own good. She typed a reply, hit send, and shut her phone off.

Beside her, Lucy remained engrossed with her phone. Something was up, but Mallory knew her friend well enough to know she would analyze, dissect, and process it from every angle before sharing.

Five days had passed since Olivia invaded the Cameron's Thanksgiving feast. He'd been so furious when he dragged her out of there. She'd pleaded with him, begged to work out their differences, to make a go of their marriage. Not bloody likely. He'd rather serve the rest of his life in some third-world backwater, fighting enemy combatants and mosquitos than to spend one more minute in the same room with her.

The day after the she crashed the meal, he'd called his attorney and initiated divorce proceedings, citing criminal wrongdoing. He had enough evidence to have the marriage dissolved and maybe even prove her culpability, but that didn't explain why she was so desperate to continue this farce.

"James, there's a man on the phone."

He looked up to find Lorraine in his doorway, which put him on instant alert. Lorraine yelled or shouted. She didn't walk back to his office to deliver messages. "Who is it, and what does he want?"

She crossed her arms, unfolded them again, looked at the floor, at the window, and finally at him. "Uh ..."

"Spit it out, Lorraine."

"It's a reporter with The Real Scoop. He's asking questions about ... you and your, uh, wife. He wants to interview you."

Not much took him by surprise. This did. "The Real Scoop? Never heard of it."

"It's a sleaze tabloid. They don't bother much with facts. You know, that fake news stuff the media is all about today."

"And why does he—never mind. Get rid of him. I'm not doing any interviews."

She looked doubtful, started to say something else, but walked away.

Where had this come from? Foolish question. He knew exactly where. Olivia had invoked the 'wronged woman' plaint. She would lynch him in public opinion. As if he cared what people thought.

Although elections were next year.

He picked up his cell phone to call his attorney again, but a knock at his door interrupted him. "Lucy? Hey, come in."

She offered a distracted smile, but remained in the doorway. "Lorraine was on the phone. She waved me back. If you have a minute, I'd like to show you something."

"I'll always make time for you." He motioned her to

sit.

Once she settled in a chair, he asked, "What do you have?"

Lucy made a few finger swipes on her cell phone and handed it to James. "I took this yesterday in Idaho Falls."

"Ah, yes. The shopping expedition. Derek said it was a success, the Mexican restaurant in particular. What am I looking at?"

"I was hoping you could pull a few strings and tell me who this is."

He studied the picture, a zoom shot of a man with dark skin and close-cropped black hair. He wore jeans and a white, loose-fitting tunic that fell to mid-thigh. "You used your cell phone camera?"

"Yeah."

"It's a quality shot."

"I have an app that lets you zoom without all the clunky external hardware."

"You have an app, or wrote one?"

Lucy was a computer prodigy with a long and colorful history of hacking for the government, creating viruses, and, most recently, writing computer games. She shrugged his question off. "Swipe left. There's more."

Several additional photos of the same man followed. In one shot, he appeared to stare straight at the camera, his eyes black as pitch. "Looks like he caught you taking this one."

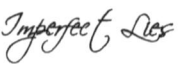

"Nope. He had no idea. I caught *him* staring. See that green patch on his shirt? Look at this." She slid a piece of paper across his desk. "I enhanced the image on my computer and printed it."

White squiggles of what he thought might be Arabic scrolled across a black rectangular field, with … crossed swords? Scimitars? Rifles?"

"Sorry about the distortion. I had to magnify the image to bring the writing up."

A soft whistle expressed his concern. "This is … You think he's connected to one of the terrorist groups operating out of Africa."

"Africa or the Middle East, I wasn't sure."

A knot of dread built as he flipped through the photos again. "What was he staring at?"

"Not what. Who. He followed us all over Idaho Falls yesterday."

James froze. "Derek didn't say anything."

She shrugged. "I didn't tell him. You know how Cassidy and Mallory turn heads when they're together."

"Yeah, I know." His trepidation increased.

"I noticed him outside one of the stores we went to. You don't see a lot of men wearing tunics in Idaho. Not even in the city."

"Go on."

"It struck me as odd when I spotted him across the street from the restaurant. Too coincidental. Later, after we got home, I uploaded the photos to my computer to study on a bigger screen. That's when I zoomed in on the patch."

"Anyone else know?"

"Wade. He told me to show you the pictures."

James nodded. "Send these to me. This one, too." He waggled the printed copy of the patch. "I'll see what I can do."

She tapped away at her cell phone. A few seconds later, his phone pinged with an incoming message.

"So, terrorist ties. Africa," she said. "Who was he tailing?"

"That's the big question, now isn't it?"

After Lucy left, James tapped out a text message to Fowler.

NEED TO TALK.

Two minutes later his phone rang, showing an unlisted number.

"Evers." He jerked the phone away from his ear when the sequence of squawks, chirps, and buzzes erupted over the line. Why'd the blasted encryption software have to be so loud?

"Sheriff."

He'd recognize Fowler's raspy voice anywhere. "Thanks for calling. I need a photo run through the facial recognition database. Suspect is wearing a tunic with what could be a terrorist insignia."

"And why does this person interest you?" Fowler had

access to a wealth of contacts, and wouldn't hesitate to make use of them when needed, but he didn't call in favors lightly.

"Because he tailed Mallory, Cassidy, Lucy, and Derek all over Idaho Falls yesterday."

"Send me what you have through the secure mailbox."

"Will do. Thanks."

The line went dead. Fowler had already hung up.

James glanced at his cell phone to check on the pictures Lucy sent, but his eyes went to the text message app. He pulled up Mallory's last text.

Our 'friendship' is for family time only. Please don't call or text me anymore.

"Not a chance, princess." She had no idea how determined and persistent he could be.

James set his cell phone down and pinched the bridge of his nose. The headache he didn't have before sprang into full force. She needed space. He got that. But not too much. And only until he unraveled the tangled knots that kept him from laying claim right now.

He turned back to his computer and started the lengthy login process. The FBI's facial recognition database contained more than four hundred million images. He had no doubt Fowler had access to even more. Given the sheer volume, a match could take months.

Of all the stuff taking up space in his head—Fowler's warning, the intruder at the Camerons, Olivia, the mystery of Jonas, his father's endgame, the reporter, Mallory's cold shoulder, and now Lucy's photos—none was more vital than ensuring Mallory's safety during her upcoming trips to Chicago and New York. He needed a plan.

As typical when faced with trouble, his thoughts turned to the men who'd stood at his side for so many years. Now he could add Wade and Jonas to that group. He needed all of them, because keeping Mallory safe could be challenging.

After a quick check of his calendar, James sent a group text to Garrett, Wade, Jonas, Kyle, and Derek. With a second thought, he added Lucy, and asked them to meet in his office at one o'clock to discuss an urgent matter. Mallory's family had a right to know of the potential dangers, and they wouldn't hesitate to ride roughshod over any objections she might make.

That decision made, he grabbed the stack of reports Lorraine left for him to review and approve. Nothing like dull, mind-numbing paperwork to help pass the time.

Garrett and Jonas arrived ten minutes early, followed minutes later by Wade and Lucy. His two deputies straggled in at the top of the hour.

Without mincing words, James explained Lucy's concerns and passed around printed copies of all the pictures she'd taken. He went on to explain the request to Fowler and how long the process could take. Only then did he broach his reason for calling the meeting.

"I don't know if this man is a danger, or even who he was shadowing. In light of Fowler's notification of an imminent threat to someone here in the area, and the intruder at your ranch, I'm concerned about Mallory's trip to Chicago tomorrow and to New York next week. She shouldn't be alone."

"She'll have to cancel," Garrett stated with all the authority in the world.

"You can't ask her to do that," Lucy retorted. "She wouldn't anyway."

"One of us could go with her. She won't like it, but … tough." Wade crossed his arms over his chest, big brother in protective mode.

Derek laughed. "Yeah, I want to be there when you tell her she has to take her brother along. She'd chop you into little bits and feed you to the fishes in Lake Michigan."

James thought his deputy was more right than wrong in this instance.

"Anybody else believe we should ask Mallory what she thinks?" Kyle, the voice of reason, posed the question James wanted to ask her, but didn't dare. To gain Mallory's cooperation, none of the solutions put forth could come from him.

Jonas sat off to one side, his attention on the enhanced image of the odd insignia.

"Jonas? Anything you want to add?"

He looked up and met James's gaze straight on. Those

deep blue Cameron eyes had turned dark, almost black …
and cold. For once, he exuded not a trace of amusement.

"Yeah. Get in touch with Fowler. Tell him we want an
undercover agent assigned to keep tabs on Mallory at all
times. He'll need her flight numbers, schedule, where she's
staying, where her interviews are scheduled, and any
names you can provide. Then *you* need to sit down with
Mallory and explain everything."

Any doubt James had about a connection between
Jonas and Fowler evaporated. "One of you will have to talk
to her. She's not speaking to me at the moment."

"Why would Fowler help?" Garrett asked. "And what
makes you think Mallory will cooperate?"

Jonas answered his brother's questions, but his gaze
locked with James's. "Because Fowler knows the big
picture, and Mallory is smarter than all of us."

Imperfect Lies

Chapter Ten

The interview in Chicago was scheduled from nine to eleven on Friday morning, but because of limited flights she had to go the night before. Garrett drove her to the airport in Idaho Falls this time to catch the noon flight.

Everything went downhill from there. A weather advisory delayed her connecting flight from Salt Lake City to Chicago. Her flight was rerouted from O'Hare to Midway, which meant no one met her when she landed well after midnight. With her bag on one shoulder and pulling a carryon suitcase behind her, Mallory followed the signs to Ground Transportation only to find heavy snow falling and no taxis. She finally managed to get an Uber to take her to her hotel.

Sleep was elusive. She gave up on it a little after five, got up, ordered room service, and left a voice mail for her contact at the newspaper to let them know she'd made it in. When no response came by seven-thirty, she made her way downstairs and asked the concierge to call a cab.

The driver got her to the building on South Wacker Drive with five minutes to spare. The receptionist greeted her, told her to have a seat, and that someone would be along soon. Soon turned into forty-five minutes. Not good since she had to leave no later than eleven to make her return flight. Too bad if they wanted her to stay longer.

She hadn't met a soul here other than the receptionist, but had already written this interview off as a lost cause.

"Would you please call Mr. Driscoll again? I have to leave no later than eleven."

"Miss Cameron?"

Mallory turned to the man who entered the reception area. "Yes?"

"I'm sorry to keep you waiting. Mr. Driscoll was called away on an emergency and asked me to fill in for him. I'm Charles Appleton, one of the staff writers. Come this way, please."

Late thirties, nice looking. Polished and professional. He led her to a small conference room where one other man and a woman waited. Introductions were made, and then the attack began. And it felt like an attack. The three threw questions her way, mostly about a shared project she knew nothing about. When they did ask a question she could respond to, Appleton would cut her off. Mr. Appleton stood at the twenty-minute mark. "Well, I believe we covered everything. Thank you for coming, Miss Cameron. Someone will be in touch."

All three of them walked out.

Don't bother, she wanted to say. Instead, she called a thank you after them, and tried to figure out what happened. Why go to the expense and bother of bringing her in when they had no serious interest in hiring her?

The two interviews she'd had couldn't have differed more. Seattle treated her with respect and courtesy. They made her feel wanted and valued. Not so much here in Chicago. They seemed put out at having to spend any time with her at all.

If nothing else, their shabby treatment simplified her decision—forget the Windy City. What would the Big Apple hold?

It took ten minutes to gather her receipts and attach them to a handwritten summary of expenses she'd incurred for this trip. They'd promised to cover all expenses, and she intended to get her money back. "Please give this to Mr. Driscoll when he returns." She dropped the receipts on the receptionist's desk and caught the next elevator, glad to be done here.

CCC

"On my way."

Heart thumping, James disconnected the call. Time to do this. He pulled on his jacket, grabbed his hat and keys, and walked out the back door with a hollered, "I'll be at the Triple C if you need me."

Lorraine gave him a thumb's up and went right back to her game of computer solitaire.

Several people raised fingers from their steering wheels to acknowledge him as he drove through town. Still others waved or tipped their hats to him from the sidewalks. Not much had changed. After all the angst and worry, the sordid details of his private life had blown over in a flash, forgiven and for the most part forgotten. The women of Hastings Bluff still invited him to Sunday dinner, the men still shook his hand at church. Crazy Mrs. Halliday still called every week and asked him to rescue her cat stuck in a tree, and old Judd Wheeler still tried to wheedle his way into getting his driver's license reinstated. Life went on despite his fall from grace.

In the venerable words of Dee Dee Guthrie, "Your faults don't make you special, Sheriff. All toads have warts."

He wasn't sure whether to be insulted or accepted. Either way, he didn't much care.

A grin slipped free. With the call from his attorney yesterday, he could at last put his nightmare past to rest. The judge had made it clear he would expedite the divorce and refer the case for criminal proceedings if Olivia didn't sign the annulment decree. Her attorney recognized a losing cause, and convinced her to sign the papers.

Another week to process the paperwork and James was a free man.

He parked in the gravel drive and climbed the front steps to the Cameron's home. The door opened before his knuckles hit the wood.

"Hey, man." Garrett grabbed his arm. "C'mon on inside where it's warm."

Jonas stood behind him, hand outstretched.

James shook both men's hands, stomped his boots on the door mat, and took off his coat. "You sure you want me here for this?"

"Absolutely. Mallory might not hold you in the highest esteem right now, but she's always listened to you when she wouldn't give the rest of us the time of day."

The brothers wanted him to explain the situation to Mallory, make her understand their concerns, and ask for her cooperation regarding their safety concerns for her upcoming New York trip. Not the best topic for their first face-to-face sit down since Olivia bombed Thanksgiving, but he'd take it. The only question was, did he follow Jonas's advice to lay it out straight and let her decide for herself, or try to guilt her into cooperating. Strong-arm tactics sure wouldn't work. He'd learned that the hard way.

"Hey, I'm going to cut out now. Good luck." Jonas grabbed his jacket and tried to slip out the front door before he even got it on.

"Hold on there, Jonas." James caught his arm. "I need you to stop by my office when you're in town. I'd like to pick your brain about some ideas."

One eyebrow lifted. "Okay." A world of wary curiosity filled that one word. And then Jonas closed the door behind him.

"Mallory know I'm here?" James turned his attention to Garrett and the reason he'd come out this morning. He wiped his hands on the legs of his jeans, unable to remember the last time his palms had been so sweaty.

"Yeah. She's making coffee in the kitchen. Everybody else is off somewhere else." Garrett motioned him to follow. "What was that about with Jonas?"

"Probably nothing, but sometimes a different take on a situation can spark some ideas. I'm hurting for leads. That's all." He followed behind his friend to the rear of the house.

Mallory sat at the kitchen counter, a cup of coffee cradled in her hands. Two other cups sat on the other side, across from her. Sugar and creamer occupied the center space between them.

"Morning."

"Sheriff."

So, she intended to play hardball. Make him work for every concession, every word, every touch. He could do that.

Garrett settled onto one of the stools and reached for a cup. "I asked James to come out because we need to fill you in on a few things that have come up."

"Is this about the intruder?" She looked at her brother, but he nodded at James.

Her gaze shifted his way, her eyes settling somewhere in the vicinity of his chest.

"Thanks for the coffee." James pulled the remaining mug to him. "The intruder is one part of what we need to discuss."

Dark blue eyes framed by thick, black lashes, flickered up, met his stare for a scorching second, but then darted right back to his shirt.

She still cared. He saw it in her expression, in the way she avoided meeting his eyes. His heart did a funny little hiccup. His mouth twitched, wanting to grin with joy. He hid it behind a gulp of coffee, and then swore silently as the hot liquid scorched his mouth.

Garrett stood and walked over to grab a glass from the cabinet and fill it from the faucet. "Here," he said, and plunked it down on the island.

James took a grateful sip. "Here's the deal, princess."

Her nostrils flared at the endearment, right before she met his stare with a glare. Mallory didn't like confrontation, but she wouldn't run from it.

"Agent Fowler contacted me before Thanksgiving. His analysts intercepted chatter from a Nigerian terrorist group that showed interest in someone in or around Hastings Bluff. No names, but it was enough to put my antenna up. The intruder here at the ranch heightened the alert. Then, on your second shopping trip, Lucy spotted someone who seemed to take an inordinate interest in your group. She snapped a couple of pictures with her phone. One photo showed a patch that is a confirmed link to a terrorist splinter group in Nigeria. We don't have identification yet, but I learned a long time ago to question coincidence."

Her beautiful eyes widened. A spark of fear flared in their depths, but was quickly hidden. "You're concerned about my trip to New York."

That flicker of vulnerability made him want to pound something. Or someone. He nodded instead. "Yes. I'm worried about you traveling alone to a strange city. We all are."

"Please don't ask me to cancel."

"It would be the best solution, but I kind of figured you'd insist on going. The second-best solution is to have someone go with you."

Mallory's chin shot up, even as the corners of her mouth went down. "What else have you got, Sheriff?"

"I had Fowler put a shadow on you in Chicago. The agent traveled on the same flights as you, tailed you to your hotel, stayed in the room next to yours, followed you to the newspaper office, and accompanied you back home." He held his hand up when she got all flustered. "Let me finish.

You never knew he was there. He didn't intrude on your space at all. I'd like to have the same agent follow you to New York, only with a team this time since you're staying several days. With your knowledge and consent, of course. They're good. Very discreet. I promise you won't see them."

Her mouth relented, and turned up in a smile. "Why didn't you tell me about Chicago? And what's changed that you're telling me now?"

Jonas was right. Mallory was sharp.

Garrett reached over and covered one of his sister's hands. "We just put it all together the day before your Chicago trip."

James leaned in. "We couldn't risk you refusing. I won't apologize for my need to keep you safe. This time, you'll be gone several days and have more free time. Knowledge will keep you cognizant of your surroundings and influence your decisions."

She took a sip of her coffee. Several seconds passed before she said, "Thank you."

"For what, Sis?" Garrett looked puzzled.

She looked at her brother, and then at James. "For treating me like an adult and not a rebellious child. You're right, of course, and I accept your offer of a bodyguard for this trip." A glint of mischief sparkled in those blue eyes. "So, what do I get if I spot them?"

Her unexpected playfulness sent a jolt of pleasure

zinging through his veins. "Princess, you spot them and I'll give you the moon. And if you don't, I'll probably give you the stars. Either way, I'm taking you to dinner when you get back."

Mallory zipped her suitcase and hauled it downstairs. The span of days since her little confab with James and Garrett about the bodyguard had passed in a flurry of holiday busyness, which left no time to worry about stalkers and terrorists.

Even better, James had been out to the house several times, and made a point of reminding her of their dinner date when she returned home.

She owed him a chance to explain. Olivia was gone now, or so she'd heard. That had to mean something. Maybe by clearing the air, they could move on and give this friendship thing a shot. But she wouldn't date a married man.

"Jonas," she yelled and dropped her stuff by the front door. "Time to go."

"Coming." His voice carried from the back side of the house.

She started that way, but drew up short when Jonas, Garrett, and James emerged from the kitchen. Her eyes honed in on the lone set of hazel ones. "Hi."

"Hi, yourself."

"All set, Sis?" Jonas bumped Garrett's shoulder. "Come help me load her stuff."

"I have one suitcase. It doesn't take two grown men to put it in the truck."

Jonas and Garrett left anyway.

"Everything is all set," James told her. "You'll stay safe, right?"

She nodded, unable to form a verbal response.

"Mallory, there's so much I want—I need—to say. I promise, when you get back, we'll talk. Okay?"

"Okay," she whispered.

He cupped her face with both hands and tilted her head up. And then he kissed her. Not a barn-burning, caveman kiss, but a barely-there, gentle brush of soft lips over hers. And then he was gone, through the kitchen, and out the door.

James's Yukon had almost disappeared by the time she pulled herself together and went out front to find her brothers.

She should be grateful he'd gone, not empty and lonely.

Jonas chuckled and climbed in behind the wheel of his fancy black truck. "Let's roll."

Garrett stared at her for a long moment, shook his head, and then took her hand and led her to the passenger side where he helped her in, and even buckled the seatbelt.

"Promise you'll be careful, baby sister."

Her wits connected to her brain again. "Of course. I'm always careful."

Garrett's only reply was to arch one eyebrow.

Chapter Eleven

Mallory followed the crowd from the arrival gate to LaGuardia's baggage claim. James was right. If someone was shadowing her, she couldn't pick him out. Better yet, she never got that uneasy feeling like she had that day at the ranch, that creepy feeling of being watched.

There, under the baggage claim sign that pointed down the stairs, she spotted a poster with her name, high above the crowd.

"I'm Mallory Cameron."

The man, her age, maybe a year or so younger, exposed a killer set of dimples. "Hey, you're cute. Not like most of the suits I meet. You check any bags?"

"Just one." Unlike the trip to Seattle where she had only a shoulder bag, and for Chicago where she'd taken a carryon, this time she checked a full-sized suitcase for her four-day trip.

"Baggage claim is down the stairs. No escalator. Sorry. Don't know why. Let me take your shoulder bag. I'm Tristan, by the way."

Mallory trailed after him, not an easy task given the sheer volume of people bustling through the airport. Thank goodness, she'd been smart enough to wear jeans and comfortable shoes for the long flight.

At the carousel, he returned her shoulder bag and grabbed her suitcase when she pointed it out.

Outside, as if summoned by magic, a dark gray Mercedes pulled up to the curb in front of them. The driver jumped out, hurried to open the trunk, and stowed Mallory's suitcase inside.

Tristan opened the rear door for her, and then got in the front passenger seat. "Hit it, Ben."

Like a thoroughbred breaking free of the starting block, the Mercedes zipped away from the curb into a space in the traffic and accelerated. She grabbed the door handle, tensed for a collision, and offered up a silent prayer. What had she gotten herself into?

"First time here?" Tristan turned sideways to look at her, a grin lurking around his mouth.

"How can you tell?"

He chuckled. "You get used to the traffic. Ben, here, he's the best. Been driving in the city his whole life."

Ben, a stout man of unidentifiable heritage, nodded

vigorously. "No worries, ma'am," he said with a lilt.

She tried to smile, but doubted either of the men in the front seat would construe it as such.

Her life played out before her eyes over and over again until Ben, of swarthy complexion and strange accent, whipped into an opening at the hotel's curb as another limo pulled away. "See. We here at hotel. You safe. No worries, yeah?" His grin spread cheer, despite the cramps in her hand.

Tristan ran a hand through his hair before he got out and opened her door. "Your palace, my lady."

She accepted his extended a hand and stepped out to a sight that took her breath away. The glass and concrete tower before her rose to dizzying heights. She tipped her head back, looked up ... and up ... and would have fallen over backward but for Tristan's steadying hand.

He laughed. "You make me see the city with new eyes."

By the time her awe subsided, Ben, the driver had already retrieved her things from the trunk and signaled the doorman for a bellhop. A young man in a red suit trimmed with gold braid hurried forward with a brass luggage cart.

"C'mon. Let's get you checked in."

Tristan might be young and more than a little flighty, but he knew his job. She'd registered, had her room card in hand, and entered the elevator in minutes.

In her room, once the porter dispensed with her bags,

Tristan slipped a discreetly folded bill into the man's palm, and closed the door.

The room, really a suite, was expansive and luxurious. And nothing like the one in Chicago. The living room area featured floor-to-ceiling windows that looked out over Central Park. Lights filled in the descending twilight, and if she tried hard, she could hear the noise of the city below. A kitchenette and wet bar filled one wall, while an open door on the other side revealed the bedroom.

"I've never seen anything like this."

"Yeah, I know," Tristan said behind her. "It really is a beautiful city. I've been here so long that sometimes I forget. Your reaction lets me see it new again."

She turned to face him. "Thank you for shepherding me through my first trip here. This country girl is more than a little overwhelmed."

"My pleasure."

The gleam in his eyes gave her pause. She couldn't be sure, but thought she detected the tiniest bit of interest there. Could she be attracted to someone like him?

Tristan wasn't handsome, not in the Hollywood sense, and definitely not like the manly-man cowboys she'd grown up around back home. His was more of an aesthetic appeal. Slender, but toned, even features, and a neatly razored chinstrap beard. He'd styled his hair in a contrived-careless-messy fashion, but his designer-label jeans fit tighter than hers did. She wanted to laugh at his black boots. They wouldn't last a day on a ranch.

Still, his posture, his mannerisms, even the way he spoke depicted someone who took care with the way he presented himself to the world. Confident and thoughtful.

When she didn't say anything more, he took a step back and rubbed his hands together. "I suppose you're wondering what's next?"

"Yes."

He walked over to the leather-topped desk and took a book from the drawer. "Mr. Ronkowski said you'd be tired from your travels, and suggested room service and a good night's rest. Here's the menu. Order what you want, sign for it when it comes, and the hotel will add it to your bill. I'll meet you in the lobby tomorrow morning at eight o'clock sharp. Dress warm. The office is only three blocks, but the wind can be pretty miserable if you're unprepared."

She nodded absently, going through the timing for tomorrow. Breakfast by seven, ready by eight. Yeah, that would work.

"Hey, you still with me?" He smiled again, showing off a beautiful set of white, even teeth that made her wonder how much money had gone toward making them so perfect. "You meet with Mr. R first, then with Dan Sharpton, one of the senior editors. He and Carol Gruber will take you to lunch, and then you'll spend a few hours in the afternoon with her. She's the HR person and will give you your schedule for the second day."

"You work there, too? I thought …"

"I do. My title is General Assistant to the Editor in Chief, Mr. Ronkowski. Translated, it means general flunky." He reached for her hand. "You got lucky. I've been assigned as your personal escort and guide."

Taking his hand was an automatic reaction. She regretted it immediately, and released it as soon as politely possible. It would be very easy to fall into "like" with Tristan. Not a good idea for someone she'd just met. And that confused her because he was nothing like James.

A disturbing thought surfaced. When had James become her standard for men?

Tristan moved in closer, crowded her until the edge of the bar pressed against her spine. He stroked her arm, eliciting a shiver.

Following her instincts, Mallory brushed past him and broke the contact. "Thanks for your help today. I'll be downstairs at eight. May I have my room key, please?"

His smile faded. With a headshake, he dropped the plastic card in her hand and turned to leave. At the door, he hesitated. "Maybe another time?"

Mallory bestowed a tight smile on him. "Goodnight, Tristan."

James tore the ticket from the pad and handed it to the

teenager. "First time gets a warning, Brett. You don't want a second."

"N-no, sir." Brett, who'd gotten his driver's license less than three months ago, accepted the written warning with shaky hands.

"Drive safe, now." James smothered a smile when the boy turned his blinker on, looked out the window to clear the non-existent traffic, and pulled out onto the road at a crawl.

Satisfied he'd put a damper on the kid's speeding, for now, anyway, James walked back to his vehicle to type up the report on his brand new customized-for-police-vehicles computer. He hit submit just as his cell phone rang.

The office number showed in the display.

Odd. Who would call him from the office? Lorraine used the dispatch radio for communication, while Derek and Kyle preferred their cell phones. Jeb Wharton, the semi-retired deputy who filled in now and then, might call from the landline, but he didn't have duty again until next month.

"Evers."

"Sheriff?"

"Why are you calling on the phone, Lorraine? Is the radio down?"

"No. There's, uh, a man here. He wants to see you."

Irritation crowded in. Why wouldn't they leave him alone? "I told you I didn't want to talk to any reporters. No

interviews. Get rid of him. If he won't leave, call Derek and have him toss the jerk out."

Silence.

"Lorraine? Did you hear me?"

"Uh, yes, Sheriff." Her voice wavered. "But he's not a reporter."

"Well, who is he?"

"He, uh, he says …"

He waited her out this time, aware that whatever came next, he probably wouldn't like.

Her voice dropped to a barely audible whisper. "He says he's your father, and he won't leave until he talks to you."

Okay, this was worse than expected. His father lived in Boston and vacationed at the family mansion in the Hamptons. He visited New York City, Washington, D.C., Philadelphia, London, and Paris once each year. That was the extent of his travels. Period. Anywhere else he deemed inferior. And yet, he'd come across the country to Idaho. To confront his son.

The end of the world must be near.

"Sheriff? What do I tell him?" A definite strain in her voice now.

"I'm out on County Line Road. Put him in my office. I'll be there in ten minutes." He disconnected without waiting for her answer, and made a U-turn.

Ten minutes. Not nearly enough time to prepare

himself. The memory of their last confrontation more than six years ago popped out of nowhere. Wonder of wonders, after all this time and all the recriminations, his father still had the power to hurt him.

James drove past the office and the shiny black Cadillac out front where a uniformed chauffeur worked hard to remove the fine layer of dust coating the car. A waste of time and energy. Dust and dirt were a part of life here.

He drove around to the back of the office and parked.

Stealth had played an integral role in his life for many years.

James eased the back door open and moved without a sound through the small kitchen until he could see his office.

A man sat in one of the guest chairs with his back to the door. He had the same graying hair, though it appeared more salt than pepper now. James had taken after his father in height and build, but this man seemed almost shrunken, not at all the robust figure he remembered.

He walked in and closed the door behind him. "Hello, Father." He sat in his chair behind the desk and rested his forearms on top of the desk.

"Hello, Son. You look well."

Shrunken didn't adequately describe his visitor. Not thin, but gaunt. Gray skin, dark circles under his eyes, and a noticeable tremble. James couldn't reciprocate the

compliment, so he got straight to the point. "What brings you here?"

"You do, Jameson. I wanted to see my son before I die. To try and convince you one last time to take over the company." He held up his hand when James started to speak. "Hold on. I want an honest, open, unemotional conversation. Then, if you're still adamant about not returning, I want peace between us. Can you do that?"

James nodded. He had no plumb line for this conversation. No grounding for a sane, calm, unemotional dialogue with his father. He couldn't remember a single discussion with him that didn't devolve into a shouting match. How many times had he walked out? "All right, I can hold my temper if you can. How about we start off with an explanation as to why you look ill."

A sad smile stretched his already thin face into a grimace. "I look ill because I am. I have pancreatic cancer. The doctors have given me four months to live, maybe more if their treatment works the way they say it will. The odds are against me, though. The disease is too far advanced."

His father's words hit James with the pointblank force of a bullet to his armored vest. James fell back in his chair and rubbed his chest, stunned by the unexpected pain. He'd been trained by the best, knew how to endure inflicted agony, but this was a crushing blow. After all was said and done, Jameson Edgar Fitzhugh Evers the Third was still his father, and the thought of such a vibrant, bigger-than-life man dying hurt more than expected. Much more.

"Shocking, I know. I'm still coming to grips with it myself. Death always seemed far off." He shrugged. "At least I have a small amount of time to right a few wrongs."

"Have you gotten a second opinion? Surely, there's a treatment out there you can take. Science is making advances all the time."

"Yes, yes, and yes to all you said. The problem is, time is a luxury I do not have, and I refuse to waste it on insurmountable odds. If you wish to know more about my treatments, we can talk about it another time. Right now, I have more important goals. Your brother is not capable of running a multi-million-dollar organization. Despite his education, Hudson is an artist at heart. He's too young and too soft for the job, has no experience, and lacks ambition. I had hoped to mentor him into the role, but that is no longer an option. And before you object, Hudson came to me. He's the one who opted out. I respect him for his candor and decision."

James hung his head. It was true. Huddy was a child prodigy, brilliant and gifted, an oops-baby. Not at all worldly. He loved music and had trained as a classical pianist from the age of eight, right up until his father demanded he attend business school. Now, at twenty-four, nine years younger than James, Hudson had a master's degree in business from Stanford and two years of working

under their father's thumb. No wonder, he wanted out. "What will he do?"

"Unbeknownst to me, your brother has continued his piano playing all along. How he kept up with school and then the work load, I have no idea. The Manhattan School of Music extended him an invitation to study there." A smile broke through his old man's composure. "He tells me it's a very prestigious offer, and one I would approve. You'll be pleased to know I gave him my blessing. Hudson will be taken care of, no matter the outcome of our talk today."

James found himself smiling. Good for Huddy, even though it meant the burden of inheritance fell to him. "You know how I feel. And besides, I know nothing about the business. What are you proposing?"

His father steepled his fingers together and pursed his lips, but took his time before answering. "Of course, you know nothing of the company's workings, but your business knowledge and acumen aren't the issue. I have smart, capable people to run the operations, but I don't have a replacement for the Board of Directors. That's where you come in, Jameson. I need someone I can trust to do the right thing, with steel in his spine and courage to make a decision to see it through. The others on the board would sell their souls for another dollar. I need you to take my place as majority stockholder."

No, no, no. He'd run away from power games sixteen

years ago. The last thing he wanted was to get sucked back into it. "You do realize I would sell the company off in a heartbeat if I thought it best."

"I would expect nothing less. In fact, I would do the same."

James couldn't believe he was actually considering his old man's offer, not for the money, though it would come with a significant paycheck, but because he'd finally found the home he searched for all of his life. How could he risk losing that? Losing Mallory? "What does the job entail?"

"I suspect you're wondering whether you would have to give up your life here. That answer is no. As Chairman of the Board, you would need to stay abreast of the company's performance and informed of any antics the other board members may get up to. You would be available to the senior management of the company as needed and make an appearance at the annual board meetings. Your time investment could be as little as five business days in a calendar year, or you could set yourself up in a fulltime office if you prefer. It depends on how deeply you wish to involve yourself. Either way, as Chairman of the Board, you will have final decision-making power."

"That's it?" James frowned. He'd been prepared to reject the offer out-of-hand, but surprise stalled him. A pleasant surprise.

His father inclined his head. "In return, you'll receive

a healthy annual salary, stock dividends, a discretionary fund, and a travel allowance. And before you object, I realize you haven't touched a dime of your trust fund. You are free to do whatever you wish with the money."

"Is this why you sent Olivia? To inveigle me into returning so you could coax me into the job?"

His father's face turned dark red, a ghastly color when mixed with the sickly hue of his skin. He leaned forward as though struggling through pain. When the spasm passed, his shoulders slumped.

"Can I get you anything? Water?" James had no idea what to do for him.

"No, thank you. The spells come and go. To answer your question, yes. Olivia came to me for help. Jeremy and Sheila Ashcroft did not teach their children fiscal responsibility. She went through her trust fund, a small fortune I might add, rather quickly. Jeremy cut her off. Told her to get a job." He chuckled. "Might as well tell a goldfish to fly."

James frowned, not liking what he heard.

"She seemed genuinely fond of you, so I suggested a deal that would benefit us both. If she could rekindle a relationship with you, I would be inclined to help her financially, but I swear, Son, I never imagined she was desperate enough to drug you."

"You knew?"

"Of course, I knew."

"But you did nothing. In fact, you looked the other way while she claimed my name for years."

"That was your poor judgment, not mine. When you let it go on, I assumed—hoped—you might actually step up and make something of the marriage. Tell me, why is it so important to dissolve the union now?"

Not a chance he would tell his father about Mallory. The old man might be on the up and up now that he was dying, but James had too many years of mistrust to open his heart. He pulled a page from his old man's book instead. Diversion. "I assume you've already drafted a proposal for the position."

His father nodded.

"Send it to me. I'll take a look and let you know."

A legal-sized envelope landed on his desk. "I like to be prepared. You'll find it very detailed, so read it carefully. Now, if you'll excuse me. I have a very long car ride back to the airport and an even longer flight back to civilization."

It took his father two attempts to rise from the chair.

James waited until he reached the door before standing. He understood that sometimes pride was all a man had to cling onto. He wouldn't take that away. "Thank you for coming, Father."

"This …" He waved a hand around the office. "Suits you. I'm proud of your service, and proud of the man you've become. Make sure whatever you decide is the right

decision for you. It won't work, otherwise. Just don't take too long."

The uniformed driver waited just outside the office. He offered an arm and supported James's father to the car.

Chapter Twelve

The day dawned bright and sunny with the only worry on her radar whether she could impress her interviewers.

As promised, Tristan and his dimples waited in the lobby when she came down. "A punctual woman," he commented when she stepped out of the elevator. "What a novelty. Good morning, Mallory."

He leaned in and kissed her cheek.

She allowed the contact, but only for a second. If he could ignore the previous night's awkward goodbye, she could, too. "Good morning, Tristan. As we say back home, daylight's wasting. Let's get a move on."

"All right, but first, a word of caution." He adjusted her bag so it hung more in front, and placed one of her hands to cover it and grip the strap. "Hold tight to your bag like this, and whatever you do, don't let go of my hand."

She took his extended hand and followed him through the revolving door.

The three-block walk to the building where her interviews were scheduled proved invigorating and eye-opening, with no time to dwell on the bitter cold. Not a hardship for Mallory. She loved wintertime. Besides, she had on her new wool dress coat and boots.

Intimidated was her first thought as they merged into the mass of people who made their way along the sidewalks. She figured out right away why he said not to let go of his hand. The strength of the crowd could easily sweep someone away.

Overwhelmed was her second reaction. Neon signs. Video displays. Horns honking. Signs. Beggars. Street vendors on every corner. Exhaust fumes. Grease odors. Rotting garbage. Only here would you find such an eclectic array of humanity. Businessmen and women who dressed in super chic suits, carried leather attaché cases, and wore ratty no-name sneakers walked with snarky young punks constantly hitching up jeans that threatened to fall down around glitzy designer tennis shoes that cost more than Mallory's entire wardrobe. Under it all, the stench of too many people crowded into one small place permeated the air.

Sensory overload and not enough time to take it all in. Mallory stared at the man coming toward her. An alien, complete with green skin and shiny, sparkly clothing.

"Close your mouth, Mallory." Tristan yanked her out of the way of the oncoming Martian, and pulled her in close to his side. "Cardinal rule. Don't stare. Don't make eye contact. Look straight ahead and go with the flow."

"Why?"

"Nothing says tourist like a gaping mouth. Every pickpocket and con artist in the vicinity will mark you as fresh meat."

She tried to do as he said, and succeeded for the most part. Until the third time she caught an elbow in the ribs from someone in a bigger hurry than her. Aggravation set in then. Men and women alike jostled, bumped, and shoved past her without apology. Anonymous and rude. And at a clip she found difficult to keep pace with.

Tristan cut through the crowd at an angle without disrupting the flow. He tugged her out of the rush and into one of the high-rise buildings. "This is us. You ready?"

She nodded, and followed him toward the bank of twelve elevators. "How big is this building, Tristan?"

To his credit, he didn't laugh at her astonishment. "I believe this one has eighty floors. We're going to forty-three. He steered her to a car that serviced Floors 40-60.

"Holy cow! The tallest building in the whole state of Idaho is only twenty stories. And we get our own special elevator?"

He did chuckle this time. "Yeah. Otherwise, imagine how long it would take if you stopped at every floor."

The elevator they rode in opened to an area with a long glass-topped reception desk. A perky blonde twenty-something looked up, waved at Tristan, and went right back to her computer.

"This way." He led her through a maze of corridors to a small office with a casual seating area for four.

A moment of panic tried to assert itself. She would need a breadcrumb trail to find her way out again.

"You'll stay in here for all your interviews. Help yourself to coffee and water. The restroom is two doors down on your right, and this—" He picked up a sheet of paper from the table and handed it her. "Shows your schedule for today."

Mallory set her shoulder bag on one of the chairs and unbuttoned her coat.

Tristan hung it for her on a coat rack near the door. "Can I get you anything before I go?"

"No, thanks." Her mind had already dismissed him and moved on to the schedule.

Three interviews, one at nine, ten, and eleven, followed by an hour for lunch, and then one more meeting. Sounded promising.

The door opened and four people walked in. "Miss Cameron?" A well-dressed man in his early fifties stuck his hand out.

She stood and shook his hand, and then the others' as he made introductions.

"I'm Dan Sharp. This is Carol Gruber, Freeman Rice, and Lila Nguyen. Rather than drag your day out, we rearranged our schedules to knock this out with one meeting. That'll free up your afternoon for sightseeing. First-timers to our city always want to see the Statue of Liberty and the Empire State Building.

Surprised, but willing to roll with the change, Mallory couldn't decide if they were being exquisitely considerate ... or just anxious to be done with her. Chicago was still fresh in her mind.

Two hours later, she crossed New York off the list, too. While not as bad as Chicago, New York couldn't hold a candle to the Seattle organization.

She took their advice. Who knew if she'd ever get here again. First, back to the hotel to change clothes and then have lunch—an authentic New York hot dog with spicy brown mustard and sauerkraut from one of the street carts.

So much to see and do here. The question was, how many sights could she squeeze in? The Statue of Liberty, Empire State Building, 911 Memorial, Madison Square Gardens, Central Park, the United Nations, for sure. Tonight, she would visit the ice skating rink and the Christmas tree at Rockefeller Center.

A bite of the messy hotdog made her groan with pleasure. Delicious. Through half-closed eyes, she caught a glimpse of a man buying a chili dog from her vendor. He paid, took his dog, and jammed half of it in his mouth as he

walked away. Another man, dressed in jeans that had seen better days and a ragged jacket, leaned against a nearby building. He stared at her, never once looking away.

Mallory shivered, the savory enjoyment of the hot dog gone. She looked around in search of the man James had assigned to watch over her. Was he here? Would he intervene if the scary guy came over? She needed to rethink this plan of hers.

She whipped out her cell phone and punched in James's number.

He answered on the first ring. "Mallory? Is everything all right? Are you okay?"

"Yes, I'm fine. No, I haven't gotten into any trouble yet. And no, I haven't spotted my watchdog, though I did see a green Martian this morning. I swear, a cow with purple spots could walk the sidewalks here and no one would bat an eye."

His laugh ignited a longing inside her.

"I called because I have some unexpected free time on my hands this afternoon and tonight. I want to play tourist, and thought it might be better if your man tagged along with me, instead of hiding. Care to introduce us?"

"The whole point of remaining unseen was to not interfere with your visit. Are you sure?"

"Yeah. The truth is, I'm a little jumpy. Being a lone female here is a bit daunting. I'd like the company, as long as he's not some overgrown knucklehead who would embarrass me."

Another chuckle warmed her insides. Too bad James couldn't show her around. Except, that would be a really bad idea.

"I'm going to put you on hold. Don't go anywhere."

"Thank you, James." She held the phone to her ear while she looked around and tried to spot her bodyguard.

"Miss Cameron?"

"Eek!" Mallory jerked around.

"Mallory," James said over the phone. "Meet John Archer."

Nondescript seemed the best description. Average height. Average build. Jeans. Hands stuffed in the pockets of a buttoned-up pea coat. Short brown hair. Chin scruff. Not handsome. Not ugly. Not one memorable thing ... until she met his gaze.

Gray eyes drilled into hers, hard, no nonsense eyes. "My name's Archer. I hear you need a sightseeing date."

The next morning, Mallory met Tristan in the lobby again, but this time she spotted Archer right off. He had a cup of coffee, and stood near the door reading a newspaper. She acknowledged him with a mere glance, but knew the moment he folded in behind her when she left with Tristan.

The close confines of the crowds didn't suffocate her

as much today. Maybe Tristan had the right of it. Maybe you did get used to the crush.

On the elevator, he informed her, "You have one interview this morning, with Mr. Ronkowski. Since you don't leave until tomorrow, I wondered if you might be up for a night on the town. I'd love to take you to dinner."

"Thanks for everything, Tristan. You've been great, but I already have plans." She had packing to do, and then a long, relaxing appointment with a bubble bath in her spa-like bathroom, but he didn't need to know that.

A tall woman dressed in a killer gray suit and sky-high designer heels interrupted them. "Miss Cameron? I'm Ava, Mr. Ronkowski's assistant. He's ready for you."

Mallory waved goodbye to a befuddled Tristan.

At the end of a long corridor, the runway-worthy assistant stopped outside a corner office, knocked, and opened the door. "Go right on in."

A heavyset man sat behind the largest desk she'd ever seen. Sans coat, with his shirt sleeves rolled up, Mr. Ronkowski pounded away at a computer keyboard, so intent he didn't speak or even look up when she stepped into his office.

Unsure what to do, Mallory edged closer to the desk. Would it be presumptuous to sit before being invited? And where? In one of the chairs by his desk, or in the seating area off to the side? She cleared her throat, hoping to draw his attention.

It didn't work.

She hovered, halfway between the door and the desk, until at last he stood and marched over to her.

"Why are you standing there. Sit down. Sit down." Mr. Ronkowski gestured toward one of the chairs near his desk, the motion more like shooing chickens than an invitation to sit.

She settled into the nearest chair.

He returned to his seat and fumbled through a mile-high stack of papers on the desk. "Ah," he muttered, finally extracting a manila folder. Several minutes passed while he sifted through the contents, and then he turned to his computer screen again.

From her vantage point she could see him open an email, but not what it said. He tsked a few times, and then closed it.

"Mallory, I'm Saul Ronkowski. Pleased to meet you. Look, I'm a cut-to-the-chase kind of guy. I've read all your stuff. I especially liked the story you did on human trafficking. You've got talent, but no seasoning. The team you met with yesterday all sang your praises, so, if you want the job, it's yours. That means you move to New York. Ava can help you find a place to live. You'll start at the bottom, of course. Entry level salary and benefits, and you'll work under supervision until you pass muster. You start middle of January. Any questions?" He gave her no chance to respond. "Good. See Ava on your way out. She'll give you the contract, fill you in on drug tests, background checks, and all the other employment stuff. Have a safe trip home."

He dismissed her with a flick of his hand before turning to his computer again.

She saw herself out and somehow found her way back to the hotel.

CCC

Mallory stuffed the last of the toiletries in and zipped the suitcase shut. The wild travel adventures had come to an end. Home beckoned. Decisions awaited.

The interviews in New York had disappointed her, but then she was stunned by the glowing praise given to Mr. Ronkowski. It didn't change her decision. New York was too busy for her, too crowded, too … much. All the sights she'd only ever read about took her breath away, bigger than life, memories for a lifetime. But never in her wildest imagination, especially after the first day with the slam-bam interviews, did she expect a job offer.

Someone knocked on her door.

She checked through the peephole, but saw no one. "Who is it?"

The man stepped in front of the peep hole, and then back a step. "John Archer, ma'am."

Mallory removed the security chain, twisted the

deadbolt, and opened the door. "You're testing me?"

His eyes smiled, but not his mouth. "Always good to be safe."

"Well, you're early, and if you call me ma'am one more time, I'm going to scream for the police at the airport and tell them you're stalking me. My mother is ma'am. I'm Mallory. Clear?"

His mouth twisted this time, his version of a smile and the first he'd offered since they met yesterday. "Crystal. Ready to go?"

"Yep. Let me do one more run through." She returned to the bedroom, checked the bathroom and then the closet, and rolled her suitcase out to the foyer.

Archer didn't take her suitcase. Instead, he opened the door and went out first. Head turning, eyes searching, he motioned her out and walked with her to the elevators. He took his job to heart.

"Need your hands free, huh?"

"Affirmative, ma—Mallory."

In the elevator, she asked, "So, tell me, did you see anyone suspicious? Any threats?"

He gave her a hard stare. "There are always threats. The risk is simply greater in a city this size. The average person doesn't notice, but they're there."

A chill washed through Mallory. Her hand shifted up to cover her heart. "You're not average, are you? What did you see? What did I miss?"

"Just the normal riffraff. Thieves and pervs who look for easy marks. You did well, Mallory. You stayed aware of your surroundings, didn't show vulnerability, and most important, you didn't make yourself a target."

"Glad to hear it, but you didn't answer my question. Do you think any of these potential threats are connected with the intruder back home? Or the terrorists James is so concerned about?"

"No, I don't. But that doesn't mean they aren't out there, only that I provided a deterrent. You don't let your guard down now, not ever. Understand?"

Wide-eyed and a little bit scared, she said, "Okay. Got it. So, tell me a little about you. Who does Archer work for?"

He gave that half-grimace, half-smile again. "Nobody. I don't exist."

ᴄᴄᴄ

"Hey."

James looked up from the never-ending stack of reports to find Jonas leaning against his door frame. He pushed the papers to one side and set his pen down. "Hey, what brings you around?"

"Reporting in as instructed. You said drop by when I was in town." Jonas gave him a snappy salute.

"Right. Come on in. Have a seat. Want some coffee?"

"Not if it's the same swill you've been making since you pinned on that badge. I have too much respect for my gut to punish it like that." He sprawled in one of the chairs in front of the desk. "So, what's on your mind?"

The Cameron brothers shared a remarkable physical resemblance. All three stood well over six feet, but where Garrett and Wade had boulders under their skin instead of muscles, Jo was lean and corded. They all had the famous Cameron temper, but instead of blazing hot and burning out fast like his two older siblings, Jonas's anger ran cold and calculating.

The question today was, how would Jonas react to having his past unearthed?

James bought himself some time by walking over to close the door. This was Jonas's story to share, or not. They didn't need Lorraine's nosy assistance.

"You're freaking me out, man. Sit down and spit it out." Jonas shifted in his chair and rested one ankle on his knee.

James resettled behind in his chair, picked up a pencil, and tapped out a cadence on his desk top. He had a knack for reading people, and one thing he knew—Jonas Cameron didn't freak. Ever. "Wade tells me you're taking some time off. I can't help but think that this might not be the best time."

Jonas's expression didn't change. He didn't blink, his pupils didn't dilate, his breathing remained steady. "Go on," he said after a few seconds.

"I don't like being a man short with this threat hanging over our heads. I worry about your sisters."

"Threats come and go, sometimes for good."

In a softer voice, James said, "And you intend to make sure that happens?"

Something dark and dangerous shifted between them, making his skin crawl with awareness.

"Need to know, James. And you don't."

"Difficult to un-know some things. Like how a bum knee isn't a legitimate diagnosis for a medical discharge. How's that knee doing anyway?"

One supercilious eyebrow arched high. "Careful, Sheriff. You're overstepping."

"I'm not asking you to break an oath. This isn't my first rodeo. I've got my own Top Secret compartmentalized skeletons. All I'm saying is you're needed here." He pulled a piece of paper from a folder and tossed it across the desk.

Jonas picked up the paper. "What is this?"

"A second threat, separate but connected. Anyone you recognize?"

"Yeah. The tall one is Toure, the piece of garbage who kidnapped Cass and Mal, and then pulled diplomatic immunity. I had a bead on him. We should have taken him out. The other one is Okafor. He's a go-between for the Nigerian government and two terrorist groups who do dirty work for them. Where did you get this?"

"Fowler sent it this morning. Toure has somehow weaseled a second chance to make good on the deal he struck with a wealthy sheik to deliver two beautiful American sisters. Twins, to be exact. I wouldn't discount revenge either."

"All the more reason for my vacation."

James studied the stony countenance across from him. Now came the part that required more finesse than he possessed. "I know about your time with Joint Special Operations Command, about AFRICOM, about the Defense Clandestine Agency. I know you're free of Fowler and his ilk now, but you can't do this on your own. We need the intelligence, contacts, and resources he commands. All I ask is you not go rogue. Give Fowler and the rest of us a chance to work some magic."

"You think he'll reinstate your task force, and send you after the Ansaru splinter group?" Jonas slammed a fist on the desk, losing a little of his iron control. "Not happening, buddy. You are not taking either of my brothers into that hellhole. None of you know squat about Nigeria. They'll snuff you day one."

"That's why I'm asking you to go with us. Fowler claims your knowledge and experience will make or break the mission."

He'd seen a lot of seemingly invincible men struggle with inner demons, but none who looked as conflicted as this youngest Cameron brother. It was unsettling, kind of like seeing one of the signs of the Apocalypse.

Chapter Thirteen

Mallory placed her shoulder bag on the conveyor belt to run through the x-ray machine, and then assumed the pose for a body scan. The doors of the glass capsule twirled around, whirred a few times, and then opened again for her to exit. She looked around for Archer as she collected her things, but couldn't find him. One minute he was right behind her, the next, poof, gone. How did he do that?

Archer still hadn't appeared by the time boarding was announced.

When her zone was called, she dutifully joined her fellow lemmings in line, held her boarding pass for the gate agent to scan, took a deep breath, and entered the 737 for the first leg to Salt Lake City. Hurry-up baby steps didn't help her jitters, but they did finally get her through the narrow aisle to her assigned seat. With quite a few flights

under her belt now, she considered herself a seasoned traveler. So, why then did flying still make her nervous?

Could it be because she'd buckled herself inside a tightly packed sardine can comprised of more than 360,000 parts, most of which were likely manufactured in a foreign country that didn't like Americans?

The flight attendant closed the door, and started the safety briefing. James said Archer would fly with her, didn't he? Guess not.

The connecting flight to Idaho was only half full, which left the seat beside her empty. She put her earbuds in and settled down for the duration. Sometime later, the flight attendant came by with the beverage cart and offered her a drink.

"Just water, please." Mallory lowered the tray in front of the empty seat next to her. With the plane only half-full, she might as well enjoy the extra room.

"And here I took you for a soda kind of girl."

Mallory looked up at the man standing in the aisle. "Archer? You're here. I didn't see you board."

"Good. It means I'm doing my job." He nodded at the empty seat. "Mind if I sit here?"

Mallory hastily moved her water and raised the tray table so he could slide in.

"In a few minutes, I want you to go to the restroom at the front. On your way back, check out the guy in 22B, aisle seat, six rows behind us. Don't be obvious."

Fear spiked through her veins. "Okay."

"Ready? The pilot will announce our descent soon. We'll talk when you get back." He stood and stepped aside to let her out.

Five minutes later, she returned, glancing at the different passengers. The man Archer had identified saw her look his way and ducked his head. A second later, eyes dark as molasses met hers, burning with hatred.

Shaken, Mallory slipped into her seat when Archer stood again. "I think it's the same guy from the picture Lucy took," she whispered.

Archer nodded. "He won't try anything with me here."

"What about on the drive home? It's a long, empty road and my brother doesn't have the greatest patience in the world."

"Your dad will pick you up this time. He's more than capable of protecting you."

"I thought—"

"Your brothers had a conflict. Don't worry, I'll make sure this guy and any other problems are neutralized."

Mallory blinked, unable to think of anything else to say.

Spotting her dad was easy. He stood a good head taller than anyone else in the crowd, and had his hat tipped back

to reveal a glorious mane of silver hair.

Mallory hurried over and threw her arms around him.

"Whoa, baby girl. What's this?" His arms came around her, one hand patting her back.

Displays of affection were not the norm for her family. They loved hard and lived big, but tender feelings were not for public consumption. "I'm just glad to see you, Dad. Glad to be home again."

"Well, we're not home yet. Let's get your suitcase and hit the road."

They walked to the small baggage claim area and got lucky when her suitcase was the fifth bag to appear. As Archer promised, nothing untoward occurred on the drive home.

Nostalgia swamped her the moment they turned down the long private drive. This trip to New York couldn't have come at a worse time. Christmas at the ranch brought its own special kind of crazy, and she'd missed part of it. "I guess you got the tree up, and all the lights and decorations done."

Dad always picked their tree out early in the year, and kept an eye on it through the summer and fall. Then, a week before Christmas, the whole family would take the horse-drawn sled out to cut it down, drag it back to the house, and decorate it.

"Nope. We're heading out first thing in the morning." He glanced at her in the passenger seat. "Can't do

Christmas without you."

Her grin left her jaws aching.

"Be warned, though." His laugh was deep and rich. "As soon as we get done with the tree, your mom plans to conscript you and the other girls for kitchen detail. She and Roseanna are fretting about getting all the food prepared."

"Roseanna could handle it all singlehandedly, if Mom would let her." Their once fulltime housekeeper had retired, but came back to help out on special occasions.

A sour thought crossed Mallory's mind. She wanted a career, adventure, and freedom from heartache, but did she really want to leave all this? Leave her family?

ᴄ ᴄ ᴄ

Mallory buttoned her jacket, pulled on buckskin gloves, and hid a yawn behind her hand. The sun had risen. Barely. She never understood why Dad always wanted to head out at the crack of dawn.

"Load up," Garrett shouted and helped TJ scramble onto the sled. "Let's go."

Sled was a generous description. More like a wagon with skids instead of wheels. Dad used to haul hay in it to the far pastures in the winter months. At some point, they added Christmas tree-hauling to the old deconstructed buckboard.

Dad climbed onto the driver's seat and reached down

for Mom's hand. One good tug and she popped up beside him.

The horses stirred, anxious to be moving instead of standing around in the cold.

Wade grabbed Lucy around the waist and lifted her onto the sled, before climbing up behind her.

Derek scrambled aboard and helped Cassie up.

"Need a boost, sis?" Jonas laced his fingers together and held them out for her.

With a hand on his shoulder, she put her booted foot in his cupped hands and sprang up and onto the sled.

"Everybody ready?" Dad called out. He'd draped a blanket over Mom's legs and pulled her close to his side to keep warm.

"Would ya lookee there." Rascal, who stood by the horses' heads holding them steady while everyone loaded up, stared toward the drive.

Mallory turned to see where he was looking.

A black Yukon made its way down the drive. It veered off toward the barn where the family had gathered.

"I didn't think he could make it," Wade said.

James stepped out of his cruiser, donned the big, white Stetson he preferred, and ambled their way. "Got room for one more?"

"Sure. The more the merrier," Garrett called to him. "Thought you couldn't make it."

James responded with a shirk of his shoulders. "Call

didn't take as long as expected." He took Wade's offered hand and jumped on the sled. "Move over," he said to Jonas.

The youngest of the three brothers chuckled, but scooted over to make room for James on the haybale— right next to Mallory.

Okay, this was awkward. "What do you think you're doing?" she muttered under her breath and moved to get up.

He grabbed her arm. "Don't. Please."

She relented with a huff.

Dad unwrapped the reins from the brake stave and flicked them to get the horses moving.

"I'm sorry, Mallory. I know I owe you an explanation, and I intend to give it. We've just got a lot going on right now."

"You don't owe me anything." She tried to pull away from his grasp, but he used the opportunity to snuggle closer.

"Yeah, I do. For now, know this. I am not married. Never was. And Olivia is gone."

Her struggles stopped. She looked up, hating the feeling of hope that kept finding its way back. How could she trust him again? Oh, but she wanted to.

"All right. For now."

The ride lasted the better part of an hour before they came to a neat stand of conifers where the foothills began

their ascent into the mountains. Each tree stood evenly spaced, in symmetrical rows, the more mature pines on the north side tapering down to saplings on the south.

"You plant these, Cody?" James gestured toward the evenly spaced rows of pine trees.

"Yep. Been seeding this acreage for the past twenty-five years. My own private Christmas tree farm. Coming out to cut one down has become a family tradition."

Pride welled up inside Mallory. She glanced at her brothers and sister and recognized the same delight she felt.

"All right, handsome," her mom said, patting her dad's chest. "Show us this year's masterpiece."

Dad swelled up like a pufferfish. "Grab the axes and the saw. Garrett, unhitch the team and get the block and tackle." He turned to tromp up the slight incline, and everyone fell in behind him.

Five hundred yards in, they saw it. Easily twelve feet tall, with thick, evenly spaced limbs, he'd tagged it with a bright pink ribbon.

Her brothers, James, and Derek all started arguing about the best direction to start the cut for the easiest fall without damaging the other trees. Once decided, they took turns with the initial axe cuts, and then worked the two-man crosscut saw—Garrett and James, Jonas and Derek, Wade and Dad. No chainsaws for this custom.

It didn't take long for the men to shed their jackets. Shirts disappeared not long after. The guys worked up a hardy sweat, and then her brothers dropped into the drifts to make snow angels.

"You're all crazy." Derek backed away, hands up to fend them off. "I'm not laying my bare skin in that stuff. It's cold."

Jonas tackled him from behind, and the others piled on.

James stood off to one side, laughing like a loon … until Garrett jumped up and lunged toward him. He almost got him, too, but James danced away and turned to run right past her.

Mallory couldn't help herself. She stuck her foot out and tripped him.

He went down face-first into a deep drift, and came up sputtering. By then, both Garrett and Wade had him pinned while Jonas scooped handful after handful of snow and buried him.

"That's coooold!" he bellowed.

"Towels and dry shirts in the wagon," Mom called. "Hot chocolate, too. Come get some before we load this tree and head home."

Derek was first to the sled, though James didn't lag far behind.

Sometime later, after the chocolate was gone, Mallory was assigned the task of gathering up all the discarded, wet shirts. She'd just scooped up the last one when James snuck up behind her and dumped a handful of snow down the back of her shirt.

"What—aiieek!" she screeched and wiggled as she squirmed out of her jacket and untucked her shirt. "You … you …!"

Nearby, Cassie, TJ, and Lucy were doing similar jigs.

"You're gonna pay for that!"

"You jerk. What'd you do that for?"

"Ooooh! It's cold!"

Flapping her shirt tail to get rid of the snow, Mallory glared at James. "Oh, you are so gonna suffer for that."

James grinned … and pegged her in the shoulder with a snowball.

Snowballs flew around her, some hitting their mark, but mostly falling apart in the air. The snow wasn't wet enough for them to stick together.

Undeterred, Mallory ducked behind a tree, scooped up a handful, and packed it as tight as she could. Peering around, she spotted James as he dodged behind a boulder. Okay, this was her turf. She knew this patch of ground better than him. Darting off to where the trees were thicker, she circled around to come at him from the other side. He'd never see her snowball coming.

Slow and careful, she made her way through the wooded area, the snow soft enough to not crunch under her feet. A quick peek to where James should be brought a frown.

He wasn't there.

Okay, she couldn't expect him to stay put. One cautious step at a time, she followed his tracks, keeping low to the ground to stay hidden. Nothing.

Laughter and squeals filled the air, a sure sign the battle was still underway. Had he gone back to the wagon? She hadn't thought him the type to give up so easily.

She stood to take another step and—whoosh! Something hit her from behind. Arms encircled her, turned her, and then she landed on the ground, cushioned by a very hard chest.

"Gotcha!" James grinned up at her. "You should know you can't sneak up on a soldier, princess."

"You cheated."

"Did not. You're just a sore loser." He raised up and brushed her lips with his.

Mallory drew back, mouth agape. She stuttered, and finally got out, "You can't do that."

"Get used to it. I intend to do it a lot more."

She struggled in his arms and against her own desires. "No. You're … you're …"

"I'm free and single and dying to see how hot this spark between us can get. Tell me you don't feel the same way."

She scrambled to her feet and stared down at where he lay sprawled on the ground. One part of her said, *what are you doing? Get back down there and kiss the man.* Another, saner part said, *run while you can.*

"I don't have to tell you anything. And I don't. Feel that way, I mean ..."

"Liar."

"You kept a wife hidden, and you're calling me a liar? Well, you can just ... kiss my foot." She stuck her lip out in a pout, something she hadn't done since high school.

A wicked smile transformed his face. He got to his feet and took a slow step forward with the lazy stare of a predator toying with its prey. "Okay."

"What are you doing, James?" She backed away from him, one step to match each of his. The quaver in her voice matched the rapid flutter of her pulse.

He didn't answer, not that she'd expected him to.

Running wouldn't work, and she dared not take her gaze off him. The man was dangerous, much faster with well-honed reflexes. She wouldn't make it ten feet before he caught her, and she couldn't win a physical battle. She'd just have to outsmart him.

The logical choice dictated she take the shortest route back to her family, the path to the right. She glanced in that direction.

He watched her with eagle eyes. When she looked at her escape path again, he smirked.

"James, enough. I'm going to leave now."

His smile became a grin, one worthy of a wolf. He held one hand out to her and beckoned with several curls of his fingers.

Her heart jackhammered in her chest. Assuming an air of regal dignity, she lifted her chin high.

"Ahh, there's my princess."

Sniffing with disdain, she took one step to the right.

He matched it.

Feigning panic, she broke into a run, spun in a half-circle, and took off in a full sprint the opposite direction.

A muffled curse erupted behind her.

He fell for it! She ran as fast as her legs would move through the snow, following the tracks she'd made when she circled around to get the drop on him. She dared not look back. It would slow her down.

She threw a glance over her shoulder and screamed.

One arm snaked around her waist, lifted her off the ground, and spun her around. A second arm wrapped around her and pulled her in close. "You can run, but know this. I will always chase you down. I'm not letting you get away now that I've found you."

He swept her up in his arms and then laid her on the ground.

"What are you doing?"

Straddling her legs with his back to her, he grabbed one leg and tugged the boot from her foot. And then her sock. "I'm kissing your foot, as requested."

James brought her leg up, bent her knee, and feathered kisses over her ankle, her arch, and then each toe.

"Stop," Mallory giggled half-heartedly. She wanted to

cry when he released her foot.

Another tugging sensation and the other boot and sock came off, followed by more caresses from his warm, moist mouth. "Can't play favorites, now can we?"

She moaned.

"Like that, princess? One day I'll show you just how nice I can make you feel."

Footsteps sounded in the woods. "Mallory, James. Time to load the tree and head back." Jonas's voice carried in the stillness of the woods.

"On our way," James hollered back.

He gathered her boots, stuffed the socks inside them, and handed the pair to her. "Climb on. I'll give you a piggyback ride."

She didn't bother arguing. Against all logic, her heart and body sided in favor of snuggling up against this man. Her man.

Chapter Fourteen

Mallory idly rubbed the sore spot on her hip where Edwina head-butted her. Rascal had a love/hate relationship with the bad-tempered old goat, and left the animal for someone else to deal with whenever possible. She'd have a bruise this time, but it was her own fault for not paying attention. You never, ever turned your back on Edwina.

She strolled back to the house after helping feed the animals, fretting about the three days until Christmas. Mom always went a little nutty during the holidays, insisting on a feast big enough to feed the family, a few special guests, and all of the ranch hands. Of course, everything had to be made from scratch. No canned stuff from her kitchen, not for Christmas. To get everything done in time, she'd drafted Mallory, Cassie, TJ, and Lucy for the full two days

beforehand. The thought of all the peeling, shelling, chopping, dicing, baking, and all-around fixing brought a groan.

Worse, it left her this one day only to finish shopping for the few gifts left on her list, make her decision on the job offers, write responses, finish an article for an online blogger friend, and get the decorations up in the barn.

Decorating the barn was Cassie's idea way back when they were barely big enough to ride. She felt sad the animals didn't get to celebrate Christmas like people, so every year the two of them would string twinkle lights along the tops of the stalls. One of their brothers would cut a tree for them, just a little one, and put it up in a corner on top of one of the old molasses barrels. They'd decorate it with tinsel, strung popcorn, and paper ornaments.

The New York trip had thrown everyone off schedule. Instead of having the family tree cut and decorated a full week before Christmas, they'd waited for her return so she could go with them. Another family tradition upheld.

She couldn't complain since it was her decision to go to New York. Even James had put off his 'talk' until she returned.

As though summoned by her thoughts, her cell phone rang the moment she stepped into the house. She had to work to keep a smile out of her voice when she saw the caller ID. "Hello, Sheriff."

"Good morning, princess. I didn't wake you, did I?"

She snorted into the phone. "Hardly. Haven't you ever lived on a ranch?"

He chuckled. "Well then, any chance you're free for lunch today?"

An insidious warmth spread through her, right before the butterflies took over. He'd been putting this conversation off forever, one she wasn't sure she wanted to have. "Yeah, I think I can make that work."

"Great. The diner okay?"

This gave her an excuse to head into town early and get some of her shopping done before she met him. "Sure. How about noon?"

"Works for me. See you then." He hung up before she could say goodbye.

"Did I hear you're going into town today, sweetheart?" Mom stood in the kitchen doorway, wiping her hands on a dish towel. "Could you pick up a few things for me while you're there?"

Mallory groaned inside. A few things by Mom's standards would take all afternoon. She'd be setting up Christmas decorations for the horses until midnight, and then get up with the roosters to start the food prep for Christmas dinner. "Sure thing. Make me a list. I'll leave right after I clean up."

Mom disappeared into the kitchen, mumbling to herself about all the things she had to do. Cate Cameron prided herself on making Christmas memories for

everyone, but she'd run herself ragged to do it—and love every minute.

Mallory took her mom's BMW. Four quick stops later, she marked off two gifts from her list, and checked off several items on Mom's. Maybe she could get to bed at a decent hour after all.

She parked in Wade's reserved spot in front of his office and stowed her purchases in the truck before going to the diner.

The smells and sounds hit her the moment she opened the door—fresh-brewed coffee, burgers sizzling on the grill, something cinnamon-y and sweet, dishes rattling, Dee Dee barking orders to the kitchen, and the low hum of conversation. She spotted James right off. Hard to miss a man so tall and broad.

The butterflies kicked up again. She hadn't been this nervous since ninth grade when Purvis Van Buren, a senior and the quarterback of the football team, asked her out. Her very first date had turned into a disaster, thanks to her brothers' self-appointed chaperonage.

A quick glance around the diner let her breathe a sigh of relief. They wouldn't be interfering today. And then she snorted. Like James would let them.

He stood from his seat at a booth near the back, the same one he and his deputies laid claim to for their weekly breakfast meetings.

Mallory stopped for a quick chat with Dee Dee, the

waitress and owner, before moving his way. Would this be the start of something wonderful and new or the killing blow for her broken heart?

James's gaze raked her up and down as she made her way to his table. A hungry, almost predatory expression took the place of his usual stoicism.

A thrill spiked through her, giving rebirth to her dashed hopes. She had a fleeting thought that this man might be more than she could handle.

"You are so beautiful, princess."

His words left her tongue-tied, but she managed to stutter, "Uh, th-thanks." She hadn't seen this side of James before. A girl could get used to it.

They ordered—a cheeseburger and fries for Mallory, the pot roast and mashed potatoes for James—and made small talk until their food arrived.

"You're in luck," Dee Dee said as she set their plates on the table. "Shea's in the kitchen today. She made strawberry-rhubarb pie, too. If you want a slice, you better order it quick."

Mallory's mouth watered. She looked at James. Nobody, not even Mom, could bake like Shea. "Want to split a piece?"

He shoveled a forkful of meat into his mouth. He nodded, swallowed, and said, "Sure."

They ate and talked about the food, about her trips to Seattle, Chicago, and New York, about Christmas, but not a word about his past or Olivia.

After Dee Dee brought their pie along with two mugs of steaming coffee, James looked over at her and said, "So."

Mallory stirred creamer and sugar into her cup. "So," she repeated.

"Guess I owe you an explanation."

She took a sip. "Guess so."

"You want the short version or the long?"

"Let's go with the long."

He turned his head and looked out the window. "My father is Chairman of the Board for Global Distribution, the fourth largest international shipping organization in the world and the only one majority-owned by a single individual. The company was founded by my great grandfather and has been passed down through the generations. I have one brother, Hudson, who's nine years younger than me. Our mother was killed in a car accident before Huddy's first birthday. He doesn't remember her. Heck, I can barely recall her face. Father has long since forgotten her. Business is all he's ever known or loved."

James pushed his coffee away. "I grew up in a very strict environment, attended the best private schools, socialized with only the wealthiest people. Manners and appearances meant everything in our social circle. Father wanted me to follow in his footsteps and eventually take over the business. He didn't take it well when I chose the

Army instead."

What an understatement. James's father was probably furious, knowing the military would change his son from the malleable heir apparent to someone who wouldn't be controlled. Mallory had seen firsthand the differences in her brothers after their time in service. They'd left as boys, but they'd returned strong, disciplined, determined, and confident men who knew what they wanted and weren't afraid to go after it. "What about your brother?"

"Huddy tried to be what Father wanted, but you have to understand something. My brother is … special. Not handicapped or compromised in any way. He's a gifted pianist, with a musical talent unlike any other. But discord upsets him. After I left, he put his passion on the back burner to do Father's bidding. Unfortunately, that same submission Father demanded made it obvious my brother would never survive in the cutthroat business of shipping and international finance. He was an angel fish in tank of tiger sharks."

"And you feel guilty for forcing him into the position you didn't want, right?"

"Yeah. At least Father realized the mismatch before it did any harm to Huddy or the business. Failure is not something either of them could bear."

The moment demanded patience. If she pressed, he would shut down. She scooped a bite of pie onto her fork and lifted it to her mouth, noting that James had yet to take a bite.

"Like I said, he has a musical gift. The Manhattan School of Music in New York wants him to study there. I suspect Father made a generous donation to encourage their interest."

Mallory tapped the tines of her fork against the plate. "Does this make you the heir apparent again?"

"Yeah, pretty much. The business has been in my family for generations."

"How does Olivia fit in?"

James told her about growing up next door to Olivia, of the rough crowd she fell in with, and how she burned through her trust fund in a few short years. "Her parents cut her off, so she went to my father for help. He struck a deal with her. If she led me back into the fold, he'd make it worth her while."

James turned away again.

"Go on. Finish it."

"I joined the Army, became a Ranger, and went on some rough missions. It's what we did. After one particularly ugly deployment where everything went wrong, my commander put me on mandatory leave. My head wasn't in a good place, and Las Vegas suited my mood. I holed up in a hotel on the strip, intending to drink my way to oblivion. Olivia, with Father's help, tracked me down. She and one of her scurvy cousins managed to bump into me in the bar at my hotel. They invited me to come out with them, and I went. She slipped something into my drink at the second stop."

Mallory gasped. "She drugged you?"

He nodded. "Yep. Rohypnol. Date-rape drug. Except in this case there was a wedding instead of a rape. It didn't work out quite like she planned, though. You see, I had a bad reaction, something Olivia didn't expect. One moment I was at the bar, the next thing I woke up in the hospital, with tubes sticking in me. The doc said I was lucky."

He had to be telling the truth. No one could make up a story like that. Could they? "But, if you don't remember, how ..."

"The toxicology reports from the hospital gave me my first clue. Apparently, I don't metabolize certain drugs very well. It made me suspicious. With help from a friend, I got copies of the surveillance tapes from all the places we went that night. One clip clearly revealed her putting something in my drink. Another showed her cousin and another dude lugging me into the Elvis Chapel. A third clip showed her signing my name to the papers."

Mallory didn't want to smile, but couldn't help it. "The Elvis Chapel?"

His lips twisted into a smirk. "Nothing but the best."

"When did this happen?"

He winced. "Five years ago."

"Five years?"

He ducked his head. "I didn't want to press charges

and ruin her life, so I tried to reason with her. She flat out refused the annulment, and then disappeared. I got orders not long after, and couldn't pursue her from Afghanistan. And every time I came back to the States, she stayed one step ahead of me. Never made any demands. Since I had no intention of getting involved with anyone, after a while, I just let it go."

He had no intention of getting involved with anyone. The words cut deep. "You said your father wanted Olivia to bring you back into the fold, but you didn't go. Did he support her all these years?"

He nodded.

"Why did he come here now? Because of your brother?"

"Yes, partly. He's been diagnosed with pancreatic cancer, so life has kind of forced his hand. Now that he's feeling his mortality, he wants to right all his wrongs."

Shadows haunted James's eyes. Regardless of their estrangement, it had to hurt to know he would lose his father soon. "I'm so sorry, James."

"It's a shock. Somehow, I never thought he would die."

"What happens with Olivia?" She hated asking about the woman, but didn't dare move forward with James until she knew for certain she was out of the picture for good.

He smiled then, happiness in his eyes. "The annulment was finalized yesterday. I should receive the signed papers within the week."

"She's gone? You're not married?"

"I'm not married. In truth, I never was."

Mallory looked away to hide the joy in her heart. "Did your father come out here to tell you all this? I have to say, he doesn't sound like the type."

"He offered me his spot on the Board of Directors."

Her head jerked up, the fleeting joy already fading. "What?"

"He says it wouldn't require me to change my life here, just to be available a couple of times a year."

"And you—of course, you're considering it. It's your family's legacy. Thank you for sharing." She started to get up, her mind whirling.

He caught her arm. "There's more I want to say."

She sank down with reluctance, but resigned herself to hearing the end of her dreams put into words.

"Fowler called last night. I had him run Lucy's pictures of the guy who followed you in Idaho Falls. Facial recognition came back with an eighty-six-percent positive match for a known terrorist. He's one of seven men identified in a group that entered the country illegally. Intelligence reported they were targeting you and your sister. All of them have been apprehended, Mallory. The threat is over. You're safe now."

She waited, knowing more was coming.

"These job offers you received are amazing, and more

than deserved. You've been sheltered here your whole life, and deserve a chance to spread your wings. It's hard for me to say this, but you need to see what life is like out there. Otherwise, you'll always have regrets and what-ifs. I'll give you a year, but then I'm coming for you, princess. You're everything to me, and if you choose to stay in the city, I'll move there to be with you. But I'm hoping you'll come home again."

Tears trickled down her cheeks. How could she leave now? How could she not?

He reached over and brushed her tears away. "Hey, I've waited for you for two years. I can wait a little longer. Just don't make it too long, okay? So, which job did you decide on?"

Chapter Fifteen

Christmas dinner was fun, loud, and boisterous as usual, but Mallory still felt a little sad. James feared it might be his father's final holiday, so at the last minute he flew to Boston to spend Christmas with his father and brother.

She understood but still missed him. James was a part of her family now. She remembered when first Garrett, and then Wade and Jonas were gone. It wasn't the same without everyone.

Garrett interrupted the revelry by clanging a knife against his water glass. He stood, raised his glass, and waited for everyone to quiet.

It took several seconds, but everyone held their glass high.

"This year, I'd like to propose a toast. To family, to loved ones, and to future generations … as in this summer." He broke into a huge grin.

Mallory, along with everyone else, stared at him before looking at TJ, who's cheeks had turned a pretty pink.

Jonas was first to connect the dots. "You, old dog. A kid? You and TJ?"

TJ's blush turned a furious rosy color.

Cassie screeched loud enough to pierce eardrums. "I'm going to be an aunt!"

Mallory sat next to TJ and was first to throw her arms around the glowing woman. She let out her own squeal.

Their mom rushed from her seat at the end of the table and squeezed the poor girl in a breath-stealing hug, while their dad made his way to Garrett's side to give him a heavy-handed back slap and then dragged him into a hug.

Handshakes, congratulations, and lots of tears, mostly from the women, took up more long minutes. Once everyone settled down, Wade stood and rapped his knife against his glass.

"Wade?" Mom had a worried look on her face.

"No, Ma. Not that. At least not yet." Wade laughed. "I know I just gave Lucy a ring, but I convinced her we don't need a long engagement. Save Valentine's Day. We're tying the knot then."

More squeals erupted. More handshakes,

congratulations, and tears. Lots of tears.

Before the excitement ended, Derek took Wade's knife and rapped again. "Uh, yeah, well, we might as well get our announcement out there, too. I asked Cassie to marry me, and she said yes. We haven't set a date yet, but I'm hoping for this summer."

"Not until after I have this baby," TJ yelled.

Cassie covered her face with one hand and held the other out for everyone to admire the sparkling diamond she wore.

"Oh, my gosh. This is so awesome." Mallory launched herself at her twin. "You didn't tell me? You kept it secret?"

"It just happened last night," Cassie whispered.

"Good luck, dude. You're gonna need it." Jonas shook Derek's hand and got a solid punch in his ribs from Cassie for his words.

When the racket died down a third time, and all eyes turned to Jonas.

"Hey, don't look at me. All I've done is buy a new mare. Hard to put a ring on a hoof."

That brought laughter all around.

"Well," Mom said with a teary voice. "There's mincemeat pie, pecan pie, a pumpkin roll, apple strudel, and my Christmas cake. Girls, if you'll help—"

"Wait," Mallory said. Guilt lay heavy on her shoulders since she sent the acceptance email to Robert Deerborn in

Seattle. She hadn't told anyone of her decision yet, much less the tight timeline he'd given her. "I have an announcement, too."

A collective hush swept through the room.

With her eyes fixed on her plate, Mallory didn't bother standing. "I accepted the job in Seattle. I'll be moving there in two weeks."

◌◌◌

On the Monday after New Year's, Mallory set her two suitcases outside her bedroom door, grabbed her carryon and coat, and gave one last look around. She should be excited about starting this new adventure. Instead, she wanted to cry.

"This it?" her dad asked.

She nodded, not trusting her voice to hold.

He lugged the bags downstairs for her, and set them by the front door. "Sure you don't want breakfast?"

"I'm sure." With her throat closed up, she couldn't possibly swallow anything.

Jonas came in the front door. "Garrett and TJ just pulled up."

Wade, Lucy, Mom, and Rascal emerged from the kitchen.

They wouldn't make it easy on her. Everyone wanted to say goodbye, even though it would break her heart. No sense in dragging this out. Taking a deep breath, she went to Rascal first. "Take care of Edwina for me, you hear?"

He folded her into a hug. "I don't know. That old goat might pine away from missing you, girl. If she does, I'll save you a bowl of mutton stew."

Mallory let out a watery chuckle, hugged him back, and moved to the next person in line. One by one, she embraced each member of her family, wiped her eyes, and blew her nose.

"Let's get this show on the road, sis. I've already loaded your bags." Jonas opened the front door and held it for her. And of course, everyone had to follow them outside.

She climbed inside Jonas's shiny black truck, and turned to look out the back window where her loved ones stood waving.

They rounded the long curve, blocking the house from sight. Fresh tears made her nose run again. She'd said her goodbyes to James the previous night. Her insides heated again at the memory. He'd lifted her chin and pressed a sweet kiss to her forehead. "The next kiss I give you won't be quite so chaste. Come back to me, Mallory."

"Cut the waterworks. You're supposed to be excited." Jonas gave her a semi-soft thump.

"Ow." She rubbed her arm. "Am I doing the right thing, Jo?"

"I don't think there's a right or wrong decision here,

Mal. If you don't go, you'll always wonder and have regrets, and believe me, those demons will haunt you the rest of your life. If you do go and it doesn't turn out the way you want, hey, at least you'll know. And you can always come home."

Almost verbatim to what James said. "Is that why you run off to the mountains every now and again? Because you have demons?"

"Everyone has regrets and demons, and everyone deals with them differently. You can't ignore, forget, or outrun them. They let you think you can, but when you least expect it, they sneak back in, stronger than ever."

Mallory studied his profile, and noticed the muscle twitch in his clenched jaw. Had his demons caught up with him? "I know you've always been closest to Garrett, but I'm here for you, too. I'm willing to listen whenever you need to talk."

He glanced over at her, a frown marring his face. "Thanks. I might take you up on that one day."

Not today, though. They rode in silence the rest of the way to the Idaho Falls airport, both lost in their own thoughts.

"Drop me at the departures curb. I'll get a porter to help me with my bags," Mallory instructed when they passed the sign for the airport.

"No can do. I promised Mom to see you through security. It was the only way she agreed to not come with us."

"Please, Jonas. Don't make this harder for me than it already is." Her voice held a huskiness she didn't recognize.

Jonas released a melodramatic sigh. "Mal– "

"Please?" She sniffled. "Don't send me to Seattle with swollen eyes and a red nose."

He didn't respond or even look at her, but he did follow the directions to the departure drop-off point. At the curb, he hopped out and retrieved her suitcases from the back, and then signaled to one of the skycaps.

The uniformed man hurried over with a cart.

"Listen, you go straight to your gate, you hear? And when you get to Seattle, you don't talk to strangers, you don't go anywhere alone, especially after dark, and you always keep your cell phone charged, powered on, and on your person. You have that can of mace Garrett gave you?"

She loved him more in that moment than she could say. "Yes, Dad. I'll be careful and aware of my surroundings at all times. I promise. Thank you."

He pulled in for a quick hug and then set her away from him. "Okay. Call as soon as you get there. And when you have an address, Cassie will ship the rest of your stuff. I'm gonna miss you, Sis. I didn't realize how much until this minute. For what's it worth, I do think you're doing the right thing. You go prove to the world—and yourself— what a fantastic journalist you are. And if this thing

between you and James is real, he'll be waiting when you come home again. We'll all be waiting. Understand? Home is where you belong."

The tears dribbled down her cheek. When had she become such a crybaby? "This is why I wanted you to drop me off, you big jerk." She dabbed her eyes with a tissue, smacked his chest, and hugged him.

He wrapped his arms around her waist and lifted her off the ground. "Love you, Mal."

"I love you, too, Jo. Now let me go."

When her feet touched the ground again, she pulled another tissue from her purse and blew her nose.

"Which airline, Miss?" the porter asked.

"Delta." She followed him through the doors, turning back only once to wave.

Jonas stood by his truck, hands in his pockets, and watched as she walked away.

Mallory gave a final pat to her cheeks and tossed her compact in the carry-on. Her eyes were still a little puffy, but her nose was no longer red.

When the flight attendant announced their descent into Seattle, she shoved the bag under the seat. Leaving home had proved more difficult than she anticipated, but she put it behind her and welcomed the nervous flutters in her belly. New adventures awaited, and no amount of guilt about leaving would stop her from embracing them. James was right. She needed this.

Jared Kinsloe waited at the baggage claim. He saw her first and gave her a hug. "Mallory, am I ever glad to see you. We had one of our staff go out on maternity leave last week, and another one announced her engagement and decision to move to Phoenix to be with her fiancé. You're going to hit the ground running. C'mon, let's find your bags. Mr. Deerborn is letting you have one of the corporate apartments for six months. It's three blocks from the office. He wants you focused, not distracted with house hunting."

A huge wave of relief flooded her. Mallory had never rented anything in her life. She had no idea about the Seattle housing market, much less where was safe and where was not. Mom offered to come with her and help her search, but she'd refused. She was twenty-six years old for heaven's sake. An adult. And this was her adventure. She had to do this on her own.

She sized Jared up as he grabbed her bags from the conveyor belt. Heavy as the suitcases were, he had no trouble hefting them. He wore another quality suit, this time with a turquoise blue silk shirt and coordinating tie and pocket hanky. GQ all the way.

He caught her checking him out, and flashed his trademark cheeky grin.

Heat bloomed in her cheeks. She dropped her gaze

first. Handsome? Check. Charming? Check. Would she go out with him? Heck, no. Mixing business and pleasure seemed a really bad idea. Not to mention that spike of electricity James always evoked was missing.

Ugh. Would she go through life comparing every man to him?

Probably. She snugged her coat closer, took one of the suitcase handles from Jared, and followed him to the parking garage.

"We'll go straight to the apartment. I'll introduce you to the property manager and concierge, get you your keys, and give you a quick tour of the place. I have to get back to work, but no need for you to come in today. Be prepared for tomorrow though. Be sure you arrive by eight sharp. Whatever you do, don't be late. Deerborn hates that."

Mallory nodded. She'd grown up on a ranch where early mornings were a way of life. She was more concerned about getting lost.

Her worry disappeared when Jared pointed out the office as they passed. "That's work. Now, see the building ahead with the flag out front? With the lion's head on it? That's your new home for the next half year. Straight shot. You can't get lost."

He pulled into the narrow entry drive, handed his keys to the valet, and motioned to the doorman. "Moving in. We need a cart, please."

The uniformed man hurried inside and returned a

moment later with a young bellhop dressed in black pants, white shirt, and black vest with the lion's head logo embroidered on it.

"Welcome to the Lion's Gate Apartments, ma'am," the doorman said. "Javier will take care of your luggage."

"Thanks, Emory. This is Miss Mallory Cameron. She'll be staying here for the foreseeable future. I'll get her checked in." He slipped the man a folded bill.

"Pleasure to meet you, Miss Cameron." The doorman inclined his head. "Please let me know if you need anything."

"Thank you," she said in return and added a smile.

Her smile widened even further when they stepped inside. Marble floors, gilt accents, and mirrors filled her vision as they made their way to the mahogany desk on one side. "Jared, this is too much. I'm sure I can't afford this, not on my salary."

"Actually, you can easily afford it. Call it a perk, if you want. It's free. Deerborn knows it was asking a lot to have you uproot your life and move here on such short notice. And he really does want you focused on work right off. Accept it and be happy. You'll earn it."

"Okaaaay."

He led her to the registration desk. "This is Miss Mallory Cameron. You have her apartment ready?"

The lady behind the desk nodded and busied herself pulling a packet of information together. "Welcome, Miss

Cameron. This is your key. I've also provided a list of important telephone numbers, a street map of the area, a list of local restaurants that deliver, and a few other bits of information. As a tenant, you have full access to the swimming pool, spa services, and gym. Housekeeping is provided once a week, on Thursdays. Please stop by or call if you have any questions or need assistance."

Jared took her arm and led her toward the elevators, the bellhop with her luggage on their heels. "This is where I leave you. Remember, eight sharp."

"Thank you," was all she could get out before he hurried away.

Chapter Sixteen

Mallory boarded the plane. Again. Flying no longer held the mystique it once did. On the contrary, she found it tedious and tiring. In the past six weeks, she'd made trips with Jared to Los Angeles, Denver, and Dallas, doing research on various stories for him.

Her phone rang. Cassie again. "Stop fretting. I just boarded the flight to Idaho Falls."

"I still can't believe you waited until the last possible minute," her sister said. "You know Lucy will be devastated if you don't make it, and weather is so unpredictable."

"Weather report shows clear skies all the way. ETA is on time, so stop with the worry all ready."

A deep huff sounded over the line. "Okay. Change of plans. Derek is picking you up."

"The most expendable, huh?"

Cassie laughed. "Something like that. If your plane is late, at least the rest of the immediate family will be there. He volunteered."

"I won't be late. Promise." She didn't understand all the fuss. She'd done the whole rehearsal thing for TJ and Garrett's wedding. How much different could Lucy and Wade's be? She'd make the wedding tomorrow, wasn't that most important? "Gotta go. They're closing the doors. See you in a few hours."

The flight arrived on time and without incident. With everything stuffed into a carry-on to avoid the wait time for checked bags, she searched for Derek ... and saw James instead.

A sensual smile formed on his face as he forged a path through the crowd toward her.

Her heart stuttered, but then picked up its normal rhythm, only faster now.

"Princess." He lifted her bag to his shoulder and took the handle of her carry-on. "Let's get moving. You have a church full of people anxiously awaiting your arrival."

"I thought—"

He was already striding for the door.

She had to hurry to keep up. "Slow down. My legs aren't as long as yours."

He looked over his shoulder with a grin, but slowed his pace until she caught up.

"I don't understand why everyone is so worried about me getting there in time. I told them I would."

"Of course, you understand. It's your mom and your sister. They over-plan everything, and you're the piece they can't control. The rest of us just nod and say, 'yes, ma'am.'"

"Got it. They will always find something to worry about."

He opened her door for her and stowed her bags in the back seat. "You need anything before we start driving? Drink? Eat? Pit stop?"

"Nope. I'm good." Mallory climbed inside. "Wouldn't want to keep the worry-warts waiting."

He laughed again and headed around the rear of the Yukon to the driver's side. Something was different about James. He seemed almost lighthearted, happy.

Her own spirits responded. She'd wondered if things would be strained between them after six long weeks with little to no contact. He said he would leave her alone, let her find her feet in a new world, and he had. But she missed him. A lot more than expected.

"So, we got about two hours ahead of us. Tell me all about your new life."

Safe enough topic. The next hour was filled with descriptions of her apartment, the new foods she'd tried, the new people in her life, but very little about her job. Not much to say there.

"Sounds like fun, but what about the newspaper? What's it like?" Not much got past James.

"It's great." She told him about Robert Deerborn's quirks, about the gossips in the pool, and a couple of the trips she'd been on.

"You seem more excited about your apartment than your job. What's going on, princess?"

"I'm excited about my job," she insisted.

"No, you're not."

"Are you calling me a liar?" Why did she have to get so prickly when he saw through her?

"No, but lies come in all shades. White, black, gray, and even invisible. Everybody stretches the truth, hides the truth, or distorts it. And most don't realize when they do it. I'm not passing judgment, Mallory. I can tell Seattle didn't meet all your expectations. Use me as a sounding board. Let me be your friend right now."

"I thought you wanted to be more." She clapped a hand over her mouth, mortified at the words that slipped out.

That growly chuckle erupted from his throat again and sent a shudder of pleasure rippling through her. She'd been surrounded by attractive, perfectly charming men for the last month and a half, but only James had the power to make her body sing.

"Oh, princess, I do want more. When the time is right. That time remains in the future for now."

"Okay, the job sucks. I fetch coffee, go pick up lunch,

file, answer phone calls, and attend meetings I'm not a part of. They give me fluff pieces to write—political announcements, special interest stories, a travel blurb for a place I've never been, a cooking segment, and even a couple of big-name obituaries. Obituaries, James." She threw her hands up and let them fall.

"Your mom mentioned you've been on a few trips."

"Yeah. Why, I don't know. It's not like I do anything or write anything about them."

"Maybe they're trying to get you comfortable before throwing you in the deep end."

"I thought so, too, at first. But I'm better than what they have me doing."

"What do you do when you're not at work?" James held the steering wheel with his left hand, and shifted on his seat to look at her.

Mallory sighed. The man saw way too much. "I went to see the Space Needle. It's pretty spectacular. I walk a lot. They have some great parks."

"But?"

"I've made friends at work, but … they're not really friends, you know? And by the time I get off work, it's getting dark, so I hurry home. I don't like being out alone at night. And the weekends are …"

"Lonely?"

"Yeah. I miss home. I miss my family. I miss the horses. I think I even miss Edwina."

He laughed. "The goat?"

She laughed with him.

"Any chance you might miss me, too?" His big hand landed on her leg.

She covered it with hers and nodded. "I think I've missed you most of all."

Mallory peeked through the door. For such an intimate wedding, an awful lot of people had crowded into the church to see Wade and Lucy get hitched.

Lucy clutched the fine lawn handkerchief in her hand, waiting to tuck it into the sleeve of the wedding dress until the last minute. Mallory's 'something blue' gift to the bride. Words adorned one edge of the linen, a short phrase, embroidered with silken thread the color of a perfect summer sky—*A Forever Love.*

How cliché, and yet it summed up Lucy's greatest desire perfectly. She'd always dreamed of a forever kind of love. How fitting they chose a Valentine wedding.

Did such a thing really exist? Her parents' marriage of fifty-years would suggest so. But, how did a person know with any degree of certainty that they truly loved and were loved in return?

Dad made an amazing stand-in as father of the bride, just as he'd done for TJ. He took Lucy's handkerchief, tucked it in her sleeve, and then folded her hand onto the crook of his arm. A quick pat on her hand and an even quicker whisper in her ear brought a radiant smile to the bride's face. Lucy stood on her tiptoes to kiss his cheek, her joy visible through the sheer veil.

A fierce longing filled Mallory's heart. One day soon, Dad would again make the trek down the aisle, this time with Cassie on his arm. Mallory wanted that same experience.

A fragment of scripture came to mind, a bit of wisdom from the New Testament. "Love is patient ... love is kind ... not easily angered ... keeps no record of wrongs ... perseveres."

Wow. If the Bible spoke the truth, then love meant selfless devotion, unconditional loyalty. Love simply was, and it endured despite a person's worthiness or shortcomings. It required no qualification, no justification, or even that the person you loved would love you in return.

Not a physical phenomenon with a quantifiable measure or a standard definition. Each person's love kept its own measure and standard.

She believed the Bible, but how did you know for sure when you found the right one? That forever kind of love?

The pianist concluded the prelude music, waited for a long, silent count, and then struck up the processional with a flourish.

"It's time," Mallory called to the others. She smoothed

the skirt of her red satin dress and glanced at the bride. Nervous and little bit teary, Lucy lifted her veil and let it flutter down to settle over her shoulders. She was an attractive girl, but today she glowed with true beauty. Breathtaking. As befitted a bride on her wedding day. Mallory couldn't wait to see Wade's face when his bride started down the aisle.

TJ took the first step in the slow march down the aisle, her barely-there baby bump noticeable for the first time in the form-fitted dress. A few moments later, the preacher's wife motioned Cassie to go.

Mallory moved into place at the door.

Two steps in, her gaze found the four men by the altar. Standing shoulder to shoulder, Wade, Garrett, Jonas, and James all looked up the aisle.

For the first time in her life, Mallory realized just how lethally handsome her brothers were, but it was James who met and held her gaze. Those hazel eyes seemed to draw her into the fire, commanded her to not look away.

As she neared the end of her walk, James raised his eyebrows and smiled. A challenge? Or a question?

The ceremony passed in a blur, and then Wade swept his new bride into his arms and kissed her until the pastor cleared his throat.

Jonas let out a piercing wolf whistle, and the congregation erupted in laughter.

The distraction worked. Wade released Lucy, who had

turned the color of Mallory's dress, while Wade wore the widest, most unrepentant grin she'd ever seen.

The recessional started up, and Wade and Lucy hurried up the aisle, their laughter contagious.

Before Mallory could take a breath, James was there to guide her hand through his arm. She looked over at Garrett who was supposed to be her escort as the Best Man, but he'd already pulled TJ to his side.

Hard muscle flexed against Mallory's hand. Heat poured through the material separating them. She held on tight, intending to savor this moment for the long, lonely nights ahead.

Next came pictures—lots of pictures—and then the reception at the ranch. Mallory had ridden with Cassie and Derek, but James didn't release her when she started toward them for the trip home.

"You're riding with me, princess." James's voice dropped an octave. And then he all but carried her to his Yukon.

She stared at the high seat and then at the dress she wore. Tight, form fitting from top to bottom. Did he really expect her to climb up there?

James solved the problem. His hands spanned her waist and lifted her without displaying an ounce of effort. "Watch your head," he said and set her on the seat.

"Th-thank you," she stuttered.

He leaned in and fastened her seat belt for her, and then

touched her face, his thumb rubbing back and forth along her bottom lip. He stared deep into her eyes with a passion that made her tremble. The veins in his neck bulged, the cords like steel. "The pleasure is all mine."

His touch, his voice, the intensity of the moment all contrived to make her heart feel as though someone had clamped a pair of jumper cables on it. The charge that sped through her was electric, unlike anything she'd ever experienced.

She wondered if he would kiss her then, but he pulled away, closed her door, and trotted around to the other side.

Disappointment never felt so sweet.

James climbed in behind the steering wheel and turned in his seat to study every inch of the woman beside him. For the first time in as long as he could remember, his confidence deserted him, left him anxious and unsure. He hated the feeling.

His eyes ran up and down her slender body, drinking in the soft curves. Those too-blue eyes had turned dark, one of her tells when emotion got the best of her. She met his stare, unblinking. The red dress fit her like she'd been dipped in liquid fabric. In a nutshell, being this close to Mallory Cameron stole his wits and ruined his power of speech. The woman drove him wild.

He let her stew in the passenger seat while he started the engine and waited for the heat to kick in, an excuse that freed him from conversation for a few moments.

His speech returned with the warm air blowing through the vents. "You are so beautiful."

Right on time, a blush made its grand arrival. A beacon couldn't glow any brighter than she did at that moment.

Chapter Seventeen

James sat in his office, his legs propped on the corner of his desk, and tried to convince himself how much he loved his job as sheriff. Today, it didn't ring true. To be honest, it hadn't for a long while. Four months to be exact. Ever since Mallory left for Seattle.

On the surface, his life hummed along, perfect, well-ordered, and under control. He had the signed annulment papers. His father had convinced Olivia to go into rehab. He even funded her treatment, and promised a lifetime monthly allowance if she stayed clean and out of trouble. Of course, James would inherit oversight on that arrangement, not something he wanted, but didn't feel he could refuse.

He'd accepted the role his father offered, and flew to Boston to work with his father two days each month for the

foreseeable future. The announcement of his position as Chairman of the Board would be made when his father felt he could no longer function … or when his battle with cancer ended, which wouldn't be far off from the way he looked.

So far, the job proved to be exactly as the old man had described.

James even made a short, three-day trip to Hawaii to celebrate Hudson's twenty-fifth birthday. That was the date established for him to take control of his trust fund, and also the day he married Carla, a sweet little flutist who played in the same orchestra Huddy had auditioned for. Even as a third wheel, James had a blast.

Derek had talked a lot of late about working at the Triple C. He had a knack with animals, and seemed especially fond of horses. His departure would be a blow, but Kyle had tendered a couple of leads as potential replacements, friends of his who'd recently left the Marines. Their background checks had come back clean, and both had strong recommendations from their former commanders.

Jonas had also suggested John Archer, the man who'd served as Mallory's bodyguard on her trips to Chicago and New York. Archer's background check turned up squeaky clean, but provided only the most basic information. The guy had to be a spook.

James glanced at the calendar on his wall, in particular

at the date at the end of month encircled in red. Elections loomed on the horizon. Time to start his campaign. With no opponent in sight, he hoped to leverage his position with the city council and hire all three men. He also toyed with the creation of a local posse for emergency situations, kind of a variation on the volunteer fire department, only with deputized locals. They'd had a need for such a group on several occasions since he'd taken over as sheriff. Didn't hurt to be prepared, and he had a good dozen names at the top of the list.

Yes, his life was in order. Except it wasn't. He had an emptiness inside him that no amount of work could fill. Only Mallory could do that, and he hadn't heard from her since Valentine's Day. Not even a text.

Thankfully, Cassie was on his side and kept him up to date on her twin's activities. Would his princess come home again?

The lazy stroll through his life came to a jarring halt when his cell phone rang. The display showed a blocked number. Dread crept in. He picked up the handset. "Evers."

The familiar sequence of squeals and squalls followed before the BII agent answered. A secure line. Fowler.

"Hello Sheriff, how are things in Nowhere, Idaho?"

"Beautiful. Until now. What kind of disaster are we facing this time?"

Soft laughter erupted over the phone line. "You think I only call when there's a problem?"

"Yes."

Fowler tsked. "Well, this time you're correct. The ThreatCon alert I sent before Thanksgiving, the one I said was cancelled? It's on again, and elevated."

James sucked in a breath. His insides seemed to shrivel when his thoughts darted straight to Mallory. Alone. In Seattle. "Details."

"Sebastien Toure has built his own army and is systematically eliminating the leaders of the drug and trafficking cartels that operate out of Nigeria. We believe he will take control and combine the three major organizations within weeks."

"That would make him …?"

"A most powerful rogue, one we have absolutely no influence over."

"You mean the government won't be able to manipulate events to your liking anymore. Go on." A sour taste settled in the back of James's throat. He reached for the roll of antacids in his drawer and popped one in his mouth. Fowler never freely shared information. When he did, you could bet a boatload of trouble was headed your way.

"Something like that. The men he's knocked off have only dabbled in the sex trade so far, mostly Scandinavian girls and other exotics, as they call them. Blondes and redheads, especially those with blue or green eyes, bring the highest prices from their African and Middle Eastern clientele. They don't poach their own people or their neighbors. But Toure's made of nastier stuff. He wants to expand into the child labor market and has already hit several refugee camps. His band of thugs snatch up children displaced by the violence, and sells them to slavers in Thailand and Laos. Chatter has it that he recently opened negotiations with the Herrera Organization."

"The group we had the run-in with here?"

"One and the same."

The magnitude of such a merger of human traffickers had catastrophe written all over it. "That's ... that would be—" He couldn't find words to finish.

"Horrendous? Yes. We didn't expect Herrera's rapid growth here in North America, and now we're paying for it. Herrera is too big, their economic influence too strong for us to completely dismantle. The best we can hope for is to contain and manipulate their efforts. Toure seems to have followed the Herrera playbook. If he succeeds in taking over in Nigeria, Sudan, and Chad, the rest of Africa will fall to him. And then, he'll be too powerful for the sheiks to stop. He'll take the entire Middle East.

James whistled.

"Eastern Asia will see the handwriting on the wall, and then we'll have a three-headed hydra that can't be killed. Human trafficking will go global with a corporate-style strategy and ... well, I don't have explain the basics to you. Suffice it to say, with that kind of money and power, there's not a nation on earth that will be able to stop them."

"Why don't the local groups take care of him?"

"These terrorist groups embody the bully mentality in its most basic and dangerous form. They react to any and everything, which is why we haven't been able to manipulate events there and contain their spread. They have no real leaders and no vision. Until Toure. He stays off their radar, no grandstanding, no show of aggression. He picks off his competition, the more astute leaders, and then absorbs the leaderless fighters into his own following. That whole region is an explosion waiting to happen."

James digested Fowler's information, not in the least surprised by the deteriorating situation in Nigeria, Sudan, and Chad. They'd all seen it coming for years. "Okay, I'll bite. What's the purpose of your call today? What does all this have to do with the Camerons?"

A pause followed that did nothing to relieve his concerns.

"What I'm about to disclose is Top Secret," Fowler said. "Need to know only. Do you understand?"

James swallowed hard. Being privy to such information would commit him to Fowler's schemes. And leave him vulnerable to prosecution if things went south. "I left that life behind."

"Even if it affects people you care about? One in particular?"

Sharp, jabbing fear paralyzed him. "Need to know. Got

it. Now spill."

"While you, Garrett Cameron, Derek Naughton, and Kyle Abbott were deployed in Afghanistan, the Defense Intelligence Agency inserted an assassin into Nigeria with instructions to take out targeted leaders. His success earned him the name, Fatalwa, which means haunted, or ghost, in Hausa. Toure is convinced this ghost is one of the Camerons. As an attaché of the Nigerian embassy to the United States, he was fully aware of the U.S. strategy employed over the past twenty years in his country. The Nigerian government condoned our actions because it afforded them protection from the insurgents. Now, Toure intends to capture, or kill if necessary, the ghost agent who kept the different groups in line. It's a show of power meant to intimidate the leaders of his country, and a warning to the U.S. It's a very smart move on his part. I would do the same in his place."

Silence again. Fowler would never name names, but he would offer enough information which would allow someone to draw their own conclusions. James ran through the possibilities while Fowler waited.

Garrett had deployed with him the last six years of their service, both in the Army and while working for the BII. Wade spent his two tours in Afghanistan, something easily proved. Neither had ever been to Nigeria, or even Africa.

Which left Jonas, a conclusion James had already

reached. "Go on."

"Toure sent the first group, all of whom we apprehended. This time he's sent a full dozen, three groups of four, each cell operating independent of the others. Facial recognition flagged two of one group and one of a second group in your area yesterday. They want the Ghost alive and brought back to Nigeria, but they won't hesitate to kill if that's the only way."

It all added up—the up and down temperament, the secrets, the nightmares, getaways to the shack in the mountains, Jonas's need to 'take a break.' "Does Jonas know?"

"Yes."

"Why are you telling me?"

"Because I need him to return and take care of unfinished business. He knows the land and the people. He's the only one with a chance to get in and remove Toure. But he can't go it alone this time. He'll need resources, contacts … and an experienced team he trusts.

"Jonas hates his past. He won't involve others."

"He will if they take one of his sisters."

⸎

Mallory looked at the pile of projects on her desk and slumped back in her chair. No matter how many hours she put in, the stack never seemed to go down. She was good at research, too good. Now, everybody wanted her help.

All that baloney about loneliness she'd spouted at Wade and Lucy's wedding changed when she returned to work. She was too busy to be lonely. Nothing but twelve-hour-days, digging and working other people's stories, never her own. Forget sightseeing. She was lucky to find time to do her laundry.

The smell of fresh coffee drew her down the hall to the break room. One thing the newspaper didn't skimp on was refreshments. You name it, they had it. Patty, one of the girls from her section held a cup under the espresso machine. She laughed as Mallory walked in.

"Guaranteed every time. Pop the espresso and half the department will follow. Want me to make one for you?"

"One what?" Mallory asked.

"Double shot espresso. The only thing guaranteed to get you through the afternoon."

Mallory shuddered. "A double shot? No thanks. If I drank that I'd be on vibrate for the rest of the week."

"Hey, you look tired. They working you too hard?"

"My own fault if they are. Being the new kid doesn't make it easy to say no, but I'm learning. The truth is I'm exhausted and I miss my family, I don't know anyone here in Seattle because I work all the time, and quite frankly I'm discouraged." Wow. Why would she unload her sob story on a virtual stranger? Patty was nice, but she didn't know her, not really.

"Mallory, there you are. I've been looking for you." Jared stood in the doorway, excitement rippling around him.

She groaned. Not another rush-rush project.

"No, no. This is good. Great even. Grab your coffee and come back to your office. I've got important news."

She took her time preparing the coffee just the way she liked it. Jared could wait. During her time here, he'd been attentive and helpful, and beyond demanding. He single-handedly accounted for more than half her workload—all for his stories.

True, he appreciated her work and gave credit when it counted. He also counseled patience, of which she had little left. His attention outside the office confused her even more. He sent all the right signals. She knew he found her attractive, but he'd never acted on it. Never invited her for coffee, or offered dinner. Not that she had the time or desire for romance in her life. Especially not after years of mixed signals from James.

She walked back to her cubicle and found Jared waiting for her. "What's up?"

"Boss wants us in his office at two o'clock."

Jared practically hummed with excitement. He was up to something. What, she had no idea. Against her better judgment, Mallory let the same excitement build inside her, praying he wouldn't disappoint her yet again.

After he left, she sat down at her desk and looked at

the time in the bottom-right corner of her screen. Ten minutes before she was due in Mr. Deerborn's office. Not enough time for her coffee to cool enough to drink. She turned her attention to closing out all the documents open on her computer. Today, she was going home on time no matter who came begging for help.

Of course, Jared was already there when she arrived. His excitement and grin remained.

"Have a seat, Mallory." Mr. Deerborn never looked up from the papers he shuffled.

Mallory took the empty chair next to Jared.

Mr. Deerborn finally set his papers aside and looked at Jared and then at her. "Baxter has been working a story on a fraudulent charity scheme out of California. I believe you've been doing some research on it."

Mallory nodded. She'd presented her findings to Emmet Baxter just yesterday. A money trail amounting to hundreds of thousands of dollars in charitable donations was being funneled from a San Diego organization to a small catholic church in the Cayman Islands. The paper trail ended there, as did the money.

"Baxter was taken to the hospital last night. His appendix burst. He had to have emergency surgery. This case can't wait, so I'm reassigning it to you two. Get your passports ready and pack a bag. You're going to the Caribbean, Grand Cayman in particular. Find that missing money. Your flight leaves—" He glanced at the big, gaudy

Rolex he favored. "In five hours. Now wrap up and get out of here." He pulled the papers back in front of him.

Mallory got to her feet, stunned by what he said. Reporters seldom recognized underlings. They wanted all the acknowledgment and glory for themselves. That Baxter had given her up as his researcher surprised the heck out of her. What surprised and pleased her even more was the trust Mr. Deerborn was showing by giving her this assignment. With Jared, of course. He'd been her watchdog and mentor all along, so it made sense they'd both get the nod.

Grand Cayman. The Caribbean. The real butterflies took flight then. Oh, wow.

Jared rose with her and rubbed his hands together. "C'mon, we need to strategize and then get out of here and pack."

Chapter Eighteen

Sunlight sparkled over the surface of the Caribbean Sea. The vastness of the ocean fascinated her, but after a while, Mallory rubbed her stiff neck, sore from staring out the window in the same position for the past two hours.

The plane banked left to begin its descent and offered the first view of the island. Grand Cayman, the largest of the three Cayman Islands, was flat with a curious blend of lush greenery, colorful houses painted in tropical shades, modern buildings, sugar-white beaches that seemed to rim the entire island, and gentle waves that kissed the shore before they receded. Mesmerizing. A tropical delight indeed.

Below, the deep blue ocean shallowed as they approached the island, paling to progressively lighter shades of aquamarine and then light green. The water

looked inviting and so clear the sandy bottom was visible from the air. She'd thought the travel photos had been touched up, but not so. The water truly was this impossible, stunning color.

The landing gear rumbled and whirred beneath the plane. Almost there. Mallory leaned forward and looked past Jared to the other side.

"You're like a kid at the circus for the first time." He chuckled. "It's actually quite endearing."

"You've been here before?"

"Yes. It's my favorite vacation spot."

She turned back to her window when the plane dipped that way again. The island grew bigger on final approach. Everywhere she looked, palm trees waved.

The postcard scenery disappeared as the small jet reached land and touched down on the runway of Owen Roberts International Airport in the capital city of George Town.

Mallory poked Jared's arm, the travel weariness of the past twenty-four hours gone. "Will we have time to do some sightseeing? And shopping? The water, the beaches, I want to see it all."

Not a vacation, Mallory. Not a vacation, the nagging voice inside her head reminded. Yes, she had an assignment, but this was her first time out of the country, first time to a tropical paradise, and Grand Cayman offered so much to see and do. She wanted to swim with the stingrays, visit the turtle farm, see the village of Hell named for its purgatorial landscape. Sunbathe on the beach, walk in the pristine white sand of Seven Mile Beach, and dip her toes in the amazing waters.

And do your job, the voice reminded.

"Of course. We'll make some down time. The Caribbean is very beautiful. I can't wait to see you splashing in the water. You did bring a bikini?"

She studied Jared as though seeing him for the first time. He wanted to ogle her in a bikini? Too bad. The only bathing suit she had was a plain, black one-piece. Unless she went shopping.

"Deerborn's assistant booked us rooms at the Comfort Suites on Seven Mile Beach. I asked for two connecting rooms with an oceanfront view." He looked away for a moment. "So we can collaborate, of course. From the property, we can walk right onto the beach. By the way, we have reservations at a nice restaurant tonight."

This was starting to sound more like a rendezvous than a work assignment. All these months he'd ignored her, and now he wanted to play? Where his peers wouldn't find out? She had to put the brakes on Jared. This assignment, her first real one, meant too much.

The door of the airplane opened and the other passengers began the slow shuffle down the aisle and into the terminal.

Mallory gathered her belongings and followed Jared

down the stairs of the plane. Outside, she lifted her nose and breathed in the clean ocean breeze. Seattle had big city congestion and pollution.

Jared rented a car, loaded their luggage, and set the GPS on his phone to find their hotel. Two blocks from the airport, she regretted not insisting on a taxi. "Watch out! Wrong lane, wrong lane." She braced her feet and closed her eyes amid a chorus of horns, shouts, and angry gestures.

"Sorry. Been a while since I drove on the wrong side of the road. I've got it now." Jared's shaky laugh did little to reassure her.

Great. Now she understood what the car rental agent meant by, "Left lane is right, and right lane is suicide."

They made it to the hotel without further mishap, checked in, and called an elevator.

On the ride to the fifth floor, Jared informed her, "Our dinner reservation is at six, in forty-five minutes. I'll get changed and come to your room." His soft laugh bothered her. "Don't worry, I'll knock on the connecting door first."

"I'm not comfortable with a connecting door. How about we just meet downstairs in the lobby at five-forty-five instead?"

Jared's frown reeked of displeasure, but he agreed with a nod.

The first thing Mallory did when she got to her room was lock the door between their two rooms. Any collaboration needed would take place in the lounge downstairs or the car.

She unpacked her few hanging items, washed her face and brushed her hair, and then changed into a simple red sundress with wide straps and a full skirt that fell to her knees. Satisfied her appearance said good taste, but no funny business, she returned to the lobby to wait for Jared.

He finally appeared, fifteen minutes late. "Sorry. Mr. Deerborn called. He wrangled an appointment for us with Father Fabian at St. Francis Xavier Catholic Church tomorrow at four."

"That's the church where all the hundreds of thousands of dollars were funneled."

"Yes, but since we don't have to leave until three-thirty, we can enjoy a night out on the town. In the morning, we can sleep in. I'll order room service and have breakfast set up on my balcony. You can wear your bikini and afterward, if we feel like it, we'll relax on the beach. Later, I'll take you to the Sunshine Grille, a very popular place with both the tourists and the locals."

Eat breakfast in her bathing suit? In his hotel room? "You know what? I'm really tired, and not much of a breakfast person, either. I get up early, like before the sun comes up early, so I think I'll opt for an early morning walk on the beach instead. How about we meet up for lunch tomorrow, at one of the little places we passed on the way here?" He might hold her career in his hands, but that didn't mean she had to put up with his cheesy seduction. Surely, he'd get the message.

That bothersome frown of his returned.

At dinner, Jared scooted into the booth beside her instead of sitting on the other side. His closeness made her uncomfortable, so she shoved her oversized travel purse between them.

"What can I get for you tonight, madam?" The waiter stood at attention.

"We'll both have the filet mignon, mine medium well." Jared said. "Mallory, how do you prefer your steak cooked?"

He dared order for her? She arched one eyebrow at him before turning a smile on the waiter. "I think I'd prefer the sea bass instead."

The waiter thanked them, collected their menus, and departed.

He wanted to talk about the nightlife in Grand Cayman.

She kept steering the conversation back to the purpose for their trip.

He ordered dessert.

She opted for coffee only, claiming she didn't care for dessert. Kind of true. She enjoyed sweets as much as the next person, but she didn't like what they did to her hips.

He wheedled and pouted in an attempt to coerce her into going to a nightclub for drinks and dancing.

She told him she didn't drink—true again—and didn't

care for dancing—kind of true. She loved dancing, just not with him. His overfamiliar, highhanded attitude grated.

He suggested coffee on his balcony when they returned to the hotel.

She declined, claiming weariness. Very true.

"Fine," he barked at last and snatched the bill from the waiter. "I'll drop you at the hotel."

Mallory manufactured a jaw-cracking yawn and covered it with her hand to hide a relieved smile, but then figured she'd better give him a sop. "Thank you for understanding, Jared. This assignment is so important to me. I want to be fresh and alert tomorrow, and entirely professional so Mr. Deerborn recognizes the value I can bring to the organization. I appreciate your maturity and experience, your willingness to share your wisdom. You're such a great mentor, almost like a surrogate father. I wouldn't be here now without you help and guidance."

Jared turned a little green. He muttered something unintelligible under his breath, signed the check, took his receipt, pocketed his credit card, and stood up. "You're welcome." The gruffness of his tone said otherwise.

Had she laid it on too thick?

The next morning dawned bright and sunny, another ho-hum day in paradise. A quick stop at the hotel desk yielded directions to several shops within walking distance where she found spray-on sunscreen, sunglasses, a beach hat, a new, hot pink bikini, a flowered sarong-style cover-

up, pink sequined flip-flops, and a big mesh beach bag for all her loot. She sneaked into the hotel to change and prayed not to run into Jared. Luck stayed on her side.

With her hair pulled up in a ponytail and a borrowed towel from the hotel's pool cabana, she set off to see the sights along Seven Mile Beach.

Two hours later she discovered that spray-on sunscreen, while a miracle invention, only worked in the places you sprayed it. Unwilling to ask a stranger for help, she'd managed as best she could—and now felt the sting on her back. Not yet ready to go back inside, one of the umbrellas by the hotel pool drew her.

Lazy, insubstantial images of sandy beaches, bikinis, and hunky men entertained her drowsy thoughts until a familiar voice shattered the reverie. "There you are. I've been looking for you."

Jared stood by her chaise, dressed in swim trunks, his lean, well-toned torso on display. He really was an attractive man, but his sleek, polished ways just didn't do it for her. "I guess you found me."

"Since you're not a breakfast person, I figured you'd be hungry by now. After we eat, I thought we could go out to the turtle farm." He grinned. "Hell isn't far from there."

The lure of sightseeing called to her. "Okay. Give me a few minutes to change. Want to meet in the lobby at twelve-fifteen?"

"Let's make it twelve-thirty. I'd like to shower first."

She could shower and be ready in five minutes if necessary, but he took half an hour? She thought about what her brothers would say and forced her lips to remain shut.

After an uneventful lunch, they made the short drive from George Town to the turtle farm conservatory on the northwestern point of the island. She loved learning about the endangered Green Sea Turtles and the attempts being made to protect their numbers, but didn't care for the almost unbearable heat or the man who seemed to follow her every step, more interested in her than the turtles. The way his eyes slid away when she looked at him set off all kinds of warnings.

From the turtle farm, she and Jared drove to the tiny village of Hell, another marvel of nature. Mallory took pictures of the jagged, spongy pinnacles of black-covered limestone and several of the signs with quotes like, "This must be what hell looks like," and "Welcome to Hell." She made several purchases in the gift shop. Her brothers loved hot, spicy food, and the Hell Hot Sauces would test their claim. She even mailed a postcard to her sister with a postmark from Hell. Cassie would love it.

When they returned to the car, Mallory noticed the same man from the turtle farm, still watching her.

With quick, surreptitious glances, Mallory memorized everything about him—dark skin, close cropped hair, shorts, a nondescript t-shirt. He didn't look like a native, or more accurately, he didn't act like a native. Tourist didn't fit either.

Garrett always told her to listen to her gut, and right now her instincts quivered with danger signs. She didn't like being so isolated with only Jared for protection. "I think we should start back now. I'd like to clean up a bit before we meet with Father Fabian."

"Good idea. I can only tolerate the tourist thing in small doses."

His callous indifference to the allure of the island played in her favor this time.

C C C

The meeting with Father Fabian didn't take long and provided even fewer answers. He did, however, offer a lead. The money channeled to St. Francis Xavier Church came in to the trustees and was redistributed, with only a small percentage designated for the Grand Cayman parish. The rest went to three different churches, one in St. Lucia, one in Haiti, and one in Cozumel, Mexico. Father Fabian had no contact information for two of the churches, but he had both a name and address for the recipient church in Cozumel.

"Father Alejandro is a fine man, and Iglesia del San Bernado is his life. I'm sure he uses the generous gifts for his people, much as I do here."

Back in the car, Jared cranked the engine, but didn't pull out right away. "What's the first rule of investigative journalism, Mallory?"

"Never reveal your sources?"

He waved one hand in dismissal. "Yes, yes. What's another?"

She thought for a moment. Numerous unwritten laws existed in journalism, some simple, others cliché—verify sources, authenticate information, simplify and exaggerate, and … "Follow the money trail."

Jared smiled. "You are such a good student."

He used his cell phone to dial a number "Hello, this is Jared Kinsloe. I need to speak with Mr. Deerborn. Now, please." He put his cell phone on speaker.

Mallory listened in as Jared filled their boss in on what they'd learned.

"Okay. Stick tight. I'll have Lucinda call with instructions." Mr. Deerborn ended the call.

"Something tells me we should head back to the hotel." Jared checked for traffic before entering the highway on the wrong-right side. Or was it the right-wrong side?

The expected return call came as they stepped off the elevator. Jared motioned her to his room.

Mallory followed, uncomfortable but without another option. Once again, he put the call on speaker. Lucinda, who handled the newspaper's travel, was already speaking.

"Your flight to Cozumel leaves tonight at six-fifty. You have hotel reservations at ..."

The rest of conversation faded as Mallory tried to take in the rapid change of events. They'd just gotten here and now had to leave? Without even seeing the island?

Jared hung up. "Go pack. We have to leave in half an hour. I'll check us out."

In her room, she stuffed everything in her one suitcase, and then hurried downstairs again. As expected, she arrived before Jared.

At this time of afternoon, the lounge area was deserted. She chose an oversized chair that looked out at the beach, and sank into its comfort. With her back to the hotel's entrance and the registration desk, she kept her ears tuned for the sound of the elevator. Jared would be down soon. They still had to turn in the rental car.

It wasn't fair, she decided. The little taste of paradise only whetted her appetite for more. One day, she vowed, she'd come back here and stay for a week. With a disappointed sigh, she turned her attention to more important things, like figuring out where—if—this money trail led somewhere. They'd found the name of the company behind the fundraiser, Midwest Distributors, but not much else, not even the name of their CEO or anyone in senior management. She hadn't pursued it since the full amount of money collected was accounted for in the distribution to the small Grand Cayman church. But why send an enormous amount of money to such a small church, and then divvy it out yet again to three even smaller churches?

A man spoke to the registration clerk. His voice held a strong accent, but not the lilt she'd come to associate with the people of the Caribbean. His was low and harsh.

Mallory peeked over her shoulder, and then jerked back out of sight.

Him. The man from the turtle farm. The one who'd followed her to Hell and now to her hotel.

Her pulse rate soared. Fear was an ugly thing. It stole your wits and left you vulnerable. She drew her feet up under her and tried to figure out what she could do. Jared would come down soon. The man would see her, and know she hid from him.

The man continued to talk to the hotel clerk, but she couldn't hear what they said. Moments later, the elevator dinged its arrival.

She dared another peek and saw him get on the elevator. The doors closed, and almost immediately, the second elevator door opened.

Jared strode out.

Relief never felt so sweet.

She hurried over to him. "What took you so long? We have to hurry if we're going to make our flight." She hustled him out of the hotel and to their car.

Imperfect Lies

Chapter Nineteen

Their flight left at 6:50 p.m., but there was no easy way to get from Grand Cayman to Cozumel. Two stops and sixteen hours later, they landed at noon on the Mexican resort island.

Mallory collected her suitcase and followed Jared outside to the taxi stand where he gave the driver the name of their hotel. She climbed into the grungy car and scooted across the seat to make room for her companion.

The island of Cozumel sat just off the mainland of the eastern Yucatan peninsula, and had the same abundance of palm trees as Grand Cayman. Instead of the lush tropical feel of the Caribbean island, though, this place seemed more arid. And hot.

No air-conditioned comfort from this driver. He coasted through the streets with the windows down, in no

hurry at all. The wind whipped Mallory's hair into a frenzy. She tried containing it with one hand, while wiping sweat beads from beneath her eyes with the other.

Jared's cell phone rang while they rode. He held it to one ear and stuck a finger in the other. "Hello." Even his voice sounded tired. "Yes, Mr. Deerborn. We're in a taxi on our way to the hotel."

Mallory let her head fall back against the seat in the ensuing silence. Her eyelids drooped. If Jared wanted to go out tonight, she would faceplant in her food.

Jared clapped a hand to his forehead. "Today? Really? We've been traveling for sixteen hours straight. We're exhausted." More silence. "Yes, sir. three-thirty. I understand."

The call ended and Jared slipped the phone back into his pocket with a sigh. "We have an appointment with Father Alejandro at Iglesia del San Bernardo at three-thirty this afternoon. We'll have to leave by three. You have time to freshen up at the hotel, but that's about all."

Mallory checked the time on her phone—almost one o'clock. She opened her mouth to protest, but closed it again. Their boss had spoken. Job first. Rest later. "We'd better get something to eat. If I stay in my hotel room, I *will* fall asleep."

For once Jared agreed with her. She just hoped for some time to do the touristy stuff.

A short time later, they arrived at Hacienda del Sol.

Not quite the same quality as the one in George Town, but it was clean, serviceable, and close to the airport. At the registration desk, she learned, to her surprise, that Jared spoke fluent Spanish.

On the elevator, he said, "The church is a twenty-five-minute drive from here. I asked the concierge to have a taxi here at three. Take fifteen minutes to freshen up and meet me downstairs."

"Okay." A shower would have to wait. A call home was in order. She'd promised to keep her family—and James—posted on her whereabouts.

Dropping the suitcase on the bed, she dug through it for her toiletries, grabbed her cell phone, and headed into the bathroom. Multi-tasking came easy to her, but she'd have to keep the call short. No time, and besides, these international rates were atrocious. She washed her face, dried it, dialed the international code and her sister's number, and put it on speaker.

Cassie's phone rang four times before she answered. "Hey, Mal. I'm with a patient. Can I call you back?"

"Sorry. I don't have a lot of time either. This will be short and sweet. I'm not in Grand Cayman anymore. We hopped a flight to Cozumel, Mexico. I'm at the Hacienda del Sol."

"What? Does Mom know?"

"That's why I called you," Mallory mumbled while she applied a layer of lipstick. "Mom likes details and I

don't have that much time. Got an appointment in five minutes. I just wanted to check-in and let someone know where I am."

"Okay. Got it. Hacienda del Sol. Cozumel. Did you see any hunky guys on the beach?" Her twin might have already given her heart away, but that wouldn't stop her from looking.

"The whole island is made up of hunky guys, Cass. I can't wait to show you my pictures."

"Okay. Have fun, but not too much."

"Love you. Bye." Mallory disconnected the phone, ran a brush through her hair, and headed back downstairs to meet Jared.

Iglesia del San Bernardo was a small, somewhat run-down church in a questionable part of town. It became painfully apparent the moment they drove up that none of the money directed their way had been used for upkeep of the grounds.

Mallory sat in silence while Jared held an amiable conversation with Father Alejandro, a Franciscan monk right down to his brown cassock, the tan cincture used as a belt, the rounded scapular covering his shoulders, and the long side-rosary that swung from his waist all the way to his left knee. With clunky brown sandals, a fringe of graying hair, ruddy cheeks, jovial temperament, and distended paunch, Father Alejandro looked every bit the part, like Friar Tuck right out of a Robin Hood tale.

It became obvious in the course of the conversation that the elderly priest thought money should be used to help the people and not for the vanity of the church. A fine man, just as Father Fabian had said. Unfortunately, he knew nothing of the charitable financial transaction that sent three-hundred thousand American dollars to his church.

"Goodness me, no. There must be a mistake. We did receive an 18,000 pesos contribution two weeks ago, but that's not anywhere near the amount you mentioned. You should speak with Señor Pedro Escamilla, an upstanding banker in our community. He is … el fideicomisario for our church. How do you say … financial person?"

"Trustee," Jared offered.

"Sí. I think he might be better able to answer your questions."

"Thank you, Father," Jared inclined his head. "How do I contact Señor Escamilla?"

Father Alejandro searched through a notebook under the old fashioned rotary phone on his desk, found the contact information, and transcribed a telephone number onto a small piece of note paper.

In the taxi back to their hotel, Mallory said, "So, we contact Señor Escamilla and try to meet with him tomorrow?"

"Yes. Tomorrow. Right now, all I want to do is fall into my bed and sleep until I wake up."

She knew how he felt. Every part of her drooped with fatigue.

The surf rolled in and then receded with a gentle sucking motion that eroded the sand beneath her feet. Gulls glided on the ocean's breezes, diving now and again to snatch an unsuspecting fish from the water. Warm sunshine kissed her bare shoulders with a promise of freckles. In the background, a persistent ringing sound disrupted the harmony of the morning.

Mallory rolled over and opened her eyes. Sunlight streamed in through partly closed drapes. She burrowed into the pillow and tried to recapture the dream.

Someone knocked on her door, jerking her awake. She looked around, confused for a moment.

The loud, insistent knocking continued. "Mallory. I know you're in there. Open up."

Jared. They'd gone to Grand Cayman … no. Mexico. "Just a minute."

Her pajamas consisted of a thin tank top and boy shorts. Not how she wanted to greet her boss first thing in the morning. Why was he up so early?

She pulled yesterday's shirt and jeans on over her

pajamas and peeped through the keyhole. Yep. Jared. Dressed in a suit.

She slipped the chain off, unbolted the deadlock, and opened the door. "Why are you up so early?"

"It's quarter past ten. I've been trying to call you for the past hour. Why didn't you answer?"

She stared at him, unable to grasp the lateness of the hour. The dream came back, the incessant ringing in the background. "I … I …"

"Never mind. Get dressed. We have an appointment with Escamilla in forty-five minutes. I need you downstairs and clearheaded in fifteen." He closed the door behind him a little harder than necessary.

She relocked the door and hurried to her suitcase, pulling clothes out like a madwoman. Fifteen minutes. Change yes, but look and act human in fifteen minutes?

The transformation took twenty minutes, but she stepped off the elevator in her gray, wrinkle-resistant suit and sensible black pumps, clear-eyed and with her hair tucked up in her usual neat bun.

Jared stood near the entrance, waiting for her. He motioned her forward and then walked out without waiting for her. He did, however, hold open the door of the taxi idling at the curb.

She climbed in after him.

"Sorry. Guess I tuned out your calls."

"I understand. Here's a tip. Turn the volume on your

phone up loud as it will go. Works for me."

"This was fast. You must have been up early to reach Mr. Escamilla."

"EcoDynamic Bank, please," he told the driver before turning to Mallory. "Credit goes to Deerborn. He's pushing hard on this story. I think he smells blood. He—"

A cell phone ring interrupted.

Jared winced and reached for his phone in his pocket. "Another tip. Turn the volume back down after you wake up. Hello, Mr. Deerborn. We're on the way to Señor Escamilla's office now. Yes, sir. One moment."

He handed the phone to Mallory. "He wants to speak to you."

"Good morning, sir."

"Good morning, Mallory. This is a golden opportunity. Not many novice reporters get such an opportunity, especially so early in their career. Follow Jared's lead, but keep your eyes and ears open. Use that inquisitive brain of yours, and find the money."

"I understand, sir. I'll do my best."

"No, you'll do better than your best. If this leads where I suspect it does, you'll want the byline."

She frowned and glanced at Jared. "Yes, sir, but what about Jared?"

Jared smiled with a slow shake of his head.

"Jared's an operations man. He's not a writer. You are. He'll get credit for the investigation, but you'll write the story. Now don't let me down."

"No, sir. I won't."

"Good girl. Now put Jared back on."

Mallory's head whirled with the confidence Mr. Deerborn was placing in her, but then she stumbled over his words—*If this leads where I suspect ...*

They were following the money trail of a charity fundraiser, a really shady trail. Close to a million dollars had been wired to a tiny church in Grand Cayman, only to be split and funneled to even smaller churches around the Caribbean. What more did he need?

She had a hunch this assignment might get ugly before they found their story.

Señor Escamilla waited for them inside the front door of the EcoDynamic Bank of Cozumel, a smallish organization from the size of the building, and one she'd never heard of.

"Mr. Kinsloe? Miss Cameron? It is a pleasure to meet you. Please, join me in my office."

The room could have passed as a supply closet. Tiny, no more than eight-by-eight, and dark, with only a desk lamp for light. He dragged in two folding chairs and gestured for them to sit.

She had to stifle a chuckle when Jared banged his knees against Escamilla's desk. The close confines forced him to slant his knees sideways.

"I spoke with a Mr. Robert Deerborn in Seattle last

night. He tells me your newspaper is doing a story on various philanthropic efforts to raise money for displaced orphans, one of which is the Eco Foundation's recent fundraiser. Is this correct?"

Mallory had to concentrate to understand his heavy accent.

"Yes," Jared answered. "It's our goal to raise awareness of this grave need throughout the United States by emphasizing international efforts in such a worthy endeavor. If you don't mind, we have a few questions for you."

"Please. I will tell you what I can, but understand that many of our donors do not seek glory. They wish to remain anonymous."

"We spoke to Father Alejandro yesterday, as you know," Jared proceeded. "He explained how the money that comes into his church is used in support of the people with very little going to maintenance of the property. He also mentioned that you handle all of the donations they receive. If you can't provide a list of the donors, could you perhaps give us a list of the orphanages that receive benefit from this money? We'd like to include a personal segment that shows the difference a monetary gift can make in the life of a child, or in this case, many children."

"I do not have specifics, but I know our investors are gravely concerned about the impact of terrorism on families and communities around the world. We try to identify those most in need by directing funds through the church to them. That way, we evade greedy politicians who appropriate our gifts for themselves."

"That's a very wise business move. Can you tell us where the funds you received were sent?"

Escamilla beamed. There was no other way to describe it. She'd first thought his shoddy office reflected the nature of his dealings. Instead, she realized he had as kind a heart as Father Alejandro. Pride shone in his eyes.

"Sí, of course. We were given a list from which to choose. Iglesia del San Bernardo selected a refugee camp for children displaced by terrorist attacks."

"Where is this camp?" Jared asked.

"In northeastern Nigeria. The Sisters of Mercy run it."

Mallory choked on a gulp. Would their boss have them chase this lead across the Atlantic? To locate these Sisters of Mercy and their camp?

"Is there a name, a telephone number, an address?"

"No, no. Just a bank account number for the wires. And a lovely thank you letter from a Sister Agatha who runs the camp."

"May I see this letter?"

Escamilla plundered through one of his drawers, opened a file folder, and withdrew a sheet of paper."

Handwritten. In English, thankfully, though the spidery scrawl was difficult to read. And nowhere did it mention any amounts.

Jared studied it for a few moments, and then passed it to Mallory.

"Thank you for your time, Señor Escamilla."

"De nada, señor, senorita."

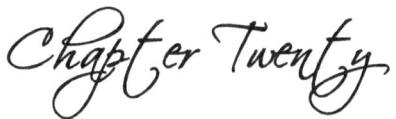

Chapter Twenty

"Thanks Cassie. Tell Mallory to call me if you talk to her again. It's important."

James hung up and dialed another number. He already knew Mallory had left Grand Cayman. He'd sent John Archer there to tail her, but then they made a mad dash to the airport and hopped a plane to Nassau. By the time Archer got to the ticket counter, the flight had closed.

That was last night.

"Yeah?" a gruff voice answered.

"She's in Cozumel at the Hacienda del Sol. How soon can you get there?"

A grumbled curse preceded his answer. "Tomorrow earliest. Sooner in a private plane."

"Hire the plane. Find her. Do whatever you have to, Archer, make contact if necessary, but keep her safe."

"It'll be expensive."

"Not a concern." What good was money if you didn't use it?

"Done." Archer ended the call.

What kind of assignment would make Mallory and her boss jump around the Caribbean like water droplets on a hot griddle? He needed to talk to her, hear her voice. She was touchy, though. She would think he was checking up on her, that she couldn't take care of herself, and she'd be right. The tough and feisty woman was no match for the rabid animals that hunted her.

He knew those dangers all too well.

"Heading out, Lorraine. Call Derek if you need anything." James clapped his hat on his head, grabbed his keys, and slipped out the back door.

The fifteen-minute drive to the Triple C afforded him time to pull his thoughts together. He needed his wits about him for the meeting with the three Cameron brothers. Jonas had a serious stubborn streak, the same one his brothers had inherited. Convincing him to go along with the plan might require all of their influence. Or, he could always play his trump card. Fowler.

James took the fork that led to the big barn. They would have privacy there.

The brothers leaned against the corral and watched him drive up.

James got out of his car and walked their way.

"Afternoon, boys. Thanks for the meeting."

Garrett waved him off. "Let's go into the office."

Wade led the way around the barn to the small office at the back. Garrett sat down at one of the two desks inside. Jonas chose the chair behind the other desk. That left the two uncomfortable folding chairs for Wade and James.

"What's on your mind?" Jonas asked. Straight to the point.

James settled into the chair in front of Jonas's desk, and decided on a direct approach. "I'm here to talk you out of your solo plan and into a better one that will give you the greatest chance of success."

Jonas stiffened, but didn't respond. His closed off expression told James everything he needed to know. This would be a hard sell.

"Fowler has eyes on the target. He's mapped out Toure's daily routine, and knows all of his bolt holes. He can provide weapons, transportation, surveillance, and intel. What he can't provide are boots on the ground. The atmosphere between the Nigerian government and ours is too hair-trigger. That's where we come in."

Jonas glanced at his brothers, with one eyebrow arched high. "Deniability."

"Yes," James said. "We'll be ghosts."

Jonas gave him another sharp look.

"We can drop you and one other into position with your equipment, feed you real time intel, and provide

extraction the moment the job's done." James crossed his legs, resting one ankle on the opposite knee. "You can finish the job. We get you out. A win-win for all of us."

"And my spotter?"

James held his gaze, eyes steady. "John Archer volunteered for the job. Said he owes you."

James didn't miss how Jonas's nostrils flared. And he couldn't blame the younger man for his reaction. According to Fowler, Archer and Jonas had worked together in Nigeria. On their last mission, bad intel had cost the lives of dozens of innocents. 'Unfortunate collateral damage,' the higher ups called it. That was enough to disgust anyone.

Jonas bolted from the chair and strode to the door in quick steps, taking James by surprise. He turned at the door with a hard look for each of them. "I have to think about this." And then he disappeared.

"Well, that went better than expected," Wade said.

"At least he didn't shoot down the idea." Garrett stood, whacked his hat against his leg, and jammed it on his head. "I got work to do. See you later."

"What are the odds he'll agree?" James asked.

Wade scratched his chin. "Fifty-fifty. Jo's hardheaded, but he's not stupid. Not any more than the rest of us. You think we should haul Mallory back home?"

James snorted. If he had his way, she'd never have left the country. Mallory was a fledgling eaglet. She needed to test her wings. But like the newborn bird, she was vulnerable out there on her own. And stubborn as Jonas. Too stubborn to admit her weakness. "She won't like it."

The laugh that followed almost made James smile. Almost. "Oh, she definitely won't like it," Wade answered. "And I'm not telling her. That's on you."

⊂⊃⊂

The rest of the afternoon dragged by. Jonas went AWOL again. A three-car pileup occurred on Route 93 halfway between Challis and Hastings Bluff claimed Kyle's and Derek's attention. Lorraine called him on his cell when the dispatch radio went on the fritz, as if he could fix the darn thing. He had money in his budget to replace it, but they'd have to give up the new armament he wanted for his men. To cap the day off, he was called away in the middle of his evening meal at the diner for a domestic disturbance. Otis Durbin had gone on another bender and came home mouthing off at his wife. Fool man. He knew better than to tick off Carolee Durbin. She topped his skinny frame by four inches and had a hundred pounds on him. And she'd done some serious damage this time, but all in a day's work.

James pulled into the driveway of the small house he leased on the outskirts of town. The standard appliances came with the place, but all he'd added in the two years

he'd been there was a sofa, a recliner, a sixty-inch flat screen, king-sized bed, and a small dinette set off the kitchen. No curtains, no pictures on the wall, no knick-knacks, no washer or dryer. Nothing to make it a home.

He dropped into the recliner and flipped through the channels until he found a ball game. Ah, the Red Sox. The Boston team still held a soft spot in his heart after all these years.

His phone rang. The display showed unlisted. "Evers."

"Found her," Archer answered. "She's tucked away in her hotel room for the night. I'll make contact tomorrow."

The knowledge that Mallory was safe and in good hands again provided much needed relief. Some of the tension slipped away. "Tell her to call me. If she doesn't, you'll have to fill her in on the threat level. Keep her safe, John."

"Roger." Archer hung up.

James had one boot off and was tugging on the other when his cell rang again. Jonas this time. "Hello."

"I'm coming to your place. Be there in five." An audible click followed.

With a put-upon sigh, James stomped his foot back into the boot.

True to his word, Jonas's black truck pulled into his driveway minutes later.

James opened the door for him. "Want something to drink?"

"No. This won't take long."

They walked into the sparse living room where Jonas perched on the edge of the couch. "Sheesh, man. You need to get some furniture, put some pictures on the wall or something. Place looks like a prison cell."

"And how would you know how a prison cell looks?"

Jonas flushed and looked away.

Curious reaction. Ignoring him, James settled into his recliner again. Might as well get comfortable. This was Jonas's show, and they'd get to the reason for the visit in good time.

And then Jonas delivered an unexpected concession. "I agree to your plan, but we do this on my timeline."

"Go on." James pulled the lever on the side of the chair and pushed into a near-horizontal position.

"End of May. We, the whole team, insert a week early at a point I designate. Treekiller and I will worm our way to the target while the rest of the team sets up base camp. You hold the rear, and call in air support as needed. We make the hit and get out."

"Treekiller?"

"Archer." A wisp of a smile flirted with Jonas's lips.

"What does he call you?" James asked.

Jonas hesitated before answering. His eyes went cold. "Fatalwa. It means ghost."

Made sense now. Fowler said Toure was looking for a ghost. "Four weeks is a long time. Lots can change. Why wait?"

"It's Democracy Day, a national holiday. Everyone in the country will be blitzed. It offers the perfect distraction. Who else is in this op?" Jonas leaned back against the sofa.

"You and Archer. Me, Garrett, Wade, and Kyle. Derek stays here to man the store. Fowler, of course, and whatever crew he comes up with. He's agreed to provide whatever we need in the way of logistics."

James had spent a lot of time thinking about the situation and had come to the conclusion that while deep cover agents burned out at a high rate, they generally lasted longer than Jonas's short tenure. Logical deduction said something had happened over there during Jonas's last assignment. Something bad enough to cause nightmares. Something he never spoke of. John Archer had offered hints, but Spec Ops were notoriously closemouthed about their work. Rightfully so. When pressed, all Archer would say was, "It's Jonas's story to tell."

"Think Fowler would let us have one of those Judas missiles?" Jonas asked out of the blue.

"What's a Judas missile?"

"Shoulder-launched, laser-guided weapon system. Fires small caliber projectiles you can custom fill with your pick of poison, or with a larger bore that will blow a hole in a brick wall. Uses facial recognition technology synced with bio data to identify the target, kind of like pointing a finger the way Judas did to Jesus. It has an accuracy range of two miles with minimal risk of collateral damage. Basically, we input the bio data, set a max range, point, shoot, and bingo. We can cherry-pick that sucker out of a crowd with one shot, and get in and out in three days."

"And if Fowler can't get it?"

Jonas shrugged. "We do it the old-fashioned way."

Technology was changing the face of war. "I'll make the request."

After Jonas left, James popped a frozen meal in the microwave and heated it. He wanted food in his belly and a hot shower before he hit the hay. Many times, he'd been cold and hungry, gone without sleep for long stretches of time, but never had he felt as tired as now. No matter. He'd take a hum-drum, predictable, and boring life of a small-town sheriff over those danger-filled days anytime. And here he was about to jump back into the fire.

With the charging cord plugged into his phone, James crawled in between the sheets. A good night's sleep could solve a lot of problems.

His phone rang again.

A weary sigh escaped as he reached for it. Better not be Mrs. Franklin. He couldn't deal with another intruder scare from her, not tonight. But when he checked the caller ID, all thoughts of sleep dropped away. "Mallory?"

"Hi, yourself. I let Cassie know where I am, but she said you needed to talk to me, that it was important."

How do you tell a woman that the very sound of her

voice made your heart skip? "Yeah, I need you to be extra cautious, more alert than ever. That threat I told you about? It's back, only graver now than before." He had to be careful speaking over an unsecured line, especially one routed over international airways.

"Oh. Okay." She sounded rattled.

"Is something wrong, princess?"

"No. Well, maybe. There was this guy."

James got to his feet and started to pace. Archer hadn't been there long enough for her to notice him. "What guy? Where? Was it the same—"

"No, not the same guy in Lucy's photo, at least I don't think so. He was in Grand Cayman. He didn't do or say anything, and yet he always seemed to be where I was. I caught him watching me a couple of times. Might be my imagination, but it gave me the shivers."

"Listen careful, Mallory. That friend I sent to look out for you before? He'll find you tomorrow. Talk to him. Get his number. Make sure you let him know ahead of time what your plans are. Will you do that?"

"Yeah, but I think we're almost done here." Her voice quavered a little.

"Are you returning to Seattle?"

"I hope so. I'm so sick of airplanes and airports. We're following a story that has the potential to be explosive. A lead took us to the Caymans, but that only led to more rabbit trails."

James scrubbed a hand through his short hair. This woman would give him ulcers before he got her back home again. "Do you know where you're going next?"

She didn't answer right away. "No, not yet."

CCC

The pounding on her door the next morning jerked her awake with a start.

"Mallory."

Jared again. The urge to bury her head under the pillow vied with the need to kill him. The clock next to her bed read 6:03 a.m.

More pounding, harder now. "Wake up, woman. Our flight leaves in fifty-five minutes."

She threw on the terrycloth robe provided by the hotel and zombie-walked to the door. When she saw Jared's face through the two-inch gap allowed by the security chain, Mallory rolled her eyes. "You've got to be kidding me."

"No time for your sass. Go throw some water on your face and get your clothes on. We need to go, like five minutes ago. Move it."

She groaned and removed the chain lock. "Please tell me we're going home."

Jared walked over to her bed and grabbed her suitcase. "Nope. Not yet."

Mallory stopped mid-stride and turned to gape at him.

"Then where?"

Jared turned her around shoved her toward the bathroom. "Get ready and I'll tell you. Now. I'm not kidding. We're out of here in …" He glanced at his watch. "Four minutes whether you're ready or not."

Mallory grabbed her jeans and a shirt, and slammed the bathroom door behind her. Five strokes with the hairbrush, another five strokes with her toothbrush, and a swipe over her face with a cold, wet washcloth got her out in record time.

Jared filled her in while she packed her suitcase.

"Deerborn has a research team that rivals the CIA. We already knew the nine-hundred-thousand dollars sent to Father Fabian's church in Cayman was split three ways, one-third to Father Alejandro's church in Cozumel, one-third to a church in Jamaica, and the final third to a church in Haiti. The interesting part is that all three churches turned around and transferred the bulk of the money to the Sisters of Mercy Mission. They kept a small percentage for themselves and sent *exactly* two-hundred-eighty-five-thousand dollars each."

"The same amount?" Mallory frowned as she tried to make her sleep-deprived brain understand.

"Yep. Turns out, three-hundred thousand dollars is a trigger point for the U.S. Treasury Department when money is transferred from the U.S. to a foreign country. And apparently, this is not the first instance of charitable donations directed to well-meaning churches outside the country. Deerborn's boys dug up a long history of similar transactions going back almost fifteen years, all originating from supposed charitable donations, which, by the way, can't be traced. This scheme involves more than sixty different churches throughout the Caribbean, Central America, and Mexico. And since these countries represent common sources of immigrant workers for the U.S., they've never aroused suspicion."

"So, this is an elaborate money-laundering scheme we're chasing? Are the Sisters of Mercy a front?" The idea of using such a desperate need to cover up corruption repulsed her.

Jared grinned and handed her a paper. "We're going to find out."

Mallory glanced down at the e-ticket in her hand. "Nigeria? I can't go to Nigeria."

His smile hardened. "Of course, you can. Unless you want to tuck your tail and run back to Nowhere, Idaho. This is your big chance, Mallory."

Imperfect Lies

Chapter Twenty-One

Mallory set her suitcase on the scale and handed her passport and e-ticket to the airline agent. A few moments later, the bag disappeared into the bowels of the airport and the agent returned her identification along with a boarding pass. "Have a nice flight, Ms. Cameron."

No turning back now. She had three changes of clothes to her name, all of them, including what she wore, dirty. Hopefully, they had laundry service in Nigeria. Otherwise, she would have to wear the same stuff again or go shopping as soon as they landed—right after she called her sister.

Her head ached at the thought of what her brothers would say when Cassie told them. Thinking of how James would react threatened an ulcer. He'd railed at her over the phone when they talked last night, going on and on about this new threat, and now she'd all but offered herself up on a serving platter.

She couldn't think about that now.

Jared led the way through security and to their gate where he promptly commandeered two seats—one for himself and one for his carry-on bag. Fastidious to a fault, he wouldn't dare allow any of his things to touch the floor.

"I'm getting a coffee. Want one?" she asked, and parked her bag on the chair across from him.

"Sure. A latte if you can find it, otherwise, get me a half-caf, sweet and light."

Really? She raised a disbelieving brow at him, but he had his phone out. Nothing short of an earthquake would break his attention now.

She walked off, not bothering to argue. He'd get whatever they had.

Not far from the coffee shop, John Archer, her trusty bodyguard and shadow, leaned against the wall. Seeing him with his own cup of joe in one hand and a newspaper open in the other added another layer of guilt. She was dragging him halfway around the world … for what? So she could dance like a puppet for a story that may or may not be there?

Archer never looked up from his reading, but she had no doubt he knew where every person in her immediate vicinity stood.

She didn't look at him or acknowledge him in any way, but uttered a few mumbled words as she passed by.

"Thanks for coming."

"No problem," he murmured, still not looking up.

As she'd suspected, the tiny coffee shop offered two types of coffee—regular and mud. She chose the lighter blend and added a liberal dose of media crema, the Mexican version of half-n-half, plus several packets of sugar to both cups.

"Thanks," Jared said without looking up from his cell phone. He took a sip, grimaced, and set the cup on the floor.

Mallory sank into the seat across from him, blew on her own steaming brew, and studied the people who bustled through the small but busy airport.

A beleaguered mother of six young kids, all who looked under the age of ten, pleaded, grabbed, spanked, swatted, and yelled at her brood.

An elderly man with a long, iron-gray beard and a cane barked his disapproval at the poor woman. She snapped back, and a heated argument in Spanish erupted. Arms flailed with dramatic abandon as the two faced off. Meanwhile, one of the little darlings took advantage of the distraction and did a fast-crawl getaway under the seats, while four of the other kids started up a game of tag in the middle of the bustling crowd. The last child, the oldest of the bunch, scaled the gate desk to investigate the computers while the agent had her back turned.

Mallory grinned. She could totally see Garrett at ten years, Wade at nine, Jonas at seven, and her and Cassie at five pulling these same shenanigans. Poor Mom.

More passengers arrived and filled the chairs around her. A few wore headphones and bobbed away to the beat of their own private concert. Others fiddled with electronic devices, like Jared, or read books and newspapers, while the majority waited with the bored patience of seasoned travelers. The overflow spilled into the waiting area of the adjacent gate, and that's where she spotted him. Brown skin, much darker than anyone else here, black t-shirt, and stocking cap. He slouched in one of the chairs, and quickly averted his face when she looked his way.

Fear unfurled inside her. But then, head still lowered, he glanced up, his gaze going straight to her.

Mallory stared back, unable to look away, paralyzed rabbit to a stalking wolf. Her pulse skyrocketed off the chart. Up to now, she'd called it nerves, edginess, and unease, but the truth was, this man terrified her.

He dropped his eyes first and broke the spell.

Had she made a foolhardy mistake? What if James was right? That this mysterious risk had targeted her?

Under the guise of buying water this time, she passed by John Archer again, stopping near him to dig through her purse for money. "He's here," she whispered. "The man from Grand Cayman."

"Where?"

"Dark skin. Black t-shirt. Gate next to mine."

"On it."

She continued to the coffee stand, purchased the water, and returned to her seat in the waiting area.

"Deerborn sent a text," Jared interrupted her disquiet when she sat down again. "Soren Reis will meet us in Lagos."

"Who?"

"Soren Reis. He's only the most renowned international freelance photographer of our time. Boss says if we can't work the corruption angle, you need to deliver a really touching human interest story. Soren can help us with that. Snap a few shots of orphans in rags, some hovels, and we're good."

She couldn't believe the callousness of his words. Did he have no compassion?

The gate agent called for boarding.

Decision time. Second thoughts about this trip consumed her. She could walk out right now, and kiss her career goodbye. Or keep her eyes open, remain vigilant and safe, and get the job done. How many novice journalists got to work with a legend like Soren Reis their first assignment out?

Choice made, Mallory joined Jared in the throng lined up for boarding. Her eyes wandered back to the adjacent gate but couldn't find her stalker. She looked around but didn't see Archer either, and that worried her.

Twenty-four long, miserable hours later, they landed in Lagos, Nigeria, where the ninety-degree temperature roasted her skin and the high humidity threatened to drown her. The taxi they hailed didn't help. It had no air conditioning.

"We have reservations at the Sheraton." Jared wiped sweat from his brow. "Soren is meeting us there for dinner. We'll figure out our plan then. Tomorrow morning, we fly to Maiduguri in the northeastern corner of the country. That's where the Sisters of Mercy are reputed to be."

Mallory nodded, too tired to formulate a response.

In her room, she set her suitcase down, plugged her phone charger in, and hooked it to her phone. First order of business, call home. It took several attempts before she reached the front desk for help with the international call before she got through.

"Hey, Mal." Her sister's voice had never sounded so sweet.

"Hey, Cass. How are things at home?"

Cassie laughed. "What? Here in Nothing-Ever-Changes, Idaho? Please. The better question is what adventure are you chasing today?"

Unexpected tears rose. Home had never felt so far away. Mallory laughed to hide the emotion her twin would surely hear in her voice. "Off on another lead. All this investigative stuff isn't as glamorous as television makes out. It's dirty, exhausting, and confusing."

"You sound like you're in an echo chamber. Where in the world are you? Pun intended."

Time to 'fess up. The moment she'd dreaded had arrived. Mallory took a deep breath, released it, and prepared to endure her twin's wrath. "Nigeria."

"What?"

Mallory jerked the phone from her ear, sure she'd be hearing impaired after Cassie's shriek.

"No, no, no. You can't be there. Tell me this is a joke, Mallory."

What could she say?

"Mal? Tell me you're not there."

"Yeah, Cass, I'm here in Lagos at the Sheraton for now, but we're off to Maidu-something or other tomorrow, and who knows after that. I'll let you know where as soon as I can. Don't worry. I promise I'll be safe. I'll be careful."

"Don't worry? How can you ask me not to worry?" Her sister's voice rose with the repeated question. "Garrett's gonna kill something when he finds out. My only hope is it's not me. I can't even imagine what James will do."

Mallory closed her eyes against the tears. She could imagine very well how he would react.

James raised his arm, ready to throw his phone at the wall. The only thing that kept him from losing his ever-loving mind and grabbing the first flight out to Africa was

the knowledge that John Archer had eyes on Mallory.

Constraint won out, but only because he didn't have time to pick up a new phone. He pocketed it instead. He couldn't believe she'd gone to Nigeria after he'd explained in explicit detail the danger there, an evil that would snatch her up and swallow her without a trace. Although, in a way, he should have seen it coming.

Mallory saw this assignment as the boost she needed to launch her career. She was brave to a fault, and smart enough to think she could get in and out of trouble, but her underlying mistake was thinking Archer could keep her safe. The man would give his life for hers, but the odds didn't favor a lone man and a naïve girl against a whole faction of fanatics led by a psychopath. If Toure knew she was on his soil …

And he would know within twenty-four hours. Probably less.

James picked up the phone and dialed the only number that could help him.

"Hello, Sheriff. To what do I owe this pleasure?"

"Operation Ghost Walk just got moved up."

Silence followed for a few heartbeats. "When?"

"Twenty-four hours or as soon as you can pull the resources together."

Another silence. "Why?"

"Mallory Cameron just landed in Lagos. She's on her way to Maiduguri, the heart of—"

"Sebastian Toure's power base. Yes, I know." A soft expletive followed. "This wouldn't be a joke, by chance?"

James didn't bother with a response.

"I didn't think so," Fowler went on. "You really need to put a leash on those girls. They're too headstrong for their own good."

"Tell me about it."

"I assume this has something to do with her job at the Seattle newspaper?"

"Yeah. She's onto some corrupt charity filtering funds through churches, money that's found its way to Nigeria in supposed support of a refugee camp for orphans."

"Ahhhh, the Sisters of Mercy Mission."

"You know about this?"

"Yes. What I didn't know was that the news media had caught wind of it. Snoops. All of them, meddling where they shouldn't. Always stirring stuff up. Call a meeting with the brothers and whomever else you deem necessary. Make it for four o'clock at the Cameron ranch. I'll fly in and we'll finalize a plan."

"Roger."

"Oh, and James. Tell Jonas he's got his Judas missile."

Immediately after he hung up with Fowler, James called Kyle, Derek, and the Cameron brothers. On impulse, he'd also called their dad, Cody Cameron. He deserved to know the danger his daughter had gotten into, and why James would be taking all three of his sons away for an undetermined time.

Next, he called his own father. James had a meeting with him in Boston next week, but this new development took precedence. His father would have to understand.

The call went straight to voice mail. Only then, did James remember the chemo treatments he'd noted on his calendar. Relieved, he left a message and promised to call as soon as possible to reschedule.

Another call went to his travel agent to cancel his Boston flight, rental car, and hotel. He couldn't bring himself to stay with his old man, not yet. And especially not with his brother living in New York now. Too many unreconciled memories in his childhood home, memories he had no desire to confront. One day. Maybe.

Paperwork and worry consumed him the rest of the afternoon. When he looked at his watch for the hundredth time, he pushed the paper aside and stood. Fowler's helicopter wouldn't land at the Cameron ranch for another hour, but he couldn't wait around any longer.

"I'm going to the Triple C," he yelled to Lorraine. "Don't call unless somebody's dead or World War III breaks out." He stomped out the back door.

Fear for Mallory consumed him on the drive, worry over what awaited her in Nigeria. They had to eliminate Toure and the threat his militants posed before she got caught in their snare. And she would. Toure was a shark circling its helpless victim, waiting for the right moment to strike.

James turned down the long, private drive in time to see a helicopter lift off and soar away over the trees. He broke out in a cold sweat. Fowler had already arrived.

Choking back a curse, he pressed harder on the accelerator and almost slid off the road. Fowler demanded punctuality, both from others and himself. He was never late. Never early, either. Something was wrong.

James parked and got out as two more vehicles rolled in behind him. Derek and Kyle stepped out of their cars. Time to kick some butt and blow stuff up. Hooyah.

Garrett opened the front door before they reached it. "Fowler's here. He brought two men with him. We're set up in the dining room."

Fowler and his men had maps spread over the table, salt and pepper shakers and other knickknacks holding them in place. A stack of eight-by-ten photos sat off to one side. "Good, you're here. Let's get started." His attention strayed to the array on the table.

The former Bureau of International Intelligence chief turned-free-agent held more power now than he ever had while working for the BII. And James still had no idea who he reported to. Someone very powerful and very high up.

Garrett, Wade, Jonas, Kyle, Derek, and Fowler's two men circled the table.

Fowler moved to one side to make room for James.

"Gentlemen, Operation Ghost Walk is officially a go.

Wheels up at 2300 hours."

Chapter Twenty-Two

Devastation came in many forms, Mallory realized as she turned in a slow circle. Unshed tears made her eyes burn. Horror left her throat constricted. The small village they passed through lay in ruins, buildings blown to bits, tarpaper shacks shredded by monsters who used devastating force. Rubble and debris littered the streets— slabs of concrete, splintered wood, shattered glass, spent mortar and ammunition shell casings, and a burned-out truck. Carts lay overturned. Rotting garbage piled up in mounds ... and a lone shoe lay in the middle of the street next to a little girl's dolly.

"Are you getting this, Soren?" Jared asked "These scenes are priceless."

Soren Reis didn't bother with an answer. He and his camera existed as one entity, taking picture after picture.

Was she the only one who saw the loss? Felt the heartbreak?

Isaac, their driver, made his way around the potholes and obstacles. He drove with slow, deliberate care and never stopped casting worried glances in all directions. "This no good. This too new," he muttered over and over.

"You said the attack happened day before yesterday, right?" Jared asked Dakan, their interpreter. "You're sure it's safe?"

Dakan spat out the window. "No one safe here. They locusts. Destroy village, people, animals, food. Leave nothing. They no come back."

A sickening wave of nausea rolled over her. A rush of bile forced her to lean out the window. Her stomach expelled what was left of the meager breakfast.

So much needless waste, so much death.

Jared handed her a bottle of water. "Are you sure this is the way to the new refugee camp? The one set up by the Sisters of Mercy?" He asked the driver.

They'd had no luck running down anyone who might be connected to the Sisters of Mercy in Maiduguri. No one wanted to answer questions, especially from foreigners. Not a surprise given the turmoil in the area. Those who hadn't packed up and scurried away grabbed whatever they could find to build barricades around their homes. A wasted effort since the still unnamed Ansaru splinter group had proven their destructive prowess many times over.

They typically targeted villages, numbers they could easily overwhelm, but they'd also hit a few of the smaller towns in outlying areas.

Locusts indeed. Devour, destroy, depart. A good analogy.

The single piece of information provided by Deerborn's research guru gave them their only lead. Two Catholic missionary nuns, who called themselves the Sisters of Mercy, had set up a camp for displaced children after the militants wiped out Enziama, the tiny village they drove through now, located in Cameroon's Neck, a narrow strip of land where the Cameroon, Chad, and Nigeria borders met.

Not the first time, Mallory doubted Deerborn's judgment in sending them to such an unstable area. She berated herself again for not listening to her instincts back in Cozumel and foregoing this mad expedition.

The driver picked up speed as they left the carnage behind. The dirt track they called a road smoothed out and narrowed as they entered a dense, wooded area. Spooky described it best.

They followed the track for an hour, maybe longer, before the trees and underbrush gave way to an open space. One small building that appeared to have been cobbled together from stray pieces of wood and metal stood in the center. Twenty or so canvas tents of varying sizes surrounded the little shack on three sides.

A cookfire stood a moderate distance from the little shack, with a large black kettle hanging from a makeshift spit. A rusted old truck stood at the edge of the clearing on the far side. From all the tire tracks leading in and out of the clearing, the derelict vehicle must still run.

A wizened old lady in a dusty black habit came out of the dilapidated building and stood waiting for them. She wiped her hands on a rag, and then pushed at the white headband under her coif. A beatific smile lit her face, a beacon of serenity in a world gone mad.

"Welcome, friends. I am Sister Agatha."

They'd found her.

Acceptance without suspicion. No condemnation, no questions.

Such a rare creature, the sister stood five feet tall, perhaps less. Nonetheless, she seemed a giantess. Age had left its mark, though. Wrinkles cut a deep tracery of lines over her face and neck, and her hands had curled into claws, gnarled and twisted from arthritis. Years of sacrifice, poverty, and hard work left its stamp on the tiny wisp of a women, but she glowed with an inner, godly serenity that could not be ignored.

Awed by the sheer magnitude of the nun's quiet authority, Mallory took her offered hand with gentle care. "My name is Mallory Cameron." She turned to the others in her group. "These gentlemen are my associates, Jared Kinsloe, our interpreter, Dakan Leban, and our driver,

Isaac Obademi. The man with the camera is Soren Reis, a photographer."

Soren, a reclusive sort who asked few questions and answered less, flitted about the camp, the camera never far from his face.

Jared towered over the tiny woman, but seemed equally impressed by Sister Agatha. Unsure whether to shake her fragile hand, he instead executed a courtly, if somewhat awkward, bow. "Sister. Thank you for your welcome."

The other two men remained at a distance, hats in hand, and heads lowered in respect.

"What brings you to our humble camp? How may we assist you?"

"Um ... er ..." For once, Jared seemed incapable of putting simple words into sentences. He inclined his head toward Mallory.

"We represent a newspaper in the United States. Stories of the work the Sisters of Mercy performs reached us. We wanted to come and see for ourselves. It is our desire to raise awareness of the desperate need here, and encourage support for your mission." An idea emerged while Mallory talked, one she hadn't discussed with Jared. "Perhaps we could stay with you for a day or two and help with our hands in some small manner, so that we might learn more of what you do here."

Jared stiffened beside her. He might kick her later, but

for now he had no choice but to acquiesce.

Sister Agatha's tranquil demeanor transformed into a wide grin. "Oh, child. You are the answer to our prayers. After the attack on Enziama, the small village southwest of here, the two women who helped us left. They fear the Mayaƙan 'yanci, the freedom fighters. The Mayaƙan do not bother with old women and babies, but we hide the young girls from them." She shuddered. "It is better they leave, but they left the little ones with only two old women to provide for them. And Akpom, of course. He carries water from the river to fill our cisterns and gathers firewood. He also drives the truck, forages for supplies, and does all the heavy lifting for us. He built this small shelter for the babies."

"How many children are here?"

"Twenty-six, twelve of which do not yet walk. Sister Mary Magdalena, come meet our guests."

Another nun, this one somewhat taller and sturdier, but of a similar age as Sister Agatha, must have been listening. She appeared in the doorway with a toddler on each hip before Sister Agatha finished speaking.

"This is Sister Mary Magdalena. She comes from Barcelona and understands more English than she speaks." Sister Agatha smiled at her friend and beckoned her forward.

The other sister blushed, but shuffled closer.

"She takes care of the youngest since my hands do not

work so well anymore. I look after the older children, those who can do for themselves. They sleep in the tents for now."

Mallory sidled closer to the nun holding the babies. One of the tots buried his face against the nun's ample chest, but the other one offered a toothless grin and lurched forward with arms outstretched.

Mallory's heart softened to the consistency of butter left out on the counter. She reached for the tot and bounced her in a slow and gentle motion. Babies were foreign to her. She knew little to nothing about them, so the coos coming from her own mouth startled her. Did all women have a natural mothering instinct?

Sister Agatha clasped her hands together and beamed at Mallory and her group. "As you can see, workers are always welcome, even if you can only stay for a little while."

◇◇◇

Breakfast ended a long time ago, and the smells from this savory stew were making her salivate. Mallory's stomach rumbled with appreciation.

She switched the long wooden paddle to her other hand and paused for a moment to wipe sweat from her face. Who knew cooking over a fire would require such hard work? Hot, yes. But her shoulders ached after working the thick concoction for the last thirty minutes.

Sister Agatha proved to be a strict, but gracious taskmaster. She sent Isaac, the driver from Mallory's group, to find Akpom, and help him carry buckets of water from the river. "Our Akpom makes eight trips to the river every day to fill two of our storage barrels. We let the water sit for two days to allow the sediment to settle on the bottom. Once done, we dip from the top and boil it in a cookpot. From there it goes into clean barrels with the purifying tablets. The work is hard and never ending, but essential for the health of us all."

She dispatched Jared and the interpreter to a wooded area to collect firewood. "Might as well stock up while we have the help."

Mallory's first assignment landed her in a lean-to attached to the side of the nursery where she cleaned and pared vegetables—onion, yams, okra, plantains, and other things she had no name for—for the evening meal. Under Sister Agatha's direction, she poured them into the large cast iron cook pot, added water, some paste-like stuff, and a bunch of seasonings she'd never heard of, and began the tedious task of watching it cook.

"Constant stirring is needed, Mallory. Otherwise, the stew will burn at the bottom. It's very difficult to clean the bottom of the pot."

Encouragement, instruction, and chiding, all in one statement. Sister Agatha had fine-tuned the art of passive-aggressive dictatorship, but she could also give James and her brothers a run for their money in the bossy category. Yet, she never asked more from anyone than what she gave herself.

Without electricity, the day ended when the sun went down, which meant the children had to be fed, bathed, and readied for bed while light remained. After that, they cleaned the camp, and yes, the bottom of the pot proved very difficult to clean.

Akpom, a simpleminded, strapping man of middle age, didn't eat with them. Though he spoke and worked with Isaac and Dakan, he seemed suspicious and uneasy around Mallory and Jared. He'd taken his bowl carved from a gourd and filled with the stew from Sister Agatha, ate alone some distance from the camp, and then disappeared before twilight fell.

Sister Agatha relocated some of the children to another tent. "You'll sleep here, dear, next to the tent I share with Sister Mary Magdalena." She turned to the men. "Gentlemen, Akpom prefers to make his bed in the truck. I hope you won't mind sleeping in yours."

Jared nodded with all the grace of an aristocrat, though she caught him scowling later. He would make her pay for this when they got home.

Just as the day ended at sundown, it began with the first hint of dawn. She woke to the sound of water pouring into the barrel near her tent. Akpom was already at work.

Must have been for some time since he had to go to the river and back again.

Mallory crawled from her tent, and groaned with the stretch of sore muscles. The sun had already climbed into the sky, bright enough to scorch her corneas and force a squint. She looked for the men's whereabouts, and then made her way to the latrine hidden beyond the edge of the jungle. This primitive lifestyle made privacy a luxury. Like clean water, something she'd always taken for granted.

Jared sat beside her on the ground to eat a small portion of fish and some wheat cakes for breakfast. His overnight beard softened what she'd thought of as a too-pretty face for a man. "Wonder where they got the fish."

Like everything else about him, he ate with finicky precision.

She was too hungry to care, and licked her fingers to clean them. "Sister Agatha says Akpom fishes in the river and sets snares in the woods."

Jared's upper lip curled ever so slightly as he tried to hide his repugnance. "You do realize we can't stay here. It's obvious none of the money made its way here, so we still have to find the connection. Sister Agatha told us last night that she'd written no letters of thanks. Without finding the money, Soren's photographs and your descriptions of this place will still make a tremendous story. Either way, we leave today, Mallory. Word gets around fast for such a backward place, and I get the feeling these people don't care much for Americans. We can't linger here. Understand?"

"Yes." Her hope of staying for another day disappeared with the smoke from the cook pit. The sisters had such big hearts and needed so much, yet they waited with smiles for God to provide what He would.

A small gasp came from the makeshift kitchen where Sister Agatha scrubbed the mornings dishes. The tiny woman backed away from the scrub pot, holding one of her hands in front of her. Soapy water dripped down her arms, mingling with blood. "Oh dear, oh dear," she cried softly.

Mallory and Jared rushed to her side.

Sister Mary Magdalena laid the baby she was changing on the floor and hurried over.

"Nothing to worry about," Sister Agatha insisted. "It's just a scratch. Quite shallow. My own fault. I was careless with the dishes."

A long gash dissected the palm of her hand and bled freely. Not shallow at all, but one that would require stitches. Carelessness may be a fault, but more likely the accident happened because her arthritic fingers no longer worked the way they should, even when she tried to force them.

Sister Mary Magdalene fussed and clucked, and wrapped the injured hand with a cloth. She gestured for Mallory to hold the compress tight while she scurried back to the nursery and fetched her sewing basket.

Mallory's stomach turned over. With no medical facility nearby, of course they had to be self-sufficient.

Sister Agatha's natural rosy complexion paled, but she sat in stoic calm while Sister Mary Magdalena sterilized a needle, loaded it with sturdy thread, and stitched her up. Afterward, Akpom, who seemed to appear and disappear at will, helped the diminutive nun over to the shade and provided a chair for her to sit on.

One thought circled round and round through Mallory's head throughout Sister Mary Magdalena's ministrations. The camp was already badly understaffed. With Sister Agatha's injury, how could they possibly care for the children, so many of them infants?

How could she leave them?

She broached the dilemma to Jared as he helped prepare the noonday meal. "I understand how you feel, Mallory, I really do. But we can't stay here. Dakan has been listening to reports on the radio. He says the militants aren't done here. Word about us will get out. We'll stay to help with lunch, but then we're leaving. It's too dangerous."

He walked away, not giving her a chance to argue.

Jared was right. He knew it, and she knew it. Danger vibrated in the air.

Mallory made her way to Sister Agatha, and sat on the ground beside her.

"Don't fret, child. Everything works according to

God's plan." She patted Mallory's shoulder with her uninjured hand. "Wait on Him. He won't lead you astray."

"How will you manage? You're already shorthanded."

"The children in this country grow up fast. They have to. Some will pick up my slack by necessity. The other things ..." She shrugged. "Circumstances dictate priorities. We'll be fine."

"And if the fighting comes here?"

She shrugged again. "We'll pray it doesn't. Either way, we submit to His divine will and trust Him to hold us in His hand. Now go help Sister Agatha while you're still here."

Imperfect Lies

Chapter Twenty-Three

Mallory wiped her face on one shoulder and then the other. Flour—or what passed for flour here—coated her hands and arms up to her elbows as she mixed and kneaded the bread for the evening meal.

Jared left yesterday, furious that she refused to go with him. He'd argued with her for the better part of an hour before he left in a huff.

She couldn't fault him. The story and Soren's pictures would create a storm of interest in the journalism world.

"One day, Mallory. That's it. As soon as we get back to Maiduguri I'm sending someone to get you, even if they have to haul you out of here in a sack."

He'd been so angry, but she couldn't leave Sister Mary Magdalena and Akpom to care for twenty-six little children, especially not after Sister Agatha developed a

fever. The two nuns had already been stretched to the breaking point. And he said someone would come for her today and bring help.

But Lord, she'd never been so tired.

Her hands moved mechanically, without thought, shaping the dough into loaves and dropping them onto the metal sheet over the fire. She wiped her hands on a rag she used as an apron and gave the stew a quick stir. This wasn't a life. These kids deserved so much more. The Sisters deserved a place where they could rest and enjoy their remaining years in comfort, not this drudgery that sapped the soul.

"I'm sorry, Father. My whole life has been one big imperfect lie. I've lived in comfort and abundance while others suffered from starvation and violence. Forgive me. I have nothing to complain about."

"Mallory!"

Sister Agatha's cry came from the small building that served as a nursery for the babies. Once they learned to walk with any degree of confidence, they were moved to the tents and assigned chores. Here, everyone worked. Everyone had to work to survive.

The truth of Sister Agatha's word rang in her memory. The children of this country did grow up fast.

"Come here, child. Now!" Stress filled the sister's usually calm voice.

Mallory flipped the bread on the metal sheet, gave the

pot another hearty stir, and then hurried to the door of the building.

The tiny nun sat at a makeshift desk in the back corner of the room, in front of an archaic radio set. She wore earphones over her coif and made frantic gestures beckoning Mallory to come closer.

Around them, twelve babies lay in box-like beds fashioned from crates. Ten slept, one played with her toes, and one cried softly, on the verge of dozing off.

"What's wrong, Sister Agatha?"

Fear looked back at her from the depths of the sister's eyes. "They're coming. The Mayaкan."

Mallory hands stilled as she wiped them on her apron again. "What?"

The nun yanked off the headphones, tossed them onto the desk, and hurried to the doorway. "Sister Mary Magdalena," she yelled.

"Sister, perhaps you should sit down and rest."

"No time child. You have to leave. You have to take the older children and go."

Okay, now she was alarmed. Either the fever had rendered her delusional … or something was terribly wrong. "Please calm down and explain. You're scaring me."

A sad smile chased the anxiety from the nun's face. "Akpom didn't make his usual trips to the river this morning. That's unlike him. And then I noticed the truck

was gone. I was worried and called to some friends at another camp. They're fifty miles away and closer to the towns. They get news much faster than we do." Her chin trembled.

Uneasiness closed in around Mallory. "Tell me."

"The Mayakan have heard of the Americans who came to see the ravages of war. They're coming for you."

Mallory took a step back. She'd often read that extreme fear was contagious and had a distinctive smell, that emotional triggers stimulated chemical signals in body sweat that could be picked up by others. She believed it. Fear permeated the small room. Hers and the sister's.

"You must flee and take the older children with you. We are too few to carry the babies and the little ones."

"No, I can't leave you. I won't leave."

Sister Mary Magdalena appeared in the doorway, a worried expression on her face. A rapid volley of Spanish flew between the two women, a conversation Mallory couldn't follow. And then Sister Mary Magdalena's worry turned to horror. She ran off, calling to the children.

"Mallory, listen, please. Even if we had the truck, the fighters are faster. They would catch up to us. Mary Magdalena and I … we are old and cannot run. Even with you to help, we are not enough to carry all the little ones. You are young and brave. You can take a few of the oldest. They have the best chance to survive. Flee into the wooded area. The fighters cannot take their vehicles there. They are superstitious and do not like the darkness. It is the only way. If it is God's will, He will spare us."

Such hard choices. The unfairness hurt so badly. "I can't do this," she whispered.

"No, you can't. But God can. Now come. We have much to do and little time." She slipped out the door, not waiting to see if Mallory followed her command.

Mallory hesitated only a moment. She didn't have the luxury of time to think her way through this mess. No time at all.

Outside, she looked for Akpom, but Sister Agatha hadn't lied. Both he and the truck were gone. Her gaze landed on the group of children huddled around Sister Mary Magdalena. They wore small packs on their backs, the oldest maybe ten, the youngest no more than four or five. The older children, the ones who could walk and "do," as Sister Agatha liked to say.

A hollow feeling settled in the pit of her stomach. She'd tried so hard to make a difference in this smallest of refugee camps, here in a barbaric land where the life of a child held no more value than a spade of dirt. The two sisters had carved out a haven of sorts for them. They begged for leftovers and hand-me-downs from other camps—ragged tents, broken cookware, blankets, and whatever scraps of food could be spared. They depended on the polluted water from the river, and the kindness of a man who'd run off at the first hint of danger.

And in the midst of this abject poverty, the sisters brought laughter and happiness, and a sense of safety into shattered lives. And now it was gone.

She looked at the children again, saw them as people with the same human rights everyone should have. A few clung to each other. Some spilled tears, but through it all, they made no sound. How sad that a child so young had to learn silence, that any noise might mean the difference between violence and living to see another sunrise. And then her eyes narrowed.

How had she missed this? Every last one of them wore a skirt. Which made all the more sense why Sister Agatha wanted them gone before the soldiers came. These were little girls, survivors every one. They had already endured terrible hardships in their short lives, and should never have to endure the bestial brutality of men who killed without conscience.

At Sister Mary Magdalena's prompting, they looked from her to Mallory.

The profound silence of the morning intruded. The laughing chatter of kids at play was gone. Birds hid in silence. And the wind … not a single breath stirred the trees. Under it all, the smell of charred bread and burning stew intruded. An omen? Or an encouragement to get moving?

Sister Agatha tugged one of the older girls from the group and brought her to Mallory. "Sister told them to obey you. This is Charri. She can speak a little English and will help you."

Expressive dark eyes the color of the native Sapele tree looked up at her, her gaze tempered by the same fear that seemed a permanent part of these children's lives.

Resolve hardened inside Mallory. She wanted the fear gone, wanted a safe haven for these kids, and the first step was to remove them from the danger that stalked. She knelt on one knee, eye level with Charri and the others. Taking both of the girl's hands in her own, she murmured, "Thank you."

Sister Agatha placed a pack on Mallory's back, and helped wind the sash around her shoulders and waist to hold it in place. "Supplies," she whispered, before tucking a compass in her hand. "Hurry. Don't look back. Go south or southwest."

Escape seemed hopeless, but she would try.

Sister Agatha gave her a gentle push. "You can do this, Mallory. I believe God sent you to us for a purpose."

Mallory touched the sister's arm, filled with a wave of doubt. So many depended on her, when she'd only ever depended on others. "Sister—"

The old nun pressed two gnarled fingers to Mallory's lips. "Shhh, my child. Sister Mary Magdalena and I have fulfilled our work here on this earth, but yours is just beginning. To save even one life will bless the Lord."

She stepped away, made the sign of the cross in front

of Mallory, and whispered a blessing. "May the Lord bless you and protect you. May He make His face to shine upon you and be gracious to you. May He look with favor on you and give you peace. And, if it be His will, I pray He will light your way, give you strength, and lead you to safety."

Tears rolled down Mallory's face. A small hand slipped into one of hers. Another pulled at her arm. She turned and started toward the jungle, with her troop of small soldiers in line behind her. Mallory didn't look back until the trees closed in around them, until there was no longer anything to see.

The relentless darkness coiled around Mallory with suffocating pressure. Panic pecked ceaselessly at the edges of her mind and tested her control and her sanity. Once more, she reached out in blindness to count those huddled around her. Her fingertips found and caressed fourteen little heads. Each one of these precious little girls looked to her to guide them away from danger.

Mallory choked off yet another sob. What a foolhardy undertaking. They had only the little bit of food and water Sister Mary Magdalena had scrounged up for them, but no shelter, no weapon.

She suppressed a snort. As if she could fight off a whole cadre of berserkers who killed without remorse.

Worst of all, she had not the slightest idea where they were or which direction to go.

She couldn't do this. She couldn't protect these children. Sweet sassafras, she couldn't even save herself. Despair plunged her into a darkness deeper than the night. Why had she come to this forsaken land? Why did she remain with the Sisters when Jared had insisted on leaving?

An image of Sister Agatha and Sister Mary Magdalena filled her head. Old and decrepit, the two aged nuns didn't deny their calling. But neither could they have covered the distance Mallory and the kids had clawed their way through today. And would do so again when the sun came up.

Were the nuns still alive? And the babies? Had she brought this disaster on them?

Silent tears rolled down her cheeks.

She brushed them away with an angry fist. No more feeling sorry and sad. They'd asked her to leave, to save a few.

"Sometimes you do what has to be done whether you like it or not." She whispered her father's words to the night. If only she'd listened to James, she wouldn't be facing this nightmare.

Maybe true, maybe not, but at least she wouldn't be here, carrying an impossible responsibility. Too late now. Way too late.

She yawned and counted heads again, more for her

own assurance than fear that one of the girls might disappear. She would do her best to get all of them to safety, but the end result lay beyond her control.

Chapter Twenty-Four

A gentle pat on her cheek startled Mallory awake. Her eyes opened to weak sunlight filtered through the jungle canopy. She brushed hair out of her face and opened her eyes to find one of the younger girls staring intently.

Mallory smiled, delighted when the girl did the same. Getting to her feet proved painful. Her joints and back complained of the night spent on the ground.

The girls huddled around her in a semi-circle, all of them awake and waiting for direction. A quick look accounted for all fourteen. Of course, they were already awake. Their typical day started with the first hint of light. Now their daily regimen was out of whack and they looked to her for what to do next.

Bathroom needs came first. She looked around the small clearing, found a good-sized stick she could use as a shovel, and started to dig a small latrine.

Charri recognized her actions, and motioned to the other girls. Small as they were, their combined efforts soon excavated a shallow trench where the girls took turns. No room for modesty in these beleaguered lives. They all pitched in again to cover the trench.

Food next. Mallory broke off a small square of bread from the supply Sister Mary Magdalena provided—no more than each girl could carry—and took a small bite. They followed her example

Water. So important. All they had was the single large bottle stuffed in Mallory's pack, along with half of a hollowed-out gourd. She carefully measured a small quantity and handed it to the girl who'd awakened her.

She stared back, unsure what to do.

"Drink," Mallory encouraged. She pantomimed raising the gourd to her lips and drinking.

The girl looked to Charri, who nodded and said something short and brusque.

The girl drank and handed the gourd back to Mallory.

She refilled it and passed it around the group, taking her sip last. Only one sip each, and yet their supply was already half gone. Mallory raised the gourd to her mouth and let the warm, chemical-flavored water slide over her parched tongue. This thirst would be their undoing if they didn't find help soon. "South, southwest," Sister Mary Magdalena said. They would find a populated area in that direction, somewhere safe. But how far? Their scanty supplies wouldn't last beyond today.

Mallory lifted the pack onto her back.

The girls followed suit.

Using Sister Agatha's compass, Mallory motioned her ragtag band of children to follow, and set off in a direction she hoped would bring them to a small town, a village, or even a farm. Somewhere the threat of the Mayakan wouldn't reach them.

The jungle grew too thick in a few areas, and they were forced to change course for easier routes. Mallory always returned to their original course as soon as the terrain allowed.

They rambled from heavy vegetation, to open tracts and sparse woods, stopping only once for the few minutes it took to drink the rest of the water. If they didn't find shelter soon—and more water—they'd be resting for a long time.

As they approached yet another open area, male voices carried to them on the air.

The girls froze, but whipped into action when Mallory motioned for them to hide.

The voices didn't recede, but neither did they come closer. And only two voices, the best she could make out.

"Stay," she whispered to Charri.

The girl's wide eyes bulged with fear, but she nodded her understanding.

More hard choices. They could seek out the men and hope they would help, or continue their hide-and-seek journey and hope to survive another night. This time without water.

With a prayer on her lips, Mallory wiped away the relentless sweat from her face, crouched low, and crept in the direction of the men's voices.

Ahead, the jungle gave way to yet another break in the thick undergrowth, but this clearing was different. Bright sunlight blazed over the open space.

She crawled closer.

Not a natural clearing. Jagged stumps littered the perimeter of the area, with neatly plowed rows filling the interior.

Six men stood in the shade of a tree at the edge of a clearing next to a harnessed … cow? They use cattle as draft animals here? How odd.

The men wore simple garb faded from use, not the heavy boots or dark green camouflage pattern the terrorist groups of the region preferred. Mallory breathed a little easier. Farmers. Defending their homes and acreage. Two held rifles rusty from age. One carried a scythe, another a pitchfork, and the fifth a stout cudgel. The sixth man held the reins to the plow. Tilling, no doubt. Not what she'd hoped for, but not a bad thing. She hoped.

Mallory backtracked to where the girls waited and motioned them to follow. Surely the men wouldn't be threatened by a lone woman with a gaggle of children. Cautious steps carried her forward again.

"Charri." She pulled the girl closer. "Call to them. Say hello."

Reluctance filled the girl's expression, but she squared her shoulders, and stepped forward. "Sannu!"

The man with the scythe spotted them first, and raised his weapon. He pointed, his voice loud.

The men conversed between themselves for a moment, gestured wildly, and then the would-be warriors raced toward them, brandishing their unsophisticated weapons.

Surely, they wouldn't attack a band of defenseless children. Had she made the wrong decision?

Mallory gathered the girls around her, pulling them as close as possible. Some clutched her legs, others held onto her arms, shoulders, back, and clothes. All of them, Mallory included, shook with fear.

One of the men with a rifle let loose with a stream of words she didn't understand. "What did he say, Charri?"

The brave little girl assigned as her helper stepped away and, with head bowed, spoke a few soft words in the same language. When the man shouted again, gesturing this time, Charri dropped to her knees and cowered face-down on the ground. The other girls followed one-by-one until all fourteen had their faces in the dirt.

Bewildered at how quickly her charges groveled before these strangers, how easily they'd abased

themselves to the will of these men, Mallory remained on her feet. "Please. Don allah." She stumbled over the unfamiliar greeting with a soft-spoken plea.

She held out a hand, palm up in supplication, and waved at the girls. "Water. Ruwa."

After a brief discussion among themselves, the man who'd spoken motioned Mallory and her group to follow.

She and the girls fell in behind him, while a second man brought up the rear.

The others went back to work preparing the field.

A rutted path made their walk easier, but a long time passed before they reached a small collection of shacks. There an old woman stood at a fire, working a long, wooden paddle in slow circles through a cook pot. She stared at the motley parade.

Mallory recognized her work, knew firsthand the effort it took to prepare the soup. What she didn't understand were the malignant stares cast their way.

Four younger women sat on the ground in the shade of the buildings kneading something in the large bowls in their laps. Half a dozen half-naked children ran amok among the hovels, while one white-haired man sat in the shade of a tree and puffed away on a slender reed-like pipe. Not far off, a dog barked.

Silence greeted their arrival. Every man, woman, and child stopped what they were doing and watched. Even the dog went quiet. The girls caught their interest, but Mallory snared and held their attention. A white woman. Alone. Her pale complexion, blue eyes, and long, brown hair that reflected streaks of fire in the sun must have been a shock.

One of the younger women approached their bedraggled group. Curious eyes looked Mallory over from head to toe, touched her hair, and ran a finger down her cheek.

Mallory understood none of the words the woman spoke, the tone of her voice struck a chord. Awe and wonder. She'd never seen a white woman before.

The old man slowly got to his feet and spoke as he limped over to where Mallory and the girls waited.

The young woman dropped her eyes to the ground and slunk away.

Charri took Mallory's hand and led her and the girls to a patch of grass well away from the huts and cookfire. There, they dropped into cross-legged positions on the ground in a circle around and tugged Mallory's hands until she, too, sat down.

The old man, apparently the chief or leader of the people who lived in the cluster of huts, rattled something to his people. Two of the young women hurried to a stone formation and dipped water into two large gourds. They brought them to the newcomers, and bade them take the drink.

"Thank you," Mallory inclined her head and handed one of the gourds to Charri and the other to the smallest girl in their little band.

The child took several long swallows and passed the gourd around until all of the girls and Mallory had drunk their fill.

Sometime later, after a visit to a communal latrine, a different young woman offered Mallory and the girls small bowl-shaped gourds of thick stew and good-sized hunks of bread. Following Charri's lead, Mallory dipped her bread in the stew and took a bite. Flavor, pungent, hot, and delicious, exploded on her tongue. She finished the entire bowl in no time, scooping the dregs out with the crust, and then with her fingers to capture every drop. A quick look around showed the girls doing the same.

Grateful for the sustenance, but puzzled by the hostility directed toward them, Mallory approached the old man with the intention of thanking him, but the old woman they'd seen at the cookpot hurried over and shook her long stirring ladle at Mallory. She screeched, obviously upset, until Charri dashed forward and grabbed Mallory's hand.

"No, Missy Malay. No, no." The way the girl wrung her hands and tried to tug Mallory back to the group suggested she'd trespassed on a cultural taboo.

When the sun sank low on the horizon, the four men who'd stayed behind to till the field returned. A few more curious glances were sent Mallory's way, but otherwise, the villagers let them be.

Mallory studied the little ones entrusted to her care.

The headcount came automatic now. Fourteen girls huddled close together in a circle around her, almost a protective wall. They didn't talk, not even soft whispers among themselves. Instead, they remained watchful and wary, as though they expected something more to happen.

Eventually, they all lay down on the ground, Mallory included. Another night without a bed. At least they had a little grass tonight. And no gouging roots.

The same two men who'd brought them to the village sat a little ways off. Keeping watch, no doubt.

Mallory didn't understand any of this. The villagers had provided much needed food and drink, but the glares, scowls, and careful avoidance made it clear the strangers weren't welcome.

CCC

A flurry of activity woke Mallory and the girls well before dawn. Someone stirred up the coals and added wood. Another someone swung the cook pot into place over the flames. The same woman who brought them water yesterday, made multiple trips from the water barrel to fill the huge pot.

Before long, the small village had become a hive of activity, with men, women, and children all scurrying to accomplish the morning chores.

Breakfast consisted of a thin gruel with a few chunks

of what Mallory took to be a vegetable. She found it pleasant, though nowhere near as tasty as the stew from the night before. Still, they all cleaned their bowls. Not knowing when or from where her next meal would come provided powerful motivation.

More water was offered and another trip to the latrine, after which the men who kept watch over them motioned Mallory and the girls back to their grassy knoll. No threats, but a clear indication to keep apart from the villagers.

Just when she decided all this waiting was not to their advantage, perhaps an hour after the breakfast meal, she heard the rumble of engines in the distance. Vehicles, moving fast.

Mallory scrambled to her feet, intent on resuming their southward trek. She'd hoped the villagers would supply them with food and water for their travel, but suspected that wasn't going to happen. No matter. They couldn't remain here. Not if they wanted to find safety.

Several of the men noted their movements and formed a loose circle around Mallory and the girls. A herding technique, one her father used during the spring and fall round-ups. A way to contain a large number of animals while leading them in particular direction. In this case, she and the girls were the horses being herded. Unbound, but prisoners nonetheless. Not good.

The motor sounds drew closer with each passing second. Birds took flight. Before long, the women in the village snatched up the children and scattered in all directions into the woods. The younger men armed themselves with makeshift weapons and became shadows in the underbrush that bordered their village.

The six men, who kept Mallory and the girls from leaving, held the containment circle until two trucks and a jeep entered the clearing. They left their post then and joined the old man, their chief, in the center of the clearing.

A dozen men in dark green camo exploded from the two trucks, weapons up and fanning around the open area.

The girls crowded closer around Mallory. She wondered if they could sense her fear, feel the frantic racing of her heart.

A man stepped from the passenger side of the jeep. Tall and fierce-looking, he exuded authority. The leader then. Was this the Mayakan she'd heard such horror stories about? Had their escape been in vain?

The village chief stepped forward and exchanged words with the Mayakan leader, their tones conciliatory. When the old man gestured toward the girls, bitterness churned in Mallory's gut even as fear kept her frozen in place. The animosity she'd sensed from the villagers was real. They'd betrayed them to the Mayakan, would give them to the monsters who'd destroyed their country, killed innocent men, women, and children in a mockery of freedom. The villagers had rescued them only to turn them over to the very devils from whom they'd run.

Helpless, she hugged her charges closer. A few shed quiet tears. All of them trembled in fear.

CCC

Hours passed. Or was it days? Mallory wasn't sure anymore. Time lost all meaning when hope deserted you.

She huddled in a corner of the windowless room, knees drawn up, arms wrapped around her legs. The door, the only entrance to her cell, fit so tight in its frame that it offered only a single crack at the top. Enough to tell whether day or night, but no more.

She shivered in spite of the oppressive heat and second-guessed every decision she'd ever made, especially those since she left home. Trusting the farmers had to rank pretty high on the worst list, but even, after all that had happened—what could she have done? The girls were dehydrated, starving, and beyond tired when they stumbled on that cursed field. Would they have found a safer haven had they skirted the farmers and gone on?

Foolish question.

Tired of chasing the what ifs on a never-ending hamster wheel, she turned to worry instead. The farmers had betrayed them. To save their own families and land, no doubt.

Could she blame them? Yes. Would she do the same in their place?

The answer, so simple on the surface, carried a weight no individual should face. How easy to take a righteous stance from the safety of distance. How different to experience firsthand the daily devastation these people faced.

Tears held in check for so long now spilled over. Imprisoned in this hovel, she lay in the dirt, her body a mass of aches and pain after being manhandled by her Mayakan abductors. Adding insult to injury, they'd clamped a shackle around her leg, and left her chained to the wall.

A screeching sound startled Mallory awake. She scrambled upright and backed away when the door opened, but forgot about her tether. The chain tightened and made her stumble.

Sunlight poured through the open door. "Agh." Mallory squeezed her eyes tight against the too bright light.

One of the Mayakan came into the room and unlocked the chain from the wall. "Come." He started for the door, chain in hand.

Mallory quickly realized she had two choices—resist and get dragged, or comply and find out what lay ahead. At least she'd be on her feet.

Blood trickled into her shoe as she followed the man

outside. The metal restraint was rough. The skin around her ankle was chafed raw. She limped her way after him, more than a little unnerved when he led to the back side of the shack.

Who was she kidding, her whole body quaked in fear. Terrible visions of what he might do filled her mind. Would he kill her? Or worse?

The Mayaƙan stopped. He pointed at Mallory and then at trench where a swarm of flies buzzed.

A latrine.

He expected her to …? In front of him? Not in this lifetime.

The man crossed his arms and barked an order at her again.

She didn't understand the words, but his tone came across perfectly clear. He hadn't hurt her—other than a busted lip and a few bruises. At least, not yet.

Her dad always counseled to pick your battles with care. Was this one worth fighting?

Nature and her all too human body sided with the Mayaƙan, and Mallory surrendered to the indignity. Here, now, with nature's insistence, there was no room for embarrassment.

When they retraced their steps to her prison, Mallory used the time to study her surroundings. The hut where they kept her was oval in shape. Its construction reminded her of Army buildings she'd seen in movies. A Quonset-like hut, made from some lightweight material. A vague memory surfaced. The wall had buckled a little when her body hit it.

More buildings stood at a distance, a compound of sorts, a collection of hovels and shacks perhaps a hundred yards or more. Were they holding the girls there?

Back inside once more, the guard reattached the chain to an eyebolt in the wall. The interior looked as austere as she'd imagined. Dirt floor. Same metal for the walls and roof. No windows. Barren.

The door slammed shut, and darkness ruled once more. In a few hours, when sun reached its zenith, the place would become an oven.

Almost immediately, the door opened again. A woman of indeterminate age entered this time. Dirty, slump-shouldered, and dressed in rags, she offered Mallory a cup of water and a hollowed gourd of watery soup. A few mysterious chunks floated in it.

The delivery lasted no more than a few seconds. She didn't wait for the dishes.

The routine repeated at twilight—latrine first, and then food and water.

"Please. More water," Mallory begged. She wanted to wash her face and clean the abraded skin of her ankle. Infection could kill her long before she starved to death.

The woman shoved the food and water—no more, no less—into Mallory's hands, and slunk away.

The guard, who'd held the door, said something then. The disgusting way he looked her up and down had Mallory backing away. He laughed, spat on the ground, and locked the door.

Her second night passed much as the first, as did the following morning. Her bathroom escort took her outside, and the woman brought more food and water. They never asked any questions. Not even her name.

Despair had become a constant companion.

Chapter Twenty-Five

"Attention all you freeloaders," a disembodied voice said through the headset. "This is your captain speaking. Stretch, yawn, scratch, grab your gear, and buckle up. ETA into N'Djamena in fifteen. That is all."

James groaned. These flyboys all thought themselves comedians. But then he looked around and had to laugh at all the yawns and stretches going on around him. A few scratches, too.

He looked out the window of the Gulfstream Fowler had provided for their flight from the unnamed air strip outside Fort Bragg. Africa spread out below them. Desert filled his view. A desolate land with nothing but dirt and sand as far as the eye could see.

The topography would change when they neared the tiny strip of land known as Cameroon's Neck. He'd studied the maps of the Nigeria-Chad-Cameroon triangle on the flight over. The arid land would roll into savannahs, with its long swaths of tall grass and areas of dense underbrush. In Nigeria, where the rainfall was significantly higher, the terrain was more green, dense enough to almost be called jungle in some places. Almost. And mountains, too, some rising to heights of 2,000 feet. Farmers were slowly terraforming the jungle-like areas and laying claim to the arable land on the slopes and between the mountains. Their progress would go much faster if they didn't also have to fight off the terrorist groups in the region.

Cameroon's Neck. That's where they'd find Sebastian Toure's lair. With borders disputed by three countries, no one wanted authority there. The perfect terrorist haven.

After the incident where Toure tried to kidnap Cassidy and Mallory, the Nigerian government decried his actions, slapped his hand, and dismissed him from their esteemed ranks. Their mistake was in not turning him over to the U.S. authorities … or eliminating him themselves.

Money wielded great power, and human trafficking was one of the largest profit sources for international crime—second only to drugs—at a staggering thirty-two billion-dollars annually. And Toure aspired to dominate the industry.

That couldn't happen. The man had no idea what was coming for him.

The airport at N'Djamena, the capitol city of Chad, lay

east of Cameroon's Neck. Easy range for a helicopter. Get in. Get out. Get the job done. Easy, if everything went according to plan.

Once they eliminated the threat, James intended to run Mallory down. She would go willingly, or he'd let his inner caveman out and toss her over his shoulder. And make sure she thought twice before putting herself in danger again.

He patted his duffel as a rush of excitement rushed through his veins. Their long, transatlantic flight was almost over. Soon the plane would land, and the plan would proceed. No more waiting.

Hallelujah, action at last. He hadn't realized how much he missed the adrenalin punch.

Across from him, Fowler pressed his headset and stared off into space. "Talk to me." He'd been talking to someone off and on the entire flight.

Silence. "Repeat."

Another, longer silence. "Roger. ETA in ten. We will standby." Fowler's face turned to stone, his expression scary.

James frowned. He hadn't seen Fowler react like this since the Honduras mission went belly-up a few years back. "What?" he mouthed, not liking the vibe coming from the man across from him.

Fowler tapped the switch on his headset again. A second later, he was speaking to everyone in the plane. "Change of plans, men. We're landing at an abandoned

airstrip sixty kilometers southeast of our original destination. Two helicopters will meet us there with reinforcements and an update on the situation. Revised ETA in thirty. We will have five minutes to clear the aircraft."

"What change of plans?" Garrett demanded.

"You'll know more when I do."

Tension filled the small cabin. James looked from Fowler, who continued to talk on the airways, to Garrett, and back again. Dread ate into his usual calm. He liked his plans well thought out, vetted, and reviewed ten times over before the first step was made. His team felt the same. Change never boded well. It was all too easy to overlook a small detail that would come back to bite you.

The jet landed on a hard-packed, dirt runway out in the middle of nowhere and taxied to a stop. One small building that resembled a toolshed stood nearby. A road led away from it and disappeared in the distance. The only indication the strip remained active was the lack of sand drifts. Someone took care to keep it cleared. Meticulous care. But it didn't even have a wind sock.

The co-pilot hurried from the cockpit as soon as the wheels touched down. He opened the hatch and lowered the aircraft stair, and then bowed with a flourish. "Thank you for flying Sand Dune Airways. Now get your butts off my plane so we can get outta here. We got no time. I repeat, no time."

Garrett led the debarkation. As soon as the last boots hit the ground, the co-pilot raised the stairs and the pilot executed a U-turn. Moments later, the aircraft roared down the runway and was soon lost from sight. From the small, unidentified airstrip, they'd fly to N'Djamena, the original destination listed on the flight plan, hopefully, with no one the wiser. There, they'd refuel and wait for the extraction call.

Five minutes passed while James and the others waited for the incoming choppers. Ten minutes passed. And then fifteen. No one moved. No one spoke. They all knew the importance of this mission, and wondered about the coming briefing.

Jonas spotted the helicopters first, two dots on the horizon, growing larger by the second. A few moments later, they felt the vibration and heard the distinctive *whump-whump-whump* of the churning blades.

Soon as the skids hit the dirt, a man jumped out of the lead chopper. Another bailed from the second chopper. Big, well-built men, wearing desert camouflage with an arsenal strapped to their bodies, they jogged toward James's group.

"Madman?" Garrett started forward, his surprise and disbelief evident. His mouth stretched into a full-blown grin. "What in the name of hades are you doing here?"

Madman chuckled and reached for Garrett's outstretched hand. "Dang, Cowboy. Is that any way to greet

the men who're gonna save your mission for you? Tell me, is that sweet little PJ still hanging with you? Cause I'm available to show her what a real man's like … if she's kicked you to the curb, that is." He waggled his eyebrows.

Garrett's grin turned into a glare as he fisted the other man's hand, forearm to forearm. He squeezed until his biceps bulged. "It's TJ, and she's my wife now. And very pregnant."

Madman's arms flexed, giving as good as he got as they tried to crush each other's hand. His grin morphed into a look of mock horror. "You went over to the dark side? Must be the end of the world, man."

"You should try it. If you can find a woman who'll have you."

Madman erupted with a deep belly laugh and broke the power struggle only to pound Garrett on the back hard enough to make him stagger.

The other guy with Madman crowded forward wearing a smile wide enough to show his pearly white teeth. "Romeo! Still loving and leaving the ladies? Hey, Dawg."

Kyle joined Garrett, sporting a matching grin. "That you, Spider?"

"Yep."

James shouldered his way in to the meet and greet, unable to pinpoint the last time he'd been called Dawg. How long had it been—six, maybe eight years? He stepped forward doing his own hand wrangling and back slapping.

"Fowler," Madman interrupted the reunion. "I know Cowboy, Dawg, and Romeo, but who're these other two stiffs looking for a ride in my choppers? They part of the team?"

Wade and Jonas hung back and waited for introductions.

Fowler stepped into the fray and raised his voice. "Enough with the lovefest, men. Our timeline is tight. Let's save the stroll down memory lane until we get to base camp."

"Right-o, then." Madman pointed to Garrett, James, Jonas, and Fowler. "You're in my bird. Crash is our pilot. The rest of you fly in the second bird with Spider. Ruby's your pilot."

CCC

A twenty-minute flight landed them somewhere in Nigeria. Ten minutes later, they'd set up a primitive camp, and sat in a semi-circle around Fowler. "Gather round," the BII agent said. "I'll make this short and sweet. From this point forward, you use call signs only. No names. Leave IDs on the choppers This is not a sanctioned mission, gentlemen. Do you understand?" He pointed at each of the men in turn. "Madman, Spider, Ruby, Crash ..."

Fowler wanted their commitment. In words. They knew the drill. The four men he named answered in turn.

"I'm in."

Fowler turned to the others. "Cowboy, Dawg, Romeo—?"

"In."

"Me, too."

"I'm in."

He raised a questioning eyebrow at Wade.

Wade thumped his chest. "Me Cochise. Me in."

A few chuckles erupted.

"Let me guess." Garrett grinned. "Cochise. Indian. Smoke-signals, right?"

Some nicknames were a variation on a man's name. Others had a story behind the designation. Wade returned the grin. "Yeah. Computers and communications. No one better."

Fowler turned to Jonas. "Ghost?"

"I'm in."

"Fitting name, little brother. Care to explain?"

"Nope."

"Good," Fowler said. "I'm Houdini and I will lead this mission."

"Whoa, whoa, whoa there, chief. I'm the leader of this team." Garrett corrected him. "You haven't had dirty hands in more years than I can count."

James stared from Garrett to Fowler. In the not so distant past, when he, Garrett, Kyle, and Derek had served on the same special ops team, Cowboy was always the leader. Wade and Jonas were the only two they'd not worked with before.

Why would Fowler pull rank now?

Steely gray eyes zeroed in on Garrett. Fowler's raspy voice dropped another octave. "Your information is flawed, Cowboy. I've led more missions in the last three years than you have in your entire career."

Madman nodded. "It's true. After you guys left, he got back in the thick of things until the new recruits got up to speed."

Garrett swore under his breath again, but didn't make any further challenges.

James blinked. Every man here had dominant alpha traits, but they all recognized the pecking order. He'd just seen a beat-down without fists, and suspected it was a first for Garrett Cameron.

Behind him, Wade whistled softly.

The others remained silent.

James waited for another challenge, but Garrett, like the rest of them, knew when to hold his tongue. Fowler had news they weren't privy to, information that dumped their carefully laid plans in the toilet. Dread reared its ugly head.

"Mayaƙan 'yanci is the name of the splinter group of the Ansaru, the ones behind the threat we're after." Fowler released a heavy breath. Reluctance roiled off him. "They've taken a prisoner. Our mission has changed to a rescue operation."

Fear coiled in James's gut. The same reaction oozed from the others who'd come with him.

"The hostage is your sister, Cowboy. They've taken Mallory."

Fowler's words left him gut-punched. James wanted to puke, but willed his heaving guts to settle instead. He reached for the void and the ice. And a little bit of fire.

Mallory. A prisoner of one of the most violent and barbaric terrorist groups in the world. They'd all feared this might happen.

Cool heads and common sense were most important now. James spoke to Garrett. "Fowler's right. You're too close to lead this one. We all are." He turned to Fowler. "What's the new plan?"

Fowler waited for Garrett, Wade, and Jonas to reorient themselves before he motioned to Madman. "Show us the photo."

"Crap, I'm sorry, man. I didn't know the target was your sister." Madman pulled a rolled paper from his pack and spread an enlarged aerial satellite photo on the ground between them.

"The target's code-name is Pixie." Fowler began the briefing. "John Archer, a.k.a. Treekiller, accompanied her on the flight over, but lost her when her group chartered a plane in Lagos and flew to Maiduguri. By the time he arrived there, they'd already hired a driver and set out to find the Sisters of Mercy refugee camp."

Fowler paused to make eye contact with each one of the team. "The Mayaƙan 'yanci razed Enziama less than forty-eight hours before her entourage went through there."

James studied the group of men as Fowler spoke. Madman, Crash, Ruby, and Spider remained silent. Even attuned to the disharmony emanating from the Camerons, this remained just another mission briefing for them.

The guys from Hastings Bluff were anything but stoic, even Kyle. Fists clenched. Nostrils flared. They fidgeted while fighting the fear in their eyes. Someone they loved had fallen into harm's way. Someone he loved.

A blood vessel in Garrett's temple bulged, the pulse too rapid.

James knew the feeling well. His own heart thudded with painful hammer blows. He suffered the same anguish Mallory's brothers shared, only multiplied a hundredfold.

"Treekiller tracked her to the Sisters' camp, several kilometers northwest of the destroyed village. They stayed the night. The next day, her entourage left. Pixie stayed."

"What?" Garrett exploded. "They left her there?"

Good. He needed to let off some steam so he could screw his head back on straight.

Fowler ignored his outburst. "The Mayaƙan 'yanci caught wind of an American woman in the area, but word

of their advance reached the sisters. Both well into their seventies, they couldn't run from the fighters. Instead, they sent Pixie away with some of the older children. The sisters knew the horrors they would face if the fighters caught them."

Garrett hung his head, struggling with the information, but managed a few curses through his clenched teeth.

Wade slammed his fist into the ground several times.

Easygoing Jonas, always a rock, went even more still if such a thing were possible.

James shoved the rush of emotions into a compartment in his brain and slammed the door. A time would come when he could unleash the rage without endangering the mission. He would drink his fill then, savor the bitter cup of revenge.

"Treekiller tracked them to a small farm," Fowler continued. "But the militants caught up with them before he could make contact. The farmers who offered them safety bartered Pixie and the children in return for the safety of their families and land."

A new emotion hammered at his mind. Ruthlessly, he shoved the panic behind the locked door and slammed it shut. He couldn't dwell on what they might do. Mallory—Pixie—didn't need a distraught mess. She needed him cold and merciless, the relentless machine he became on missions. Emotional reaction would get all of them killed.

James leaned over and whispered in Garrett's ear, loud

enough for Wade and Jonas to hear. "Get it together, man. She doesn't need her brother right now. She needs hardnosed warriors to yank her out of this mess."

Quick as a heartbeat, the brothers morphed into hardcore, professional soldiers. Duty first. No questions. No second guessing. And no emotion.

Fowler must have seen the metamorphosis. He nodded once and continued with the briefing. "Treekiller has eyes on the place where they're holding the target. So far, to the best of his knowledge, she remains unharmed."

"Let's keep it that way. How soon can we move?" Garrett asked, his tone flat and even.

Some of the tension dissipated with the simple question. Every soldier hated waiting. They all knew with each minute Mallory remained in enemy hands, her chances for survival diminished.

"Glad you asked. The last satellite pass shows a large armed contingent here." He pointed at the larger of two red circles drawn on the map. "Intelligence reports increased terrorist activity in the last week. We don't know if it's Mayaƙan 'yanci, Boko Haram, or Ansaru. Let's keep our heads down regardless. Our primary goal is retrieval of the target. Do you understand?"

"What about Toure? If he's in the area, we could—" Jonas asked.

"Negative. Toure's whereabouts are unknown and irrelevant to this mission," Fowler snapped. He stared long and hard at Jonas, before continuing. "Our goal is to retrieve the target. If we can snatch her little friends without endangering the primary goal, we will. If you have a problem with these orders, speak now."

James held his breath.

Jonas had perfected stoicism to the highest degree. Other than a grin or an occasional curse, he seldom revealed any emotion at all. But now, with his arms crossed over his chest, his forearms and biceps bulging, tension radiated off him in waves. By slow degrees, Jonas slowed his breathing, and finally nodded.

The others in the group released a collective breath.

"Our target is being held here." He traced a line from the larger circle to the smaller one. "Nineteen kilometers away. It is now 1433. At 1800, Crash and Ruby will fly us to the LZ, five kilometers southeast of this point, far enough they won't hear us coming. Treekiller will meet us there at 1825. From that point on, headsets are on and keep communications to a minimum."

Fowler pointed out three different locations on the picture map. "Alpha Team—me, Dawg, and Ghost—will circle south of the compound to where Pixie is being held. Our objective is to extract the target."

James glanced up at Fowler's words. Funny how the call signs felt comfortable after so many years of not hearing them. He returned his attention to the map and committed every tiny detail to memory. Now that he was so close to finding Mallory, anxiety consumed him. Of all his past missions, none held more importance than this one.

"Bravo Team—Madman, Romeo, Cochise—set up here, on the northeast perimeter nearest the children. Your objective is to retrieve as many as possible and get them back to the LZ."

Wade and his group exchanged chin nods.

"Charlie Team—Treekiller, Spider, Cowboy—move into position here, one kilometer northwest of the compound."

"Do you have an estimate of how many enemy and their weaponry?" Garrett asked.

"Treekiller reports fluctuations in the number of Mayaḱan in the camp, with a minimal presence at night. As of 1200 hours, he reported nineteen men, heavily armed, and three trucks in the compound. Also, six women, camp followers, most likely, plus Pixie. He couldn't give an accurate count of the children. According to the sisters, fourteen girls left with Pixie, all between the ages of four and eleven."

Garrett nodded.

"Charlie Team will recon the area, ascertain the current number of enemy in the camp, as well as the surrounding area." Fowler went on. "I want each team in position and reporting in by 2200 hours."

More nods, from each member of the task force this time.

"At 2215, Charlie will set off the diversion, a series of flares previously discussed, intended to draw some of the Mayaƙan away from the compound. Alpha and Bravo will then wait for a forty-five count, before extracting the targets. Once you have your targets, return to the LZ."

"Roger," Spider, Madman, and Wade answered in unison.

"Charlie team, after you set off the diversion, take a circuitous path to the northeast before turning south. Our extraction window is small, 2345 to 2355 hours. You'll have to book it double-time."

"No problem," murmured Spider.

"Listen up, this is important. The choppers will not wait. I repeat, the choppers will not wait. Avoid engagement with the enemy if at all possible. It will only delay your return. Any questions?"

Too many variables, too many unknowns. Neither Kyle nor Wade would ever leave a child behind. Madman either, from what he knew of him. And the chances of Charlie Team avoiding enemy contact were slim to none. Alpha Team had the best chance of making it out without a skirmish, but it would crush Mallory if they lost anyone during her rescue. He didn't even want to think about what losing the girls would do to her.

"All right, gentlemen. You know the rest of the plan details. Sync your watches."

Chapter Twenty-Six

"Ow." Mallory drew in a breath with a hiss and rubbed her poor, abused knuckles. She counted to one hundred, waiting to see if the guard had heard her cry and come to check on her.

He didn't.

The fear receded. She felt for the eyebolt again, pinched it tight with her sore fingers, and twisted again. And again.

She ignored the sting where the unforgiving edges of the screw had shredded her skin. What was a little pain there when her whole body throbbed—her right cheek and busted lip where her captor had hit her, her ribs where he'd slammed her against one of the flimsy hut's support struts, the raw patch on her left ankle where the shackle had rubbed the skin away. But most of all, her heart grieved for

the girls in her care that she'd lost. And the sisters and babies she'd left behind.

Her fingers slipped again, this time from motion. Had the eyebolt moved at last? She went back to work, listening for any sounds from outside. It wouldn't do to let Scarface discover her work. The sadistic monster would pound her into ground beef, and she'd never escape, much less find and rescue the children.

The guard struck fear in her heart. The hideous scar that stretched from his ear to one corner of his mouth was the stuff of nightmares, but when he grinned, the leer gave him the look of a demon. And he grew bolder with every latrine visit, touching her hair or running his sandpaper hands down her arm when he returned her to the cell.

Mallory shuddered. The memory brought a wave of repulsion … and she wracked her fingers again.

Tears sprang forth unbidden and unwelcome, but they wouldn't help. Anger helped force them away. She grasped the eyebolt again, and this time it moved.

Excitement surged through her.

With renewed hope, she attacked the bolt again. A few quick twists and she felt the nut holding the bolt in place come free with a soft plunk to the outside ground. Unscrewing the bolt came easier after that. Faster now, a few more turns … and the eyebolt worked free.

Yes! She was right. The hut's thin material didn't offer adequate support to anchor such a heavy bolt.

Suppressing a shout of triumph, she peered through the peephole left behind, but flinched away. Eyes used to complete darkness couldn't bear the blinding light. A starburst remained behind her lids, imprinted on her retina, even with her eyes squeezed tight.

Slower now, Mallory allowed her vision to adjust until she could see through the tiny hole.

The sun sank low on the horizon. The guard would return soon for the evening ritual. A moment of panic gripped her, but then her heart leapt. Two little girls stood outside a building some distance away. Whether hers or not, she couldn't say, but her spirits soared.

And then reality returned. She could now move about the room, but freedom still eluded her. The locked door and the brutal guard remained. Still, the small victory kept her hopes alive. Insignificant as it was, she'd reclaimed a small measure of power. Her family, James, would be proud of her.

Just like that, the tears crushed her. Did her family even know she was missing? Would her brothers come looking for her? Would James?

Yes, of course, And they would. But not in time. She had no one to depend on but herself. Tears would have to wait.

She quickly pushed the eyebolt back into its hole.

Not long after, her bathroom monitor arrived and led her to the rear of the hut. This time, though, Scarface

watched with avid curiosity, talking the whole time. She couldn't make sense of his words, but the tone of his voice fired her imagination. Scarface frightened her.

She finished quickly and hurried back to the front of the hut, not waiting for him to yank her chain.

He laughed, and used his bigger body to pin her against the door.

Mallory's heart thudded out of control. This encounter had only one outcome. She would fight him. And he would hurt her.

A shout from someone near the other buildings jerked Scarface away, but not before he squeezed her bottom and shoved her inside the cell.

Mallory went sprawling on the dirt floor. Pain shot through her in an undulating wave of agony—her ankle, ribs, hands, and face. She pushed to a sitting position, appalled at the weakness in her legs and arms. Time had become her enemy as much as the monsters who'd taken her.

Scarface ran the chain through the eyebolt, engaged the padlock, and hurried off.

She had to get away. Soon. Before he found the courage to do more than touch.

Sometime later, the door opened for the women to deliver the meal of slop-soup.

"Sloup." Mallory snickered.

Locked in again for the night, she once again removed

the bolt, a plan forming in her mind. With her new freedom of movement, if she stood with her back to the wall beside the door when the groper-guard returned in the morning, perhaps she could get behind him while his eyes adjusted to the dark. She could slip the chain over his head, around his neck, and choke him until he passed out. After that …

Her plan fell apart at that point. Mallory had no idea where they'd taken her or in what direction safety lay, if safety even existed anymore. Her only alternative was wait and see what happened next, which was no option at all.

Despair, always hovering in the back of her mind, tried to assert itself, but she refused to give in. She'd rather die trying to escape than passively wait for death's embrace.

Sleep came as it had the previous night, a fitful stirring that offered little rest. Sometime later, a noise woke her. Distant shouts. Feet thudded on the ground. Running. More shouts. Vehicles roared to life. Tires screeched. And then a peculiar silence, as though the night held its breath.

A sense of urgency pressed in, and Mallory once more worked the eyebolt free. She peered through the pinhole, but found only more darkness.

As she looked, a light flashed in the distance, bobbed up and down and side to side, twin lights bouncing, moving. Soon, she could make out the sound of an engine.

A vehicle was coming. It grew louder with each second, until it stopped beside her door, motor still running.

The key scraped in the door lock.

Mallory turned from the pinhole, gathered up the long length of chain, and scrambled into the corner nearest the door. Adrenaline rushed through her veins. The constant fear amped higher. Her time was up. She had to act. Now.

A silhouette stood in the doorway, a big shadow against the blacker, starless sky. He grinned, and his teeth made a slash of white in the darkness.

Scarface had come back for her.

Mallory tensed, her lungs frozen. She waited. And hoped he couldn't hear her pounding heart.

He leaned down, hands searching over the ground for her.

This was it. Maybe her only chance. Before his eyes could adjust to the darker interior, she pounced. The chain slipped around his neck. She yanked it tight. Tighter.

He reared back, hands working at the chain cutting off his oxygen. He staggered upright, pulling Mallory off the ground.

Mallory kept her grip on the metal noose, though. Her life depended on it.

But then he reached one hand over his head and tangled his fist in her hair. A mighty yank sent her flying over his head.

Fire erupted in her scalp. A second later, her back hit the ground. Every molecule of air exploded from her lungs. Stunned, unable to breathe, she watched in horror as he threw off the chain. Scarface outmatched her in both size and strength, and in physical altercations like this, physics won. Every time.

He grabbed her by one arm and leg and lifted. With a roar, he threw her against the wall.

Pain exploded in her head. Fiery slashes of agony pierced her side. Stars swam in a frantic dance as her vision dimmed.

She fought off the darkness only to realize Scarface had grabbed her leg and dragged her away from the wall. He turned her onto her back, his hands rough as he tore at her clothes.

"No!" She screamed, though no sound emerged. She pushed at his chest, flailed fists against his face, a gnat against a boulder. "No!" She managed to get out this time.

He stopped long enough to backhand her.

Blood filled her mouth. Fresh pain made itself known. And still she knew and felt everything happening. Even the chain gouging into her hip.

She lay still … let his hands roam … and pulled at the length of chain. Why did it have to be so long?

At last, she reached the end, found the bolt, gripped the rounded portion. And stabbed.

Scarface jerked away with a howl. He fell to one side, rolling around and clawing at his neck.

Mallory scrambled to her feet and stumbled to the door, but had to stop in the doorway when the chain pulled tight. She stopped, looked back, and had to retrace her steps to the figure on the floor. The liquid, gurgling sound he made, the way his hands moved slower and slower, weaker, until they fell by his side, the macabre way his legs twitched after he stilled both mesmerized and horrified her.

Scarface lay spread-eagled in the dirt, arms wide, chest not moving. A thin shaft of moonlight penetrated into the room to reveal the eyebolt … in his neck … where she'd stabbed him.

Her legs collapsed, sending her to her knees. She'd killed a man.

No. She killed a monster. Regret and guilt would wait. Desperation intervened. She had a shackle on her ankle with a long chain attached to it, and now to a corpse. The door was open. A battered truck, like none she'd ever seen before, idled right outside. She had to get out of here while she could.

Gathering her courage, she threaded a finger through the eyebolt, and tugged. The bolt came free with slurping, sucking sound. One hand slick with the guard's blood, Mallory gathered up the chain, limped out to the truck, and threw it inside onto the floor. She climbed in behind the wheel.

Standard shift. On the column. No problem. Growing up on the ranch, there weren't many vehicles she couldn't drive. The truck started forward only to stop after a few feet. Two little girls were in one of the other buildings. She couldn't leave without them, without at least trying to find the others.

Letting out on the clutch again, she moved at turtle speed toward the other huts.

No one came out to see who was driving in the middle of the night. Other than a small jeep, there were no other vehicles. Was that the commotion that woke her? Had the rest of the men gone?

Mallory shoved the gear in park, and jumped from the truck, but had to stop and wrap the chain around her waist.

The first hut was unlocked and empty.

The second hut had a padlock on the door, but unlike her cell, this one had a window. Joy surged when she spotted four little bodies huddled together in a corner of the room, their wide eyes a sea of white in the night.

Breaking the glass would be a cinch, but first she had to see if any of the guards remained.

The third and fourth huts were also locked, but their windows revealed more of the girls. The fifth, a much larger hut, opened with a turn of the door handle. Empty, like the first.

Assured that none of the Mayaƙan had stayed behind, Mallory returned to the first hut and used the chain to break the windows, and clear away the jagged fragments. She whispered to the girls and motioned them to the window. "Come quickly. Hurry."

They recognized her voice, and hurried to help each other through the window. Mallory had to pull the last one

up and out, the effort taking her breath away. Sharp, stinging pain burned through her ribs.

The second and third huts went easier with the girls calling to each other. Quiet as a summer breeze, she herded them to the truck and helped them climb into the back. The canvas cover would shield them from sight.

Ten. She counted only ten little heads. Where were the other four? Where was Charri? She couldn't leave without looking one more time.

Mallory hurried back to each of the huts, and searched every corner.

No more girls.

Anguish made her legs weak as she returned once more to the truck. Unshed tears made her eyes burn. With a hardness she didn't know she possessed, she shook off the pain and failure, and settled herself behind the wheel. Time to go. Time to save those she could.

James hunkered down in the brush beside Fowler and Jonas. Theirs was the shortest route to get into position, but it meant waiting longer while the others reached their positions. He covered his watch face and checked the time. 2310. Five more minutes before Charlie Team set off the flares.

He stood slowly, his movements masked by heavy

underbrush and the darkest sky he'd ever seen, and he slung his M-4 carbine over his back. Close quarters called for a smaller weapon. He patted the K-bar holstered to his thigh. A wicked knife could do as much damage as a Glock. More, sometimes.

Counting down the minutes and seconds, James perched on the balls of his feet. A forty-five count after the flares went off and they'd move. At last.

Beside him, Fowler and Jonas tensed as well.

"Eight-seven-cover your eyes," Fowler whispered. "Three-two—"

The sky erupted in a ball of dusky reddish-pink light. Even with his hand over his eyes, the glare made him squint.

He counted the seconds in his head. Forty-five. Not even a minute, and yet, an eternity.

Jonas's loud whisper came at last. "Let's roll."

Running low, ten yards apart, James forged his way to the right side of the small building, while Jonas went left. Fowler swung well wide of James, to provide a lookout between them and the collection of shanties in the distance, the greatest point of danger.

Right off, James knew something was wrong. Intel, both aerial surveillance and Archer's report, showed Mallory in this small, isolated building. It had no windows and only one door on the side facing the other huts. Now, the door stood wide open.

James and Jonas met at the door, backs to the wall on either side of the opening. James pointed at Jonas with a downward motion, and then at himself with an upward gesture.

A nod from Jonas was the only warning. He crouched and went in low and to the left.

Not even a second passed before James followed, going in high and to the right. His eyes swept the room, his arm and the Glock he held moving in sync, registering everything. Shadows. A man down. Unmoving. No others. No enemy. No Mallory. Too quiet. And the metallic stench of blood. Fresh. And a lot of it.

James knelt by the man's head and shined his penlight. He felt his neck, searched for a pulse, but found blood instead. The man had a nasty gash in his neck. He'd bled out from a punctured jugular.

Had Mallory done this? His princess who loved horses and dogs, and rescued stray goats?

"She's not here," Jonas whispered. Worry filled his voice.

"Let's get Fowler and help Bravo search the other buildings."

They'd just made it to the first hut when Wade's voice came over the headset. So much for radio silence. "Mallory's escaped in a stolen truck, but she's going the wrong way."

"Well, stop her!" Fowler responded.

"Hold on. Madman's trying to hotwire an old jeep."

Vroom. An engine started up behind one of the buildings. Headlights appeared, coming fast.

James took off at a run, just as the jeep reached him. He grabbed one of the windshield struts and swung himself into the passenger seat as it passed him. And did a doubletake.

On the other side, Jonas dove into the empty cargo area behind the driver.

The man really was a ghost. James hadn't seen or heard him running.

The engine roared as Madman speed-shifted through the grinding gears, and pulled every ounce of power from the jeep. A few minutes later, they spotted the truck's taillights ahead.

"Pull up alongside. I'll jump." James shed his rifle, and positioned both feet on the runner, ready to leap.

Jonas crawled to the right side of the jeep, intent on doing the same. "Mallory won't be expecting us," he shouted over the roar of the engine. "She'll think we're the bad guys. You go down the right side and open the passenger door. When she looks at you, I'll grab the wheel. Move fast, so she doesn't roll the truck."

"Roger."

"Get ready, boys," Madman yelled as he maneuvered the jeep up to the left rear bumper.

A little more, another six inches.

Jonas jumped first, fingers clawing into the canvas cover for a handhold.

James leapt seconds later, clinging like a monkey to the braces that formed the canopy.

The truck careened from one side to other. The little minx had seen them and was trying to throw them off.

James got a foothold on the tailgate and was halfway across the back when a tire iron whacked the top of his boot. What the heck?

Whoever swung the iron didn't hit nearly hard enough to do damage. Thank goodness for reinforced boots.

He leaned down and peered inside … and almost lost his grip. Children. A mosh pit of tangled arms and legs, piled up against the backside of the truck cab, all but the one who dared swing the tire iron at him again. She aimed for his leg this time.

He yanked the tire iron from her, and tossed it to the side of the road. No time to deal with the kids. He continued his step-by-step way across the back of the truck to the right side, and on to the front.

Across from him, Jonas was already in position behind the driver's door.

James reached the cab and nodded once at Jonas. In one continuous motion, he opened the passenger door and dove inside. "Mallory, slow down, baby. You're going the wrong way."

She screamed. Her whole body jerked to the right

when she turned to stare at him. So did the truck.

His still open door snapped off when they sideswiped a tree.

With nothing but the dash and the seat to hold onto, James found himself on his knees on the floor ... with a foot coming at his face.

He threw his arm up and scuttled backward to avoid the kick aimed at his head, and almost fell out.

"No!" Mallory screamed again, but this time anger tempered her fear. She aimed another kick at his leg this time.

"Whoa, princess. Stop. It's me, James." Where the heck was Jonas?

The driver's door opened, and the man of the hour grabbed the steering wheel and used a little hip action to shove Mallory over.

The truck careened from one side to the other as Mallory fought him for control.

"Mallory!" James scrambled up on the seat, wrapped her in an embrace, effectively pinning her arms to her side. "Princess. Stop fighting. It's me, James. And Jonas."

Mallory went still as a grave. "James? What are you doing here?"

"Yeah, baby. It's me. I'm taking you home."

Imperfect Lies

Chapter Twenty-Seven

James buzzed with relief. He'd found Mallory, had her in his arms. His world righted itself. *Thank you, Jesus. Thank you, Jesus. Thank you, Jesus.*

"You ready to go home, kid?" Jonas asked from the other side of the truck.

She whipped around. "Jonas?" Her voice quavered, on the verge of breaking.

Her brother grinned. "Hey, sis."

She touched his arm, his face. "You came?"

"Of course, we came." Jonas sounded indignant. "All of us did—me, James, Garrett, Wade, even Kyle. Not Derek, though. James made him stay and play sheriff. You didn't think we'd let you have all the fun, did you?"

"I hoped … I prayed so hard, but … they found us. They took the girls."

"But you got them back," James said

She looked at him again. "What … how?"

"Saw them in the back. One of them tried to break my leg with a tire iron."

A horrified expression spread across her face.

James kissed the top of her head. "Don't worry. Takes more than a forty-pound kid to drop me. Brave little thing."

"But I only found ten of the girls. I lost the other four." She buried her face in his chest. Sobs wracked her slender frame.

Oh crap. He hated when women cried, and Mallory's tears were the worst. They ripped him apart. "Shhh, baby. I've got you now."

Society viewed a man's tears as a sign of weakness, while a crying woman was lauded for letting their guard down enough to release pent-up emotions. Just one more double-standard, this one favoring women.

His first reaction was to fix whatever made her sad, to do something to make her stop crying, but he couldn't undo what had happened. Helpless and confused, he stroked her hair instead. Held her close. And whispered foolishness in her ear like a love-struck idiot.

Because that's what he was— in love, and completely at her mercy.

"And another one bites the dust." Jonas sang a little off-key, his fingers drumming on the steering wheel.

James wanted to knock the smirk off his face, but

decided to table his aggression for now. That's how men handled emotional overload. Through aggression, or by shutting down their emotions to deal with at another time.

He closed his arms even tighter around Mallory and stroked her hair, his focus on her needs. Her body shook with spasms as the sobs subsided. And then came the snuffles. Relief never felt so good.

"You found ten and got them out, and against ridiculous odds," he cooed. "You're strong and brave, and won't take crap from anybody. I hear you roar, woman. You're amazing."

A tiny giggle broke through her weeping.

"Fowler called you a warrior," Jonas encouraged. "A regular Amazon. He brought a half-dozen men with him to get you back. You've got your own Army now, Mal."

She rubbed her eyes.

"Hang with me, princess." James grinned when she wiped her nose on her sleeve. "We'll get you and your girls out of here, I promise."

He needed her to stay strong a little longer, to tap that core of inner strength all the Camerons possessed. They weren't safe yet, not by a long shot.

She responded with a long, shuddering breath and a nod.

The complex equation of Mallory Cameron turned him on like no one before her. She had no idea how beautiful she was, inside and out. Here she sat covered in dirt, blood,

and snot, hurting more than most people could bear, and she worried over the four missing girls. Hard and soft at the same time. Strong, but vulnerable. "You know, I may never let you out of my arms again."

"I'm okay with that."

Jonas turned the steering wheel hard to the left, eased forward, whipped the wheel in the opposite direction, and reversed. After repeating the short, jerky motions a few times, he got the truck pointed back in the direction they'd come, and picked up speed.

"What are you doing?" Mallory struggled in James's arms, manic with fear. "We can't go back there. We have to get away."

"You were going the wrong way, baby. Trust me. We got this." James rubbed his hand up and down her back. He hated her distress. *Please Lord, help me keep her safe.*

CCC

The truck bumped and bounced over the road, waking up all of her injuries. Each jolt sent an ice pick stabbing into her ribs, while a blacksmith hammered away inside her head. Her cheek was sore where the guard's knuckles had landed, one eye swollen almost closed. Worst though, was her ankle. Try as she might to ignore it, the raw flesh under the shackle throbbed and burned. She refused to complain, though. Nothing to be done until they escaped this terrible place.

James must have sensed her distress. He feathered light caresses over her face and neck. "Just a little longer, princess. We've got a doctor waiting."

Mallory embraced the comfort he offered. She'd gone through hell and come out on fire, but here, in his arms, even though reason insisted the danger remained, she felt safe for the first time in forever.

The truck slowed.

"Why are we stopping?" An edge of hysteria crept back into her voice.

"Gotta pick up the help," Jonas said, his tone light.

A face appeared at the open passenger side. "She okay?"

"Wade?" Her eyes widened.

"Yeah, Mal. I'm here." He leaned through the open door around James, and hugged her. "You scared us half to death, baby girl."

A chorus of soft squeals erupted from the back.

"Hey, there's kids back here," a deep voice called from the rear of the truck.

"The girls." Mallory tried to climb over James to get out. "I need to see to them, make sure they're all right."

James held her in place.

Another man joined Wade at the door. "Miss Cameron? I'm Agent Kevin Fowler. You, ma'am, are an amazing young woman."

She stared, open-mouthed, at the infamous agent who commanded an equal measure of both respect and scorn from her brothers and two new sisters-in-law.

Fowler patted her arm. "Don't worry about the girls. I speak a little of their language, and I'll take care of them."

"Why is he here?" she whispered after Fowler walked away.

"He made this rescue possible. We wouldn't have gotten here in time without him." For once, Jonas didn't make light of a situation.

"But does he know anything about children?"

James pulled her against his chest again. "Fowler and his wife have six adopted kids. I'd say that makes him uniquely qualified. I promise, he'll protect your girls with his life."

Someone pounded on the back of the cab.

"That's our signal." Jonas forced the grinding gears to engage, and drove for perhaps twenty minutes before the truck started to sputter. "End of the road for this old wagon Everybody out. We got thirty minutes to hoof it from here to the LZ."

Mallory lifted her head from James's chest and looked at him. "The what?"

"Landing zone. We didn't exactly come through the front door. The Nigerian government will blow a gasket if they find us here. Can you walk a little way?"

"Define a little way."

"One and a half kilometers. Not quite a mile."

She groaned. Under ordinary circumstances, half an hour would allow more than enough time to cover the distance. But she was beaten down, sore, injured, weak … and lugging an eight-foot chain. And that didn't take into account the girls in the back, all under the age of eight, and with much shorter legs. Once again, her choices amounted to no choice at all.

James slid out and reached to help her down. When the chain rattled across the floor, he picked it up and followed it to her the shackle on her ankle. "What in blue blazes is this?"

Jonas appeared at James's side. "They chained you, Mallory?"

"Yeah, they did. But I worked the bolt free and— Oh God." Her knees almost gave way. "I killed the guard with it." She covered her face with both hands.

"I'm sorry you had to do that, princess." James pushed her hands away and cupped her face, so she had to meet his gaze. "I'm also thankful you found the courage to do it. My only regret is you didn't leave anything for me. He got off too easy."

Fowler interrupted. "Save the gab fest for another time, people. We have a bird to catch, and a large group of very volatile insurgents to avoid. Gather round."

James walked her to the rear of the truck, the chain looped over his arm.

When the girls spotted her, they scurried over and wrapped little arms around her legs.

Mallory stooped down to hug each one.

"Listen up," Fowler continued. "We have six men, one battered woman, and ten little girls. Ghost, take point. Romeo, cover the rear. Dawg, Cochise, Madman, and I will help the girls. Let's vacate this place." He leaned down and swung one of the younger girls onto his back for a piggyback ride.

Mallory tugged on James's sleeve. When he leaned down, she whispered in his ear, "What did he call them?"

He smiled. "Tell you later."

The trek took longer than it should. Besides Fowler, Wade and the huge guy James called Madman also carried a child. They didn't get far before two more girls fell.

Wade and Madman grabbed them up before Mallory could.

"They're exhausted," Mallory said to James. "Give me the chain. If anymore falter, you'll need to help." She fastened the length around her waist.

James hoisted another stumbling girl onto his back. Before he'd gone a step, she had her arms around his neck, head against his back, and had closed her eyes.

The sight melted what was left of Mallory's heart.

Fowler insisted they maintain the torturous pace, even though it meant the children still able to walk took three and sometimes four steps to match the adults.

"Keep moving. One foot in front of the other, Miss Cameron," Fowler encouraged. "Help will arrive soon."

Another girl dropped.

James grabbed her, leaving two still on their feet.

If they went down, Fowler could take a second child, but Mallory wasn't sure she could carry even one. She had enough trouble keeping herself upright.

Step by step, just as Fowler directed. Numb to the pain in her body, Mallory would do what was needed. The safety of the girls took precedence. And if she made it home, she was never leaving again.

Home. The word never sounded so sweet.

Before long, four more men joined their party. Two hoisted the remaining girls onto their backs. Heroes, all.

One of the newcomers swooped in and grabbed Mallory. He swung her around in a circle. "I've died a thousand deaths worrying about you, Mal. Mom would never forgive me if we came home without you."

"Garrett," she squealed. "Too tight. You're crushing me." Definitely cracked ribs. Nothing could hurt this bad and not be broken.

"She's injured, man. Go easy," James yanked on one of Garrett's arms.

Garrett released her like he'd been burned. "Sorry, sis.

I'm just so happy to see you in one piece. Or mostly one piece." He held her chin, studied her face, and then, nostrils flaring, he looked at James. "Tell me the dirt bag who did this is no longer breathing, Dawg."

"Nope. Toes up. She took care of him herself."

Not much took Garrett by surprise, but that piece of information did. One eyebrow arched high as he looked from James back to her. "Mmm."

"How far?" Fowler barked.

"Clearing's not far," Garrett said. "Choppers due in three minutes. The Mayakan are maybe seven minutes behind us."

Mallory looked around, amazed at how fast the men moved, most of them carrying two girls. The fourth member of Garrett's group made his way to her side. "How you holding up, sweetheart?"

"Archer?"

"Yes, ma'am. You are one tough person to keep track of." He grinned.

"Gotta move faster. Double-time." Fowler broke into a trot.

Up ahead, Jonas was running back toward the group "Birds incoming. Get these kids on board now." He took one of the girls from Wade and sprinted back the way he'd come.

Archer grabbed another child from Madman and raced after Jonas.

Not a minute later, Kyle came barreling up from behind the group. "They found the truck. We'll have company in five minutes, maybe less." He took one of the girls James held and set off at a dead run toward the landing zone.

Everyone ran, Mallory included. Thankfully, James matched her stride and caught her upper arm with his free hand. His steadying grip was the only thing that kept her from toppling over.

Whirling rotor blades kicked dust and debris into the air. Their thumping sounds rattled the air with vibrations that Mallory felt in her bones.

Jonas reached the bird first, before the skids hit the ground, and wrenched the door open.

Archer followed close on his heels, and together they thrust their burdens inside. Arms freed, Archer motioned the others to hurry.

"Give us your ammo," Jonas yelled.

Half the group stayed with Jonas at one helicopter, while the other half followed Archer to the second bird. When the children were safely inside the chopper, they stripped off their ammo—clips, cartridges, belts, a few grenades—and handed them over before climbing inside.

Mallory's heart sank as she watched Jonas stuff his pockets and the web vest with the extra ammunition. She understood his intent, but asked anyway. "What are you doing, Jonas?"

Gun shots echoed through the night, coming from behind. Instinct made her duck, but she soon realized the enemy was not yet in range. Soon, though. Too soon.

"Everybody on board now!" Fowler yelled before he turned to Jonas. "You know the plan."

Jonas brushed Mallory's cheek with a kiss. "No time. Gotta go."

She watched until he and Archer melted into the underbrush on the other side of the clearing. Ghosts.

James grabbed her waist and lifted her up.

Kyle pulled her inside and dumped her out of the way just as the chopper lifted off.

Her stomach plummeted with the dizzying take off, even as panic overwhelmed her. "Wait!"

Her scream went unheard in the noise of the straining engines. Paralyzing fear gripped her as she watched the man she loved struggle for his life.

James had both arms inside the door, elbows spread wide, but his lower body still dangled outside.

Fowler and Garrett each grabbed one of his arms and hauled him in, and then Kyle slammed the door and secured it.

"Get us out of here!" Fowler yelled to the pilot.

Her ribs flared in agony. The ragged breaths turned to groans. They'd gotten everyone on board, safe. Everyone except Jonas and Archer.

Relief and guilt, pain and exhaustion made a bitter

cocktail.

James scooted to her side and draped a scratchy blanket over her. The engine noise made conversation impossible, but his closeness provided a measure of warmth and comfort.

Exhausted, Mallory burrowed closer for the furnace of his body and reassurance of his touch. She needed him.

CCC

James took the headset Fowler offered, slipped it on, and tapped the intercom switch. "See if you can find something to remove this shackle."

Fowler nodded before crawling to the other side of the cabin. He returned a moment later with a small zipper case and a larger plastic box with a red cross on it. He held out a penlight to James. "Here, hold this so I can see."

The agent lifted Mallory's leg and rested her ankle on his knee, lock side up. "A little more to the right," he instructed.

Using a pair of thin, metal implements from the case, Fowler set to work. Less than thirty second later, the shackle snapped open.

A man of many talents, for sure, but a lock-pick set? In his go-bag?

Fowler tossed the shackle aside and opened the first-aid kit. "Hold her leg," he instructed James. "This might sting,"

He soaked a sterile gauze pad with antiseptic, and cleaned the abraded skin.

James winced, but Mallory never flinched. She didn't move at all.

"I called up Sawbones for this op," Fowler said as he worked. "A just-in-case precaution. He'll meet us in Lagos."

"We're stopping in Lagos? Why not Virginia? I want her out of Nigeria." James tried to suppress his anger.

Fowler's expression said he didn't succeed. Even more surprising, the man who never explained anything offered several reasons.

"One, we can't remove the children from Nigeria without papers. Two, if we take them to the States, we'll draw unwanted attention. Three, we cannot afford said attention because of the sensitive and somewhat illegal nature of our mission. Four, said attention might also shine a spotlight on the ongoing mission Ghost and Treekiller are pursuing. Five, Mallory requires medical attention now, not after a transatlantic flight. Six, she came to Nigeria on a U.S. passport. Failure to return to the States on that same passport will send up red flags in the State Department. Seven, we can offload the children in Lagos and put them into the care of someone who will ensure their safety and find them suitable homes. And eight, the nuns, I have dispatched a team to bring Sister Agatha, Sister Mary

Magdalena, and their kids to Lagos. They have Mallory's personal belongings, including her passport. Now, is that enough, or do you need more reasons?"

"What about Jonas and Archer?'

Fowler didn't say anything at first, but neither did he turn away. "The original mission is still a go. However, the time constraints have been lifted. It may take longer than first anticipated. Ghost and Treekiller made the decision to see it through. Call it unfinished business for them. That is all I can tell you."

"No timeline?"

"No. You'll just have to wait and see like the rest of us. They will make contact at the appropriate time."

"What if they don't?"

Another pause. "Then they don't."

"You know the Camerons won't accept that."

The moon filtered in between the clouds and illuminated Fowler's face long enough to reveal his smile before he turned away. "I know."

Imperfect Lies

Chapter Twenty-Eight

The helicopters set down on the same isolated airstrip southeast of N'Djamena.

James exited first, and held his arms out to take Mallory from Kyle. He carried her to the same Gulfstream jet that brought them here, and sat in one of the captain's chairs with her cuddled on his lap. The jostling movements didn't wake her. Neither did the screaming jet engines, or the sound of ten little girls whimpering with fear. She didn't stir during the entire flight to Lagos.

Worry ate at him. He'd bathed her face using feather touches over her bruises, a difficult task given how much rage flowed through him. Five minutes. That's all he wanted with the animal who'd done this. Five minutes he would never get because Mallory had already dealt with him. He kissed her forehead. "You are so awesome, princess."

The other members of his team washed and fed the children, and settled all ten of them on the small bed at the back of the plane. There, they curled around each other like a litter of puppies and drifted off to sleep.

He thought about laying Mallory on the loveseat where she could stretch out, but couldn't bear to let her out of his arms. Had she squirmed or indicated the slightest discomfort, he would have relinquished her. Instead, she snuggled against him, letting out little contented sighs from time to time.

Contentment. Yeah, that described him. A man could get used to the feeling.

She woke after the plane touched down in Lagos and the doctor came aboard and started prodding her.

"Ow." Drowsy, she swatted at the hand poking at her ribs. "That hurts."

The doctor chuckled. "There she is. Hello, Mallory."

"Good morning, princess, wakey-wakey," James coaxed with a gentle shake. "This is David Sallijay. He's a doctor and an old friend. We call him Sawbones."

Her eyes held a look of confused irritation as she struggled to throw off the fog of sleep. "Who?"

"Call me David or Doc, if you want."

She tried to sit up, winced, and relaxed back into James's arms instead.

"Here, let me help," Doc said. "Give me your hand and

pull yourself up. It will hurt less if you do it yourself instead of someone else pulling."

It would hurt either way, but she did as he instructed.

"There. Better? Ribs are tricky things. An upright position puts less pressure on the injury."

"Semantics," she said. "Still hurts."

David turned to James. "Why don't you get Mallory a nice cup of something hot and sweet. She could use a sugar jolt. You prefer tea or coffee, Mallory?"

"Water first," she croaked, and then said, "Coffee."

"Water and coffee, it is. And Dawg? How about you wait in the galley while I examine Mallory's injuries. I'll call when we're done."

"Not a chance." James crossed his arms, not about to leave Mallory's side for more than a few minutes. But then he cut his eyes to Mallory, saw her blush, and reconsidered. "Uh, Mallory? Baby? You want me to leave?"

She cast her eyes down and nodded.

He smiled. This was a side of his princess he hadn't seen before. Modest and embarrassed. Cute. Time would take care of that problem. He'd make sure of it. "Okay. Just don't take too long."

David shooed him away.

In the galley at the front of the plane, James started a pot of coffee and poured cold water from the bottle in the small fridge into a plastic cup.

Garrett came with him. "How's she doing?"

"She's awake. Doc's checking her over. They kicked me out."

Garrett slapped him on the back and laughed. "Don't take it personal. Females are funny that way. Just chalk it up to crap women say or do that doesn't make any sense. You'll keep your sanity longer."

James snorted at the homespun wisdom and changed the subject. "Girls taken care of?"

"You know, every time I think I've got Fowler figured out, he goes and does something I don't expect. The man has contacts everywhere, in every conceivable walk of life. He whipped out his phone when we landed, and bam! He had the Chairman of the Board for some international adoption organization on the phone. Fowler arranged for the girls to stay at this guy's home. They'll receive medical care, and eventually be placed in foster homes. Dude's got some serious pull."

"We wouldn't have gotten Mallory back without his help."

"You're right. By the way, thanks for taking care of my sister. I owe you."

"You don't owe me anything. She's my responsibility from now on." There. He did it. Claimed her. Declared his intentions. Her mother already loved him, so all he had to do was get her father's blessing, beat the tar out of her brothers if they messed with him, and convince Mallory to see things his way.

Garrett's expression changed in rapid succession—surprise, curiosity, concern, annoyance, and a hint of anger before settling into disapproval.

Tough. James braced his legs in a wide stance and dared the eldest Cameron brother to complain. He wouldn't back down, not with his future at stake.

Some of the tension drained away when Garrett's glower changed to a smile. "I can see I don't have much say in this."

"None at all."

"Then, welcome to the family, Dawg."

"They call you ... Dawg?"

James turned at the sound of her voice.

"That's a terrible name." Mallory stood in the door with Doc right behind her. "It's a guy thing, right? Like the ridiculous, secret hand shake you guys made up back in high school?"

Garrett laughed, but looked uncomfortable. "I ... uh ... need to check on something. Back in a few. Glad you're feeling better, Mal."

James stared and drank her in. She'd changed into the t-shirt he left for her and brushed her hair into a high ponytail. Even with the bruises on her face and arms, she was the most beautiful sight he'd ever seen. But then, her comment sank in. Terrible? He liked his name. "Hey, it's a good name. Strong."

Doc choked off a laugh and backed away. "Uh, think

I'll go help Garrett with whatever he's checking." He disappeared down the aircraft stair.

"Strong, huh? Are you sure you weren't named after an over-amorous hound dog?"

James felt the heat flare in his cheeks. His player days ended the moment he arrived at the Triple C Ranch ... and met an angel named Mallory Cameron. Why hadn't he realized that before now?

With understanding came shock. And then amusement. His subconscious had recognized right away what his head had denied. Mallory had ruined him for all other women.

James patted the back of one of the chairs. "Why don't you come over here and have a seat before you fall down?"

"I'm not a ragdoll. Don't treat me like one." She made her way to the seat anyway.

He handed her the cup of water and sat beside her. "For your information, princess, they're not nicknames, they're call signs." He emphasized the proper designation. "In our line of work, real names pose a danger to both the soldier and those close to him. We don't carry anything on missions that could reveal our real identity."

"That's awful. How does your family know—" Her mouth snapped shut.

He had to laugh at the dumbfounded look on her face. "How does your family know if something goes wrong?"

She nodded.

"They don't," James explained. "The government doesn't sanction what we do most of the time. We don't exist."

"But—"

"There are others who notify the family with discretion and secrecy, but only when it's safe to do so. It's the nature of the business."

"Well, it's a terrible business, if you ask me."

"So, you're really okay?" He wanted to change the subject. She didn't need to know about the ugly side of his life—or her brothers' lives.

"David said I have a couple of hairline rib fractures, but there's not much can be done to treat them. Only pain meds. He's not concerned about the flight home." She ran her fingers over her bruised cheek. "These will fade. For my ankle, he gave me antibiotics and a tetanus shot, and told me to follow up with Doc Burdette when I get home."

"David, huh?" The little green monster raised its head. Had he not known Doc was married and madly in love with his wife, James might have said more. And embarrassed himself. Instead, he rubbed his fingers down her arm, and smiled when goosebumps pebbled her skin.

She peered up at him from lowered eyelids, a frown of displeasure on her lips.

"Coffee's ready. You want something to eat? Or a bath?"

The light in her eyes sparked, but then dimmed. "Yes,

to all of it, but what I want more than anything is to know what happened to Sister Agatha, Sister Mary Magdalena, and the babies."

Her sadness gutted him. Mallory gave so much of herself to others. He wanted to give her the world.

"I believe I can answer that." Fowler's head and shoulders appeared in the doorway as he climbed the stairs. He handed a backpack to Mallory. "I believe this is yours."

Her sorrow turned to hesitant hope. "How did you get this? I left it—"

James stared at the former agent, stunned when Fowler's face softened.

"Your Mr. Kinsloe went back to the camp for you. By the way, Sister Agatha and Sister Mary Magdalena send their regards. It seems the Mayakan 'yanci had no interest in two elderly nuns and a passel of crying babies. They couldn't get out of there fast enough. Didn't even relieve them of their paltry food supplies."

"Jared came back for me? The sisters are well?"

Jared? He didn't like the sound of another man's name on her lips, or the joy in her expression when she spoke of him. The worthless coward left her alone and unprotected in the squalid camp.

Mallory flinched when his muscles flexed. Concern etched lines in her forehead. "James? Are you okay?"

He eased his hold, but refused to let go. No, he wasn't okay. He fought to control a fierce desire to find this Jared guy and beat him to a pulp. Jealousy packed a hefty wallop for someone unused to such emotions. "Yeah, baby. I'm fine. Still reeling from the danger you fell into."

She relaxed against him, her cheek over his heart, one hand on his belly. Could she hear the thunder in his chest? Feel the way his blood pounded? "I'm safe now, thanks to you and the others."

"Alrighty then. I see now why the others are wandering around outside. Now that you have your passport, Mallory, we can depart. You've got forty minutes before the others return."

James smiled. Maybe Fowler wasn't such a bad guy after all. Forty minutes might be enough to get him in trouble, but then again, it could also be the beginning of the rest of their lives. With a finger under her chin, he tilted Mallory's head up and let his gaze roam over every inch of her face. "I think I fell in love the moment I laid eyes on you, Mallory Cameron."

◌◌◌

With the children offloaded, James convinced Mallory to rest on the bed in the aft cabin. Ten minutes after takeoff, he grinned at the soft snores she made in her sleep and covered her with a blanket.

Fowler stood in the doorway when he turned to leave. "She's a strong woman."

"That she is."

"Care to join us for a debrief?" Fowler inclined his head toward the front.

James nodded and followed him out, closing the door behind him.

The others sat in the chairs, gathered in a circle—Cowboy, Cochise, Romeo, Madman, and Ruby—everyone except Spider and Crash who piloted the plane. And Ghost and Treekiller, who they'd left behind.

"Sit, Dawg. None of us like leaving men behind, but it was necessary in this case. And those two wouldn't have listened had I ordered them out."

James took one of the last remaining seats. "Why? What was so important about that band of insurgents?"

"Not just any band," Kyle said. "Toure led the group that chased us. I saw him."

Tension escalated among the group. Their original mission's goal was to remove Mr. Toure from power, but Mallory's abduction changed the priorities. Now they learned after the fact, Toure was in reach the entire time they were on the ground, right up until the helicopters carried them out of range.

"So, we left two men behind to execute a plan meant for ten. With no support, no backup, and no extraction options."

"No," Fowler replied, his voice like iron. "We left two men to accomplish a one-man mission. Those two have more resources available to them than you can possibly imagine. Your job here is done."

"You expect us to just go home and wait?" Garrett asked, his voice low and dangerous.

"That's our brother out there," Wade added.

James remained quiet, marveling at the emotion of the two Camerons. He'd seen Garrett angry, and wouldn't wish his rage on anybody. Wade, on the other hand, always conducted himself with the utmost control. The man never raised his voice. Until now.

"Ghost is a highly trained, exceptionally skilled operative. He, above any of you, has the best chance of completing the mission. Don't underestimate him. He will succeed. He will survive."

"You can't know he'll come home," Garrett argued.

"And you can't know he won't," Fowler fired back. "Have faith. Trust him."

Neither Garrett nor Wade responded, which James construed as unwilling acceptance. Good thing, too. Fowler wouldn't hesitate to lock them both up somewhere no one would find them, at least until Jonas resurfaced. James suspected Garrett knew that, too.

"Your job, gentlemen, is to keep your home and your people safe until Homeland Security can root out and round up the cell Toure sent to spy on your family. I'm sending Madman and Spider with you, to beef up your defenses. You can make them volunteer deputies, or hire them on as

hands at your ranch, whatever works best. Your call."

"Will you keep us apprised of the mission in progress?" James asked, disguising the demand as a request.

Fowler scowled, his annoyance obvious. "Yes. I will notify you of any developments, good or bad, Sheriff. This meeting is adjourned."

Each man nodded in response to Fowler's glare before he grabbed a chair and stalked off. Back rigid, he settled as far away from the others as the small enclosure allowed, and opened his laptop.

Chapter Twenty-Nine

"Sweetheart? Come into my office please. I'd like to talk to you."

Mallory froze, the potato in her hand only half peeled. When her mother used that tone of voice, she meant business, and no argument or plea would sway her.

"I'm getting the potatoes ready for dinner. Give me five minutes, okay?" Anything to delay the inevitable.

"Put what you've peeled in a bowl and cover them with water," Mom instructed. "Dinner will keep. This conversation won't."

Okay, no reprieve this time. She'd dodged the dreaded 'talk' for weeks now. Apparently, Mom had had enough.

Grabbing a bowl from the cupboard, she dumped the peeled and half-peeled potatoes in, added water, and rinsed her hands. She took her time drying them with the dishtowel, knowing if she delayed much longer it would push Mom's limits.

The walk from the kitchen to Mom's office at the front of the house had to be the longest of her life.

"Come in, dear. Shut the door and have a seat."

No witnesses meant no nonsense. Not good.

The door closed with a soft click. The chair squeaked when she sat on it. All these little details claiming her attention were important. They kept her mind focused on mundane things, away from the memories.

"You've been home a whole month, Mallory."

"Yes, it's good to be back. I missed all of you. And this place, too. I've decided I'm not ever leaving again. This is home. This is where—"

"Stop."

Mallory's voice choked off.

"One month, Mallory. And not once have you stepped outside. You won't go into town, you don't ride anymore, you won't even go to the barn and collect eggs for me. It has to stop, dear."

Mallory closed her eyes.

"I know you still have nightmares," Mom went on. "I know about the panic attacks, even though you're very good at hiding them from your dad and brothers. And you hardly speak to James anymore."

"I just need time."

"No, what you need is help. Time will only strengthen

your fears. You have to confront them, deal with them. You need professional help."

She looked at her mother in disbelief. "You think I'm crazy?"

Her mother didn't answer, but her eyes glistened with unshed tears.

Some of the tightness in Mallory's chest eased with the realization she wasn't the only one hurting, wasn't the only victim. Her whole family worried over Jonas's absence, not knowing if he lived. They shared in her torment, too. The nightmares and panic attacks.

Mallory's tears rose to the surface. Her throat tightened, making it difficult to force words out. "I don't know what to do."

"Here." Mom held out a business card. "Francine Eberhard is a friend of Doc Burdette and a doctor of clinical psychology. She specializes in treatment of PTSD."

Mallory studied the card, her eyes going straight to the address. "This says her office is in Idaho Falls. I ... can't."

"Dr. Eberhard is willing to come here for your first few sessions, but you have to make the call. You have to do this for yourself."

"I don't know if I can." Heavenly day, she hated the way her voice trembled, hated the nightmares, the fear, the panic. "I'll try."

Mom smiled and wiped her eyes. "That's all I ask, dear. That you take a chance and try to find your happiness

again."

C C C

Mallory lay awake most of the night trying to convince herself why she couldn't make the call to the psychologist. The distance was too far for Dr. Eberhard to come here. Too far for Mallory to go there. If she couldn't talk about what had happened with people who cared for and loved her, how could she bare her soul to a stranger? Besides, she didn't really need help. She could kick this nonsensical terror on her own, given enough time.

Who was she fooling with all these lies? Fed up with her cowardice, she rose with the first crow of the rooster, got dressed, and made her way down to the kitchen. *Don't think, just do it.*

The coffee called to her. After filling the basket with grounds and adding water, she set out the ingredients for pancakes. *Don't think, just do it.*

A glass of juice sounded good, a piece of toast. She washed the dirty dishes … and recognized her tactics. More delays. More excuses.

The sun had risen high by the time she stuffed her feet into her boots by the back door, and grabbed the egg basket. This time she followed her own advice and emptied her mind—*don't think, just do it.* The door opened, and closed with a bang. The egg basket swung wildly on her arm. Her feet carried her two-thirds of the way to the barn before the panic set in.

Just as she was about to turn tail and run for the safety of the house, a vehicle drove down the drive. The black Yukon veered away from the house and headed her way. And here she stood, unable to move forward, unable to go back. James would see her reality, a proverbial rabbit frozen in its tracks.

He parked and got out, but the hat shading his face couldn't conceal the smile he wore. "Hey, princess. Glad I caught you. Got something in the mail yesterday, and thought you'd want to see it."

If he noticed her inability to move, he didn't show it. Instead, he took her by the arm and led her to the open door of his car.

She went with him, docile as a lamb and amazed by the way he made her fears disappear. Funny how he did that.

He reached inside, grabbed an envelope from the dash, and handed it to her. One line was scrawled across the front: *Destroy this after Mal sees it.*

Intrigued, she took the envelope. The writing seemed familiar, almost like ... She looked up at James, encouraged by his excitement. Could it be?

Hands shaking, Mallory ripped the envelope open. A single thick piece of paper lay inside. No, not paper, a photograph. With fingers both reluctant and eager, she slowly pulled it out … and released a gasp. Tears flooded her eyes. Four little girls stared back at her from the picture. Skin dark as ebony. Eyes of darkest brown. Short, inky-black hair. And smiles that showed lots of teeth. What thrilled more was the man who knelt on the ground between them. Jonas, wearing his own grin, and a twinkle in his eyes. His arms enveloped them, as they snuggled into him.

"Jonas? He found them?" Her voice sounded hoarse even to her own ears. Clutching the photo in one hand, Mallory launched herself at James, threw her arms around his neck, and held on for dear life.

He laughed, a long, deep belly laugh that released something inside her. Tears poured down her cheeks. Not the miserable kind either. This weeping was filled with joy, excitement, delight, and freedom.

James hugged her tight and swung her around in circles until they both grew dizzy. He opened the tailgate then, lifted her to sit on it, and crowded in close beside her. "Did he mean it? That we have to destroy it?"

"Yeah. Jonas took a big chance sending it, even through diplomatic channels. It not only compromises him, the girls' connection to him puts them in danger, too. But he knew you'd worry." James took a lighter from his pocket and flicked it. The flame surged high. He held one corner to the fire.

Mallory's tears continued to fall, bittersweet now as

the flame consumed the photo, leaving only ash behind. Jonas was safe. He'd found the girls. "Is his mission done? Will he come home now?"

James's smile faded. "I don't know, princess. I hope so. You know you can't tell anyone, not even your parents."

She nodded. Agent Fowler drummed the secret nature of Jonas's mission into her. But at least, she knew for the moment he was safe.

"You collecting eggs this morning?"

She smiled for what seemed like the first time since returning home. "Yep. You want to help?"

After James left, Mallory washed the eggs and stored them in the refrigerator.

Mom had already made the pancakes, cooked the bacon, and even loaded the dirty things into the dishwasher, so it looked like breakfast was over … except for the lone plate on the stove with the clean towel draped over it.

Mallory zapped the leftovers in the microwave and ate. She could claim the trip outside this morning as a step forward, mainly because of James, but the anxiety remained. A breakthrough, not a cure, but an incentive to regain control of her life and emotions. She had a brother to welcome home … and a lover to claim.

After rinsing the dishes, she went upstairs to her bedroom. For this call, she wanted privacy.

"Good morning, Dr. Eberhard's office. This is Anita, how can I help you?"

"This is Mallory Cameron. Dr. Eberhard asked me to give her a call."

"Please hold. I'll see if she's available."

Elevator music played over the airwaves, something soft and mellow. And boring. The wait lasted about two minutes.

"Hello, Miss Cameron? This is Dr. Eberhard. I'm so glad you called. Doc Burdette speaks very highly of you."

"Yeah, uh, I …." She had no idea what to say.

Dr. Eberhard's soft chuckle took away some of the tension. "I understand. You'd like to set up an appointment, but you're not sure you really want to do this or not. Let's make it easy. How about I come to your house on Friday?

"It's a two and a half-hour drive. I can't put you out like that."

"I don't hold office hours on Fridays. And don't worry, your insurance will cover the expense of house calls. Anyway, Doctor Burdette tells me your mom makes a mean chicken salad. Think you could talk her into making some for lunch that day?"

Mallory smiled, completely charmed by the easy conversation and soft voice. "Friday is good, and yes, Mom would love to make her chicken salad for our lunch. Thank you for making this easy for me."

"No worries. I'm going to connect you back to my receptionist. She'll give you my email address. Send me directions, and I'll see you on Friday around eleven. Okay?"

"Okay. Thanks."

After getting a confirmation email from the receptionist, Mallory hung up and decided to venture out this time. Just a stroll around the house. She missed the fresh air and sunshine, the smell of freshly mown hay and horses.

She hesitated on the doorstep, still nervous about venturing anywhere alone.

Mom came around the corner of the house wearing old jeans, one of Dad's denim shirts, and the heavy-duty gardening gloves. To her credit, she didn't make a single 'atta girl' remark, or even blink at finding her reclusive daughter outside. "Want to keep me company while I work on my roses? Helps pass the time with someone to talk to."

Mallory forced the uncertainty away, grabbed the little tool box Jonas had made back in high school shop class, and followed her mom to the front yard. She wasn't dressed for digging in the dirt, but that didn't stop her. She'd discovered that occupying her hands and mind played a key role in overcoming her fears. With trowel in hand, she attacked the weeds that had grown up since last fall's pruning.

They worked side by side in silence for a long while before Mallory spoke up. "I thought you wanted someone to talk to."

"Only if you want to. Forced conversation is boring and painful." Mom rose up on her knees, pressed a hand to her back, and stretched. "Old bones don't work the way they once did."

"I called."

Her mom went still. "Called who, dear?"

"Dr. Eberhard."

"And?"

"She's coming here. On Friday. Doc Burdette told her about your chicken salad. She asked if you might make it for lunch."

Mom's smile lit up the day. "Well, of course, I will. What time?"

"Around eleven. She sounds nice."

"Well, I hope so. Don't suppose I could talk you into running into town for groceries?"

"Mom."

"Okay, okay." She held her hands up in surrender. "Baby steps it is. Thanks for getting the eggs this morning."

Mallory hid her smile. She should be thanking Mom for the push. "You're welcome."

Waiting always seemed to make the time drag, right up until it ran out. Friday morning arrived, bringing another bout of panic. Deep breaths helped. A little.

Her mother had been a godsend, planting little suggestions to keep Mallory busy.

"Would you run out to the barn and tell your father dinner's early tonight?"

"Could you feed the horses for Rascal this morning? He has a dentist appointment in town."

"I need you to check Edwina's hooves. That old goat has been hobbling around the last few days."

"My rose bed needs a good drenching. Would you grab the hose and water it down?"

Mallory did it all with a smile. She'd been outside more in the past four days than in the last month. Mom never grumbled when she declined, just kept coming up with new ideas. Today's idea was the best yet.

"I thought since the weather's so nice, we should have our lunch outside. Would you sweep off the patio, wash down the table and chairs, and set the table, please?"

Piff, just like that the morning disappeared.

"Mallory, dear. Dr. Eberhard should be here in fifteen minutes. You might want to get cleaned up," Mom called from the kitchen.

"Oh, crap." Where had the time gone? Mallory tweaked the place settings, wiped a nonexistent speck of dust off the table, and hurried inside. "Thanks for the

warning. Guess I lost track of the time."

Her mom beamed and shooed her away. "Go on now. Hurry."

Right on time, the sound of tires crunching gravel announced the doctor's arrival. Mallory swiped on a neutral shade of lip gloss, smacked her lips together, and hurried downstairs to join her mom as the doorbell rang.

"Hello," Mom said, offering her hand. "You must be Dr. Eberhard. I'm Cate Cameron, and this is my daughter, Mallory. Come in."

Dr. Eberhard shook Mom's hand and then took Mallory's. "It's a pleasure to meet you both. Dr. Burdette speaks very highly of your family."

"That old codger? He'd better." Mom's chortle destroyed any anxiety Mallory had. "Let me show you the family room. No one's home but us, so you can use it, or if you prefer something smaller, I have an office you can use." She gestured toward the small room off the foyer that served as her writing refuge.

Dr. Eberhard looked at Mallory. "Which do you prefer? Big and open, or small and intimate?"

"A hole to crawl in?" she retorted, more than a little serious.

"The office it is, then. Lead on."

At the door, Mom spoke again. "Lunch is ready anytime you are. Just come into the kitchen. Can I get you anything? Coffee? Water? No, okay then, I'll let you get to it. Mallory can show you where the bathroom is."

"Wow," Mallory said after the door closed. "She's more nervous than I am."

Dr. Eberhard laughed out loud. "Mallory, I think you and I are going to get along just fine."

An hour later, Mallory agreed. For a stranger, and a shrink at that, Dr. Eberhard was remarkably easy to talk to. They covered a lot of ground, with Mallory telling much of the story of her trip to Nigeria, by the time they finished.

"You did well, Mallory. With your desire to get better and willingness to do what's needed to get there, I think I can help you through this … we'll call it a rough patch. I propose two visits a week for a start. I'll come here on Tuesdays and Fridays for the next three weeks, and then we'll reevaluate. Sound like a plan?"

Mallory nodded.

"Good. I can't wait to taste your mom's chicken salad."

Imperfect Lies

Chapter Thirty

June ended in a drought with a wildfire burning its way through the middle part of the state. Fortunately, the blaze didn't reach the Challis/Hastings Bluff area, but the heatwave and lack of rain produced its own problems. Farmers fretted over crops, while ranchers and farmers pulled in every favor owed to truck in hay and water.

The soaring temperatures affected everything, crops, animals, people—her hair. Mallory smiled at herself in the mirror and tightened the ponytail. James touched her hair every chance he got. Said he loved the weight and feel of it. Not today. Two minutes outside and he'd end up fondling a sweaty mess.

A quick swipe of lip gloss followed by a hearty smack and, "Ready or not, here I come."

Lunch with James at the diner in town. No big deal,

right?

Wrong. Today represented a turning point, the day she took back control of her life. Three long months of intensive, soul-baring therapy ended yesterday, although Dr. Eberhard promised she would always be available if needed.

Dr. E credited early detection and treatment for their success. "Post-traumatic stress disorder victims demonstrate clear biological changes, as well as psychological symptoms, Mallory. Some of these trauma survivors return to normal in time. Others, like you, often fall into a cycle where they relive their experiences through nightmares and/or flashbacks. Sometimes certain sights, sounds, or even smells can trigger a panic attack. Depression and isolation often complicate the problem. Any of this sound familiar?"

Yes. She possessed intimate knowledge of the symptoms Dr. E described. PTSD, incurable, yet manageable, was not just for soldiers.

Mallory looked at herself in the mirror and lifted her chin. Those were her symptoms, her downward spiral. Irrational fears still lingered, popping up at the most inopportune times. Dr. E said in all likelihood they always would, but the paralysis they invoked held no power over her anymore.

Enough. Too much alone time in her head exacerbated the problem. She opened her mental toolbox instead—

breathing techniques, muscle relaxation, grounding exercises, and recognizing when she needed help and asking for it. *One foot in front of the other, one step at a time.*

Coping mechanisms made powerful allies, as did family and friends. And James.

She skipped down the stairs and passed her mother on the way to the kitchen. "I'm having lunch with James at the diner. Mind if I take your car?"

"Help yourself. Keys are on the kitchen counter."

The smile on Mom's face alone made all the sessions with Dr. E worthwhile.

"You need anything while I'm in town?"

"No thanks. Enjoy your lunch."

Mallory kissed her mother's cheek and headed to the barn.

The blue BMW started with a *vroom.* With the top down, sunglasses on, and ponytail whipping in the wind, she sped down the drive. The panicky moments sometimes crept up on her, but the therapy sessions had helped her recognize triggers and take steps to prevent them from turning into a full-blown panic attack. The trick was to replace the fear and dread with tangible, everyday images that would anchor her in the present. Simple things like mailboxes.

She counted seventeen by the time the diner came into view.

CCC

James leaned against the wall outside the diner and waited for Mallory to park her mother's car. She didn't get out right away, reluctance evident in the way she held herself. Wariness was there, too, obvious in the way her head stayed in constant motion, her eyes wide as though she expected someone to pop out of nowhere. Even with the threat against her and her family neutralized, fear held her with an invisible tether.

Dr. Eberhard had worked wonders, though, and in a relatively short amount of time. James had friends, soldiers who'd survived a warzone but couldn't live a normal life in the civilian world because of the crippling effects of PTSD. Maybe there was something to the hype about early diagnosis and treatment. Or perhaps Mallory was just stronger than most.

The frown on her face reflected intense concentration as she sat frozen in place. One hand to tap the top of her head. A finger touched the inner point of one eyebrow … her temple … beneath that same eye … the philtrum under her nose … and then the center of her chin under her lip.

EFT. Emotional Freedom Techniques. Several of his friends had utilized the stress therapy exercise.

Mallory's demeanor changed the moment she spotted him. A radiant smile spread across her face.

He did that for her. No one else.

James started toward the BMW, opened her door, and helped her out. Unable to stop himself, his fingers tugged her ponytail free and spread the long, wavy mass around her shoulders. "I love your hair."

Roses blossomed in her cheeks. Her head tilted down.

"Hey, now." His hands cupped her face, thumbs rubbing along the angle of her jaw, nudging her chin back up. "Look at me."

Incredible blue eyes fringed with long, inky lashes looked at him.

"Be forewarned. I'm going to kiss you, and not like your brother's best friend."

A frown line creased her forehead. Her eyes moved left and then right. "What? Here? Now?"

"Yes, ma'am. Here, now, in front of God and anybody who might happen by. Do you want that?"

Their gazes met and locked. Her nostrils flared ever so slightly, and then her lips parted with a breathless, "Okay."

Her answer ignited a fire he'd kept carefully banked for way too long. James leaned in.

The kiss started with slow, sweet, barely-there touches over her soft lips. He nipped the lower one, prompting a gasp. The kiss turned harder then, deeper, until the flames inside him threatened to rage out of control.

Ragged breaths prompted a break for air, which allowed him to take a step back and put some much-needed

space between them. "I knew you'd be my undoing the first time I laid eyes on you."

Mallory pressed a finger to her swollen lip and gave in to a smile.

"That kiss was a promise, Mallory. I want to see where whatever this is leads us. Tell me you're with me."

All the trust in the world resided in her expression. "Yes, James. I want this, too."

Pulling her tight against his chest with her cheek pressed against his heart, he buried his nose in her hair. This is what he wanted. Mallory. Everyday. For the rest of their lives.

The door of the diner opened behind them, and four old codgers spilled out onto the sidewalk—Fred Robertson, Gene Flowers, Virgil Yancey, and Stan Butterwick.

Mallory tried to jerk free, but James slipped an arm around her shoulder and kept her close to his side. He'd declared her his with their very public kiss, and soon the whole town would know.

"Howdy, Sheriff." Fred tipped his cap. "Miss Mallory. Good to see you out and about again."

The other three offered similar greetings, and old Stan even took his hat off.

"Afternoon, boys." James smirked. "The rest of the Romeos inside?"

"Nah," Virgil laughed. "They already left. Gene here had to have a second piece of Shea's coconut pie. Good to see you, Mallory, sheriff."

"Romeos?" Mallory whispered as she stepped through the door James held for her.

He laughed. "That's what Polly Prescott calls them. Claims all they do is eat and gossip, eat and carouse, eat and tell jokes. She meant it as a slight, but they took a shine to it. Stands for Real Old Men Eating Out."

Mallory clapped a hand over her mouth to smother her giggles.

Shea Townsend waved to them from behind the counter. "Mallory! Where have you been? I haven't see you in ages. Are you back for good?"

"Hi Shea." Mallory's cheeks turned a rosy tint. "Been back for a little while, but haven't gotten out much. Catching up on some work."

Mallory's quick response surprised James, not that he let it show. What she said was true, just not the whole truth. No one knew about her trip to Africa, only that she'd taken a job with a newspaper in Seattle. When she told Kinsloe she wouldn't return to Seattle, he'd asked her to stay on and work from the ranch. She had been busy. But she didn't answer the question of whether she was home to stay, and that bothered him.

"Sheriff's booth is open in the back." Shea waved them toward the rear of the diner. "I'll be with you in a minute."

James steered Mallory toward the rear where he and

his deputies always sat when they met here. Sheriff's booth, huh? Sure enough, it sat empty. Now that he considered it, he couldn't recall ever seeing anyone else sit here. The thought made his lips twitch.

"What's the smile for?" Mallory asked.

"Just thinking what a funny little town this is—and how much it feels like home."

He took the seat across from her, the better to watch her expressions. So far, he hadn't seen any regrets over their kiss.

"You're staring at me." Mallory looked down.

"Look at me, princess. Not the table." James reached across and took one of her hands. His breath hitched when she did as he directed. Yeah, he wanted this.

Shea strode over at that moment, menus in hand. "What can I get you to drink?"

"I thought you worked the kitchen on your shifts. I don't believe I've ever seen you wait on customers before. Did Dee Dee finally take a day off?" James asked.

"She … uh, had some business out-of-town. She figured I'd do better out front than Jerome." Shea blushed. "I'm not so sure. I've screwed up more orders today."

"We saw Gene Flowers and his cronies outside. They said you had coconut pie. Can you save me a piece?" Mallory asked. "And I'll have water."

"Make that two slices of pie and two waters," James added.

Shea nodded. "I'll set them aside right now. Only have three left. Say, Mallory. I was wondering …" Her voice dropped to a whisper. "I haven't seen Jonas for quite some time. Is he hanging out at the ranch? Catching up on work?" By the time she finished speaking, the rosy blush had darkened to a deep pink.

James studied the waitress/chef as she and Mallory talked and noticed how her eyes lit up when talking about Jonas.

"He … uh …" Mallory stumbled over her words while she searched for a suitable answer. "Went on vacation. He needed some time off."

"Oh." The single word held a world of surprise and disappointment. And hurt.

Shea had confided her past to James when she first came to Hastings Bluff. He understood why the blonde bombshell didn't date, at least not since she landed here. Beautiful, friendly, and an angel of generosity, she drew the eye of every male who walked through the door. And to a man—young or old, ugly or handsome, rich or poor, married or single—she fended them off with ease. Shea maintained a strict 'no-fly zone,' and yet managed to turn their ardor into devoted friendship. Heck, everybody in town loved the woman.

Jonas didn't date either. The last unattached Cameron brother had a reputation for his encounters of a one-time nature.

A frown pulled at the corners of James's mouth. Before they'd rescued Mallory from the Mayakan, he recalled seeing Jonas here at the diner several times. Always with Shea. Chatting, eating, laughing … flirting?

Shea and Jonas. Not a good mix. He'd have to keep his eye on them when Jonas returned. If he came back.

"Earth to James."

He blinked. Shea had returned with their drinks and asked for their order. "Sorry, what?"

"Do you need more time?" Pen poised over the order pad, Shea waited for him to choose.

"Give me a burger, fries, and a lemonade. And the pie. Don't forget the pie."

She nodded and scribbled on her pad before turning away.

"I can't tell you what it's like to do something normal for a change." Mallory let out a long sigh. "How good it is to get out of the house."

When she squeezed his hand, James realized he hadn't let go the entire time Shea talked to them. Good. He wanted people to know she was his.

They made lighthearted small talk while they ate, until finally Mallory shoved half of her coconut pie across the table. "Here, you finish. I can't remember when I last ate that much. My stomach hurts."

The way she patted her belly—adorable. "I love you, Mallory Cameron."

A medley of reactions flickered across her face.

Her surprise and what he hoped was desire teased him. He could work with those. "I know you love me, too, but I don't expect you to say it back. Not until you're ready."

Concern spread across her face. "I don't know ... I mean ..."

"No rush, princess. We'll take this slow and easy. We'll get to know each other first, the real us. I'm talking about long walks, movie nights, dress-up dates, dinner, and lots of conversation. No pressure for anything more. I know you need time. I know you're conflicted with your brother MIA. And I'm not going anywhere. Are you?"

She looked away, and his heart sank. When she looked back, her gaze was strong and steady. "I thought I wanted a big city career, with lots of exciting assignments and exotic travel. I don't. I enjoyed Grand Cayman and Cozumel, and even some parts of Africa, but that's not me. One thing I learned through all this, I'm a homebody. I like my life just fine here on the ranch in Hastings Bluff. I'm not a big city kind of girl."

His grin grew wider with each word she uttered. "You have no idea how happy that makes me. Don't get me wrong, if you decided to live in Seattle ... or New York ... or Timbuktu, I'd follow you in a heartbeat. I can't let you out of my sight again, but neither would I stand in your way if that's what you want. But don't forget, we also have Garrett's and TJ's kid to usher into the world. From the size of her belly, she's got to be close."

She reached for his hand this time. "Four weeks. And I wouldn't mention her size if I were you. Not if you want to keep all your parts in working order."

"I have one more piece of news to share. It's something you'll like, I think. Mostly."

Her anxiety hadn't gone completely away, but curiosity tempered by hope erased a large chunk of it. One of those sexy brows arched high. The woman had no idea what that did to him.

"Okay, what?"

"All's well that ends well."

Confusion lasted a full ten seconds before understanding dawned on her beautiful face. "Fowler's last message. Is it really over?"

He nodded. "Mission accomplished."

"And Jo, is he okay? He's coming home?"

"Physically, he's fine, but I'm not sure what's going on in his head. He went off grid again. The last time he disappeared for two years."

A single tear trickled down her cheek, but she smiled and wiped it away. "So, the wait continues. That's fine. I've gotten good at waiting. The important thing is, he's alive. Which is a heck of a lot better than the alternative."

"You can't tell anyone. Fowler's a hard case that way. He'll send word to your family when the time is right."

"And yet he made sure I knew."

"Even hard cases have soft spots." James pulled her hand across the table, leaned forward, and pressed a kiss to her open palm.

Her breath caught, but she didn't pull away. "Thank you, James. For everything. I don't know how I can ever repay you."

"You can't, princess. Love doesn't have a price. It's given freely, with no expectations. Although I wouldn't mind a little loving in return."

In a flash, her seriousness turned naughty. "Only a little?"

"Or a lot. When you're ready, of course."

"Of course."

We hope you enjoyed

IMPERFECT LIES.

If you did, please consider
returning to the Amazon page
and leaving a review for the author.
Keep an eye out for book 5
of The Camerons,
IMPERFECT PROMISES,
coming soon!

Acknowledgements

I've always been an avid reader, but never gave much thought to the writing process before I attempted my first book. What a shock to learn that writing is the easy part. The true test of commitment comes with the long hours of research, poring over critiques, working through edits, additional edits, and then more edits, the bared heart as the manuscript is submitted to the publisher. And that's *before* it goes to the publisher, where it's scrutinized under a microscope.

Yeah, writing the story is the easy part. Getting it "reader-ready" is the true labor of love.

With this said, it is my privilege to thank all the wonderful people who helped bring Imperfect Lies to print: my critique groups; my trusted beta readers—Emily Grey, Shari Nardello, Brenda Curtis, Vicki Mobley, and Barry Thomason; my gracious publisher, Marji Laine Clubine and her team of editors; and last but far from least, my patient and loving hubby, Paul Noyes, without whom none of the military and tactical scenes in my stories would come to life. Thank you.

About the Author

Elizabeth Noyes is an award-winning author of edgy, action-packed, romantic suspense. Her best writing comes while cruising the Caribbean, visiting National Parks, riding trains across Canada, bumping along on tour buses around Europe, or tucked away in the sunroom of her home in suburban Atlanta (when she and her hubby return from traveling, that is).

A Letter to My Readers

Post-traumatic stress disorder (PTSD) is a real and growing concern in our nation, especially among our military veterans. By including this topic in my story, I hope to encourage a greater awareness.

The most common documented causes of PTSD are war, rape, violence, terrorism, physical assault, and threat of death or grievous injury. Milder symptoms of PTSD include (but are not limited to) anxiety, nightmares, avoidance, hyperarousal/reaction, social withdrawal, depression, flashbacks triggered by stressors, emotional numbing, and even a multitude of addictive behaviors. In many cases, the sufferer may experience psychosis, reliving of events, and even physical symptoms such as headaches, migraines, chest pain, digestive disorders, difficulty breathing, dizziness, and extreme fatigue. Ignoring these signals won't make them go away, and in fact could lead to more serious medical conditions.

> Fact: An estimated 70% of adults in the United States have experienced a traumatic event at least once in their lives. As many as 20% of these people develop post-traumatic stress disorder (PTSD).

Another psychological concern of PTSD is known as 'survivor's guilt.' This occurs when a PTSD sufferer doesn't understand why they survived an event when others did not. (*Why me?*)

> Fact: It is estimated that 1 in 13 adults in the

United States will develop PTSD during their lifetime. Women are twice as likely as men to develop PTSD.

Early diagnosis and treatment of PTSD is very effective when combined with strong support from family, friends, and co-workers. Assessment by a mental health professional is essential, and treatment options may include psychotherapy, exposure therapy, desensitization exercises, remembering and reliving stressor situations, and in some cases, prescription medication. The treatment is a slow process.

Fact: Stress caused by trauma can affect all aspects of a person's life, including mental, emotional, and physical well-being.

It is important to understand that PTSD is not a disease like, for instance, cancer. Whereas a surgeon might excise a tumor through surgical means and eradicate remnant cells with chemotherapy or radiation, the cause of PTSD—a traumatic event—can never be eliminated; the memories can never be erased. What treatment can do is help reduce PTSD episodes and the extent to which the symptoms affect and interfere with the many facets of daily life—home, relationships, work, school, and social interactions, thereby restoring a semblance of control to the suffer.

For more information about PTSD visit www.PTSDUSA.org.

For immediate help, contact one of the numerous Hot Lines/Crisis Lines available in your state, or call:

PTSD Foundation of America
1.800.717. PTSD (7873)

Veteran Crisis Line
1.800.273.8255

National Veterans Foundation Hotline
1.888.777.4443

Rape, Abuse, Incest National Network
1.800.656.4673

National Domestic Violence Hotline
1.800.799.7233

National Council on Alcoholism and Drug Dependence Hope Line
1.800.622.2255

Gulf War Veterans' Hotline
1.800.796.9699

Read about All the Camerons

The last thing Garrett Cameron needs is another woman interrupting his life, but when the feisty vixen that blew his mission two years ago shows up at his ranch running for her life, what can he do?

Evil stalks TJ McKendrick. Only faith in God and trust in each other can overcome the deadly odds they face.

Sometimes past and present collide.

Scarred by childhood tragedy and then abandoned by a mother who couldn't handle a gifted child, Lucy Kiddron survived foster care to become a computer analyst for the government ... until her final assignment goes horribly wrong.

Wade Cameron understands betrayal. The two risk everything as they muddle through a minefield of danger, distrust, and a burgeoning attraction that won't be denied.

Cassidy Cameron's life is in a tailspin. Her estranged twin sister hates her. Worse, the arrogant town deputy who stole her heart wants more than she's willing to give ... or is she the one who wants more from him? And now she's being threatened by a pair of unsavory ruffians.

Derek pulls out his guns instead when Cassie stumbles into a maelstrom of illegal arms deals, illicit drugs, and human trafficking.

Recent Releases from Write Integrity

What would you do if you discovered, by accident, no less, that the President of the United States was attending your daughter's wedding in less than two weeks?

Panic. You'd panic, I tell you.

That's what the parents of the bride, Pastor Hugh Foster and his wife Melanie did. Talk about a faux pas!

Well, good luck with all that, Pastor Foster.

Oh, and Heaven help the president.

In early spring of 1955, Annabelle Cross and her daughter-in-law, Connie have nearly made it through the first winter on their own. Annabelle begins to dread Connie's upcoming marriage and removal to Sutter's Landing, which will leave Annabel alone for the first time in her life.

Connie's doubts increase when Alton's bigoted brother Jensen uses every opportunity to drive a wedge between them. Is she doing the right thing? Did she move too quickly?

Imperfect Lies

**Thank you
for reading our books!**

Look for other books

published by

Write Integrity Press

www.WriteIntegrity.com